SHADOWS ON THE RIVER

BY

LON D. HADEN

This book is a work of fiction. Places, events, and situations in this story are purely fictional. Any resemblance to actual persons, living or dead, is coincidental.

ISBN: 1-4107-3566-4 (e-book)
ISBN: 1-4107-3565-6 (Paperback)

Library of Congress Control Number: 2003092665

This book is printed on acid free paper.

Printed in the United States of America
Bloomington, IN

1stBooks - rev. 09/12/03

PROLOGUE

This story is fictional, the characters are fictional, the locale and many of the landmarks are real. The Ferris Caves carved in the Dakota sandstone bluffs on the Smoky Hill River, southeast of Kanopolis, Kansas are still there. Scarred and defaced by those that do such things, they shall endure and will stand the test of time for many generations to enjoy.

The Hummel Bridge has been torn down, declared unsafe by those that make such decisions; replaced by a sign stating it was there.

This brings us to the Smoky Hill River, a narrow strip of running water that winds its way west to east, across three fourths of the state of Kansas. Many have forgotten the important role this almost unknown river played in the settling of the Western United States.

The Smoky Hill River Trail, which followed the river, was the main route used by the early settlers to cross Kansas as they made the long journey to Denver, Colorado and on west. Water was always a worry for these early pioneers and the river provided water, even though at times, one might have to dig for it in what seemed to be a dry river bed.

Towns and army forts sprung up along the Smoky Hill River. Fort Harker, Fort Hays, Fort Ellsworth and Fort Wallace were established to protect the settlers and drive the Indians from the prairie. The Indians didn't give up easily, but eventually, they where overcome and forced to live on reservations, all in the name of PROGRESS.

Lawmen and badmen followed the Smoky Hill River Trail. Bill Hickok, William F. Cody, Bat Masterson, Frank and Jesse James, Ben and Billy Thompson, Wyatt Earp, and George Armstrong Custer just to name a few.

The railroad came and it too followed the Smoky Hill River as it moved west.

Buffalo by the hundreds of thousands lived along the river and the prairie grassland that run on either side and provided food, warmth and shelter for the Indians. As well as food for the railroad workers and sport for those that would eventually ride the rails.

Those days have long since past. The war cry of the Comanche and the Sioux have been replaced by the roar of two hundred and fifty horse power tractors and combines that can chop down a thirty foot swath of wheat in one swipe.

The council drums of the Cheyenne and the Apache no longer echo up and down the river, having been superseded by the rumble of jet planes that pass overhead at the speed of sound.

The thundering herds of buffalo are gone, in their place Angus, Hereford, Simmental, and many other breeds of cattle continentally graze on the Kansas prairie.

This is only as a reminder of the significance the Smoky Hill River played in the early settling of the Great American West.

CHAPTER 1

NORTHWEST OKLAHOMA 1953

Jumbo's first experience with pain and the pure cursed meanness of mankind was when he was a six month old pup. It was a hot July evening, when he found himself on the wrong end of Orie Shank's blacksnake whip. Again and again the braided rawhide ripped and tore into his back, sides, and legs.

He screamed as the whip cut into tender virgin flesh, leaving red welts that covered his blue-grey coat and opened lesions that dripped blood about the pen. The flogging finally stopped and when it did, he lay in the corner of the pen bruised and battered, afraid to move, wondering if the pain would ever stop.

Shank stood over the quivering pup. He weighted, at best, one hundred and seventy pounds and stood a mere five foot five. However, he looked like a giant to this frightened son of a Pit Bull mother and a father of unknown ancestry.

"Ya bastard, next time I tell ya ta shut-up ya best be a shuttin' up." Perspiration dripping from his round red face, staining a well worn blue chambray shirt. His beady brown eyes looking down on the terrified pup.

He spit tobacco juice on Jumbo before he turned and walked away, carefully closing the gate and making sure it was latched.

Jumbo watched through half closed eyes as Shank wrapped the whip in a neat circular package. The last thing he remembered was Shank draping the instrument of his suffering over a twelve inch limb that stuck out from a hedge post that supported one corner of the pen. Orie Shank could have cut the limb off when he set the post, but when the post was set it stuck out about chest high on Orie, just the right height to hang anything he desired, on it.

Jumbo lay in a state of unconsciousness for sometime. He awoke to the tender stroke of a small hand as it caressed his broad flat head. He opened his eyes and slowly wagged his tail, as he recognized the soft symphonic female voice. Armella Shank knelt beside him. With a clean rag and warm water she began to clean up his bloodstained body. He tried to raise his head.

1

"Just lay still, don't try to get up. Boy, he really worked you over. But you'll be alright, I'll take care of you."

Jumbo trusted her and laid his head back down. If there was a bright spot in Jumbo's life it was this pretty, petite, eleven year old girl, with medium length dark blonde hair tied back in a pony tail. Her hazel eyes began to fill with tears as she worked diligently on his pain wracked body. Armella was his caretaker. It wasn't a job she had been given, it was a job she had taken because Orie Shank, her Grandfather, was neglecting his care.

She understood Jumbo's suffering, for she too had suffered at the hands of Orie Shank's surly disposition. Her mother had died in a car accident shortly after she was born, leaving her to be raised by her grandparents. It wasn't a job Orie and Lois Shank chose, but they had little choice in the matter, not knowing the whereabouts of her father. Orie was drunk most of the time and never thought of anyone but himself. Born of wealthy parents, he had never learned to work and at fifty years of age, he had nearly squandered the family fortune; nonetheless, he didn't plan on changing his ways anytime soon. He entertained himself by finding ways to cause someone else grief, pain, and suffering—it seemed for now, Jumbo was his fervor.

Lois Shank was at least ten years younger than Orie, stringy straight gray hair hung limply around a plump homely face. She stood a good six inches taller than Orie and out weighted him by over a hundred pounds. Her weight problem, along with her squalid nature, certainly made her less than desirable to most men. She didn't particularly like Jumbo, but he did serve a purpose; when Orie had Jumbo on his mind, he wasn't abusing her or Armella.

Armella worked on Jumbo until almost dark. He stood up and playfully tried to lick her hands and face when she had finished. He felt better now and as she left, he whimpered, trying to coax her back. She turned to face him a weak smile on her lips. "I have to go now. Be quiet, before he comes back and beats you again.".

Jumbo turned his head to the side, as if he understood. He lay down in the middle of the pen, hoping he would never get a thrashing like that again. He was certain he could not withstand another one of Orie Shank's beatings.

Shank's goal was to create a monster that would be feared by all of mankind, a savage animal, so dangerous, so fierce that it would be feared by all creatures large and small, those that walked on the earth and those that flew in the air.

He wanted a sideshow freak, an animal so bloodthirsty he would destroy all that dared to enter the fighting pit with him. The whippings didn't stop and by the time he was a year old he had been beaten several more times. He had toughen to the bit of the whip; instead of crying out—he barred his fangs, showing glistening white teeth, held in place by powerful jaws that could crush the hardest of bones. Instead of whines or whimpers an angry growl would form deep in his throat—an admonishing not to be taken lightly. Jumbo no longer feared the whip—now he challenged the whip.

The trees began to drop their leaves as summer turned to fall. Jumbo had grown into a magnificent animal. His huge frame carried a mass of rippling muscles that bulged under his scarred blue-grey hide.

Onlookers came to see the ferocious beast, always staying their distance, as he charged the fence again and again. On two points they all agreed, he weighted well over one hundred twenty five pounds and they wanted no part of him.

Shank's plan was going array, he had not expected Jumbo to get this large. His plan was to put him in the fighting pit, but no one in his right mind would pit his dog against a giant like this.

Orie Shank had created the monster he wanted, but now, what was he going to do with his charge. Jumbo hated every man he met, every animal that walked the earth. He hated everything that lived; with one exception, Armella, whom he trusted and loved.

Armella's main concern, for the time being, was shelter for her ward. He had outgrown his dog house and certainly needed protection from the cold winter winds and the snow that was sure to follow.

She approached Orie about the situation one morning as he watched her feed him. "Grandpa, this dog needs a house for the winter."

"He don't need nothin' . . . gets more now than he deserves."

"But he'll freeze to death, with no house," she pleaded.

"He can dig a hole," Orie snapped.

"There's no way he can dig a hole. You laid wire all over the bottom of the pen, so he couldn't dig out."

"I'm not spending money on a house fer no damn dog. He'll just have to do the best he can."

"Couldn't I just put some straw bales in there for him to lay in?"

3

"Oh! I guess. Don't be askin' me ta help ya." Orie started to walk away, suddenly he turned around to give Armella a warning. "Don't you dare leave him outa that pen . . . if ya do I'll use that whip on ya." He pointed to the corner post of the dog's pen.

Armella spent the better part of the afternoon building Jumbo a dog house out of straw bales. She stacked the bales two high in a rectangular shape, leaving an opening on one end. Behind the barn, she found an old piece of plywood that was used for a roof.

She patted Jumbo on the head and gave him an affectionate hug, as tears run down her cheeks. "I done my best . . . I hope it's good enough."

The winter was a trying duration in time for Jumbo. The daylight lasted only a short time; the nights were long and cold. Armella would come to feed him in the morning before she went to school. The pads on his feet became hard and callused as he paced back and forth on the hard frozen ground, vigilantly waiting for her return in the evening. She was his custodian, the only person who had ever shown him any kind of human love or kindness. He looked forward to her gentle touch as she ran her hands over his sleek velvet coat. The soft words she spoke as she stroked his head or scratched his ears. The warm embrace when she arrived; the passionate hug when she left.

To Orie Shank cold weather was a curse. The arthritis in the joints of his hands and legs would almost incapacitate him at times. He spent most of the winter in the house by a warm fire.

Spring finally arrived with warm days and cool nights. Orie's joints began to loosen up and by early summer he was back to being his sordid contemptible unrestrained self.

Orie slammed the kitchen door as he swaggered out of the house. Jumbo knew what was about to happen as he watched, Orie strutted toward his pen. He had seen the walk before as well as the wild in the eye, half crazy look on his face.

Jumbo moved to the back of the pen as Orie lifted the rawhide whip off the post at the corner of the pen. The whip had hung out in the elements all winter and spring; it was stiff and unmanageable.

Orie removed a oil soaked rag from the hip pocket of his overalls. He ran the rag from the handle to the very end, again and again; carefully working the braided leather until it became pliable and soft.

Satisfied, he grasped the handle and flipped the savage weapon behind his back. He raised his arm over his head and with one quick over head motion the lash sprung to attention; cracking like a dead tree limb that had just been broken in half.

Jumbo quivered at the sound.

Orie stepped into Jumbo's prison, carefully closing the gate. "Now I'll show ya who the boss is . . . ya blue devil."

Jumbo allowed himself plenty of room to maneuver, as he moved to the back of the pen, dark eyes alert, unblinking, ivory white fangs exposed by snarling lips, tail tucked, hair standing on his back, ears laid flat on his head. Jumbo growled a deep threatening rumble from deep in his throat, as he watched the whip that lay motionless behind Orie Shank.

The lash snapped at Jumbo; so quick it was only a brown blur. The winter's rest had been a blessing, he had healed, there were no sore muscles, his reflexes were lightning quick. He jumped to the right, as the whip cut through the warm morning air.

Jumbo waited for the next blow, it came, even quicker than the first. He didn't try to avoid the pain that he knew was coming. Jumbo struck with the quickness of a viper, jaws agape, teeth sharpened to a keen edge, catching this instrument of torture in mid-air, jaws slamming shut like a steel trap, so fast Orie Shank never realized what was happening.

Orie Shank was horrified as the big hound began to drag him around the pen. "Damn you Jumbo—turn loose, damn-it!" Jumbo shook his powerful neck and head as he locked his jaws even tighter around this instrument of horror.

Shank was mortified, terrified, fearing for his life. He tried to move toward the gate while still hanging onto the whip. Jumbo planted his feet. It was useless, he couldn't drag the big hound. He was no match for the demon he had created; the energy was quickly leaving his body. The color had left Orie Shank's ordinarily red face, his eyes were wide with fear. He had lost control of his prodigy. In order to save his hide he turned loose of the handle and gave Jumbo complete control of the blacksnake whip.

Armella watched from the kitchen window as Orie escaped through the gate. She feared what might happen next. She knew her grandfather too well, he would retaliate, there was no way he was going to accept this defeat.

Jumbo had moved to the middle of the pen, tossing the whip in the air, pouncing on it, like a cat playing with a mouse, tearing at it with razor sharp teeth, slowly reducing this instrument of punishment to a pile of useless leather.

Shank stormed around the pen as he watched in disbelief. "Ya, blue bastard, I'm gonea kill ya," he swore. Hastily he returned to the house, entering the front door in a rage.

"I'm gonna kill 'em . . . that blue devil." He announced to Armella, as she retreated to her bedroom. The color had returned to Orie's face, it was beet red, covered with a determined evil look. His hands were shaking so bad that he could barely pour a drink from the whisky bottle that set on the kitchen table. Holding the glass with both hands, he gulped down his drink.

He would drink himself into a drunken stupor and then carry out his dastardly plan; it had happened before.

Lois Shank had gone into town early that morning, leaving Armella home with her Grandfather. Armella understood the gravity of the situation as she paced nervously in her bedroom.

A plan began to form in her mind; perhaps she could open the gate, turn Jumbo loose and convince her Grandfather that he had not latched the gate.

She quietly slipped out the back door. Once outside she raced to the dog pen.

Jumbo was entertaining himself by chewing on the small strips of leather that were strewn about the pen. He watched as Armella opened the gate; pushing it wide open—leaving it open.

He began to wag his tail as she approached. "Jumbo you have to get out of here. He means to kill ya."

He didn't move.

She wrapped her slender arms around his massive neck as she tried to pull him to his feet. "Come on! You have to get up and get out of here. Please!!"

Armella's plea went unheard as he tried to lick her face. The front door slammed. Armella turned at the sound.

Orie Shank was tottering on the front step; rifle in hand.

Jumbo came to attention, sensing danger, he jumped to his feet.

Armella's face was pale, her heart fluttered, a lump formed in her throat, she felt sick to her stomach. She tried to speak but could only mutter a whisper. "Run Jumbo run . . . he means to kill you. Please run!" The frightened girl ran to the gate hoping he would follow. Orie, even in his drunken state, realized what was happening.

"Close that gate, don't let him out, damn you Armella," he screamed.

Now Jumbo understood the urgency in Armella's voice. He bolted out the gate, nearly knocking her down as he passed.

He was free at last. He raced from his man made prison, enjoying this new found freedom, not realizing the mortal danger he was in.

He stopped some fifty yards behind the cage that had held him captive, turning toward Orie Shank who was now standing to the side of the lockup.

"Don't shoot!" Armella cried out, as Orie raised the rifle to his shoulder.

The rifle banged as the hammer struck the primer igniting the powder. The bullet cracked as it sped past Jumbo's ear, just inches from certain death.

To Jumbo it was a freighting sound, he turned to run as Shank jacked another shell in the chamber. A stinging burning pain spun Jumbo around when Orie fired the second shot. The thirty ought six bullet ripped through muscle, hide and flesh as it plowed a five inch long, quarter inch deep furrow out of his lower left shoulder. He wanted to stop and lick his wound, a third shot quickly changed his mind as the bullet kicked up dirt at his feet.

He forgot the pain as he tried to outrun an untimely death. The adrenaline was pumping, his animal instincts and will to live had taken over. He had to get away someplace where Orie Shank would never find him.

A tree grove loomed ahead; he could hide there. The rifle cracked again, the bullet went wild as Jumbo disappeared into the woods. He stopped behind a dead tree to check his injury, licking at the blood dripping from the horizontal wound that was slowly turning the ground red under his feet. The pain was getting more intense, as the wound began to throb, forcing him to lie down. He was alone, confused, and afraid, the only world he had known was a twelve by thirty foot prison. Jumbo was in a world he never knew existed.

He watched in amazement as a squirrel jumped from tree to tree. He felt the coolness of the shade, something he had never felt before.

His ears stood at attention when he heard the scream, a loud piercing cry that came from the Shank place. The hair raised on his back at the sound of the second shriek, a gut wrenching wail that ripped at the very core of his heart. Jumbo lay motionless, as if paralyzed, he had never heard an outcry like this before, but he knew—it was Armella.

Orie Shank was taking out his vengeance on the one person that had befriended him. The only human being he had ever loved and given love in return. It wasn't a love of passion, but of caring; a love entranced in trust.

He stood up on unsteady legs, after several shaky steps, he gained control of his body, rushing from the security of the tree grove into the open area from where he had just found safety. He had forgotten the pain that had forced him to the ground just moments before; his own safety wasn't even a consideration. He was quickly closing the distance between himself and Orie Shank. Recklessly charging across the open field, a savage fury building in his mind, a turbulence out of control, with no thought of consequences.

He was crossing the field in huge leaping bounds at a speed he didn't know was possible. He looked in aghast at Orie Shank standing over Armella's motionless body; her face and clothes covered with blood.

Orie was about to strike the hapless girl again, when out of the corner of his eye he caught a glimpse of the blue streak that was about to attack. He quickly turned to retrieve the rifle that was leaning against the corner post of the dog's pen. The same post he used as a hanging place for his whip. He was raising the weapon to his shoulder as he turned to meet Jumbo's attack.

Jumbo launched his assault with powerful hind legs that catapulted his huge body into the air, his full weight landing on Orie Shank's shoulders and chest like an out of control, flesh and blood battering ram. The rifle fell to the ground as Orie slammed against the corner post with a dull thud, emitting a sickening moan as the air was forced from his lungs.

Jumbo came down hard, landing on his feet, immediately coming up on his toes, ready to continue the fight.

Shank's face had already turned ashen, horror stricken eyes, wide-open, not seeing, pale and cold, blood trickling down the corner of his mouth, arms dangling limply at his side, a small circular spot of crimson forming on his shirt—where the limb he used to hang his whip had just barely protruded through his chest as it passed through his heart.

8

Orie Shank was no longer a threat. Jumbo's attention turned to Armella, slowly he walked toward her, whimpering as he looked down on her battered body. His eyes heavy with sadness as he began to lick the blood from her face with his ruff tongue. Her face was badly bruised, one eye nearly swollen shut.

She stirred ever so slightly as a car turned in the driveway. Jumbo watched as the red and white Ford came to a stop in front of the house. Lois Shank was struggling to get her obese body out of the car when she looked toward the scene that had unfolded earlier. Horrified, she became hysterical, screaming and crying as she rushed toward a lifeless Orie.

She stood in front of Orie, tears running down her face. Jumbo was still standing by Armella. She gave him a wicked look. "You killed him. I know you did. I knowed ya was trouble the first time I laid eyes on ya. An' what have ya done to that poor girl," she sobbed.

"I hate you Jumbo. I always have." She picked up the rifle that was laying at Orie's feet. I hate you! I hate you!" She screamed, as she raised the gun to her shoulder pointing it at Jumbo. "I'm going to end this right now."

Jumbo was wise to the rifle, understanding now that it meant pain and was more dangerous than the whip; it could reach out much further to cause the suffering.

He turned and ran to the opposite side of the pen. Lois Shank fired one shot; it sailed well over his head, as he raced for the tree grove that had offered him safety before.

His shoulder was getting stiff and very sore, but he knew he had to get far away from this place. He worried about Armella, but for his own safety, he had to push on.

Jumbo needed help but he certainly wouldn't find it here. He was on the run, it was a long winding path he would follow, trusting no one, foraging off the land, living like a wild animal, trying to survive in a hostile world he did not know or understand.

CHAPTER 2

The sun was just coming up as Jumbo took refuge beside a down tree, east of Kanopolis, Kansas, on the Smoky Hill River. He had been on the trail for exactly six weeks. His shoulder healed with no permanent damage and if it wasn't for the nasty scar, one would be hard pressed to know anything had happened.

Living off the land had been a feat; unlike anything Jumbo had ever expected. He left the tree grove heading west crossing the Cimarron River near Freedom, Oklahoma. He moved slowly, his shoulder was sore and he walked with a distinct limp. His animal instincts were already beginning to take over as he realized if he wanted to eat he would have to find his own food. Hampered by his injury and a lack of experience, it was nearly impossible for him to catch anything that would feed an animal of his size.

On the fifth day of his pilgrimage he reached Buffalo, Oklahoma, with gut drawn tight to his backbone, he started following Highway 183 to the North. He quickly learned two lessons that he would never forget. The highway could provide food, it was there for the taking, struck down by the trucks and automobiles that raced by in either direction.

Lesson number two, beware of the danger that lurks along the roadway. He learned this quickly, when he was nearly pancaked by a truck as he tried to eat an armadillo in the middle of the road. The armadillo's hard shell was a challenge even for his puissant jaws. He would carry his meal off the road from now on and try to find food more to his liking.

Jumbo crossed the state line into Kansas on the twenty-first day of his journey. He would continue to follow Highway 183 to Kinsley, Kansas. There for some unknown reason, he would leave the highway and follow the Arkansas river to the northeast.

He liked the river; although food was more difficult to find. He was getting around better on his sore shoulder and catching game wasn't as difficult. Jumbo was once again drawn to the north when he reached Great Bend, Kansas. He followed Highway 281 to Russell, Kansas where he would meet up with the Smoky Hill River.

The Smoky Hill River wasn't the largest river in the state of Kansas, nor was it the most picturesque; it was a slow easy going river and many times only ran two to three feet of water. In many areas it ran on a bed of sand and numerous sandbars were always present to fish from or to have a family picnic.

The Smoky, as it was known in the area, got its start in Colorado, just a short distance from the Colorado-Kansas line. The river started with two forks in Colorado. The North fork passed about fifteen miles south of Burlington, Colorado and wound its way into western Kansas, drifting slowly east and south, near Russell Springs, Kansas it would meet the South fork. The South fork also started in eastern Colorado, some twenty miles west of Arapahoe.

The Saline River would join the Smoky near Solomon, Kansas. It would make its way into eastern Kansas, where the Smoky would enter the Republican River near Junction City, thus ending its journey across the state.

The Smoky Hill River's peaceful beauty had a mystical effect on Jumbo and he began to work his way east down the river.

Buy the time Jumbo reached the Smoky, he hunted and searched for food like his ancestors of many generations before him. The senses that he seldom used before, had become more acute. His eyes picked up the slightest movement; ears harkened to the faintest sound. He depended on his nose more than anything else; a tool he had never used while locked up in Orie Shanks jail. His nose helped him to find food that would have otherwise been overlooked and warned him of danger that silently lay ahead.

He had learned to travel at night under the cover of darkness. Man was seldom out at night and Jumbo wanted nothing to do with man. He avoided towns because the smell of man was too strong.

****

The sun was high in the sky when Jumbo awoke from his nap. He was in the shade when he went to sleep, but now the sun was beating down on him unmercifully. He stood up, already panting.

His stomach told him it was time to eat; but first he would go down to the river and get a cool drink of water.

Stiff from sleeping in a curled up position, he stretched while sniffing the afternoon air. Jumbo picked up a strange scent on the wind; a strong, powerful, pungent odor. The river was suddenly very quiet.

The rat-a-tat-tat of the Redheaded Woodpecker's chisel like bill hammering on the old dead elm no longer echoed up and down the river. He sat quietly on the side of the tree, his meal interrupted by something roaming in the timber.

Its presence had suppressed the mournful call of the nesting turtle doves. Their timid nature causing them to scrunch down tightly on their nest; hoping not to be noticed.

Absent was the melodious whistle of the western meadowlarks that were so plentiful in the grassland that run along the timberline of the river. It was as if a great plague had passed through and struck them all down.

An ill-tempered unpredictable rattlesnake lay sunning himself on the Dakota sandstone bluff that housed the man made Ferris caves. He sensed the danger as he coiled up, ready to strike; changing his mind, he slithered under a large rock.

The Mississippi Kite hung motionless in the sky high above; his watchful eyes surveying the stage, waiting for the drama to begin.

A fox squirrel raced ahead, traveling on the tree tops, leaping from tree to tree; his sharp bark a message for all—beware.

The hair stood up on Jumbo's back as he looked around—it surely must be an evil force if its very presence could change the serenity of the river and all the creatures and birds that lived on and around the river. He jumped up on a log for a better look. His keen eyes scanned the area, searching for a movement, there was none. His ears were alert, standing up, straining to hear anything that would tell him what had entered the neighborhood.

He heard a limb snap down river; something was there. What was it? It wasn't a man, it didn't smell like a man. It must be an animal. He turned his head to the side, curiously listening, watching, waiting to see what had disrupted the harmony of the river.

Jumbo was about to meet Ol Razor, a feral boar hog that had roamed the river for nearly two years. Razor took refuge on the river in the daytime, staying out of sight in the timber and heavy cover. At dusk he would begin to roam the prairie, searching for food, destroying crops, gardens or anything else that struck his fancy. He had no fear of humans for at one time he had been raised by man. He understood their habits and way of life. He was their tormentor and every farmer in the area hoped to put a bullet in him and stop his rein of terror. He was the King of the river and knew no fear.

Jumbo and Razor had one thing in common, they both lead a solitary life.

Jumbo watched and listened as Razor continued to move closer. Jumbo could see him now; the old boar was unlike anything he had ever seen before. He was huge, at least four times bigger than Jumbo.

He recklessly crashed through the brush and trees, using his huge head with four inch tusks that protruded from his lower jaw to move anything that got in his way. His dark red boar bristle hair was covered with dry dirt and mud.

Razor stopped short, just a few feet in front of Jumbo, who left out a warning snarl. Razor returned an intimidating grunt.

Jumbo was still standing on the log, watching, as Razor moved closer. He stopped again, his cold calculating eyes looking up at Jumbo.

Jumbo wasn't giving any ground. He barked twice, loud and threatening.

Razor couldn't comprehend this, everything else ran when he confronted them. Surely this creature wasn't going to challenge him. He lowered his head and moved closer.

What was he up too? Jumbo watched as he pushed his callused nose under his vantage point. Razor snorted and with one powerful motion, lifted the log up, rolling it over, dumping Jumbo on the ground.

Jumbo scrambled to his feet, wide-eyed and ready to fight. Razor wasn't waiting, charging straight at a dog who barely had time to plant his feet. Jumbo leaped to the side as Razor passed, slashing out with a well honed tusk. Jumbo spun around as he passed, mighty jaws snapped at his back side, Jumbo missed, chasing after the old boar catching him by the rump on his second try. The thickness and toughness of Razor's hide surprised him. He had a good hold, but his hide seemed impregnable.

Razor squealed as he spun around trying to shake Jumbo loose. Jumbo hung on but lost his grip when Razor slammed him into a small cottonwood tree, breaking two ribs. Jumbo, dazed from the blow and in incredible pain from the broken ribs, was trying to get on his feet when Razor hit him, hooking a tusk in flesh and hide, with one quick upward thrust he ripped a seven inch gash in a just healed left shoulder, passing through the center of the scar left by Orie Shank's bullet.

13

Lon D. Haden

Jumbo was branded, just as sure as if someone had taken a hot iron and laid it on his blue-grey hide. The wound would heal, but when it did he would carry the mark of the inverted cross; not a symbol of the godly, but a mark of evil, a sign of the unjust—the devil's sign.

Jumbo was seriously injured. He knew he had to retreat or find a place to make a stand. Razor charged again, blood still dripping from a freshly used saber. Jumbo left a bloody trail as he retreated into the timber before Ol Razor could do any more damage.

This was an animal he did not know or understand. Perhaps they would meet again, but for now, Jumbo hoped he could recover from this battle.

CHAPTER 3

The Barnes' house had been abandoned for years. No one knew much about the Barnes family, except they had lived there during the Great Depression. Hard times had befallen them and when fire destroyed part of the house, that was the final blow. They loaded up what they could and left for parts unknown, never to be heard from again.

The farmstead sat in prime Kansas grassland, it was badly overgrown with weeds and trees that had sprung up here and there. A trail lead up to the house from the east, kept open by young lovers who wanted to get away, for a short time from the rest of the world. The trail led to the front of the house where a small patch of buffalo grass had taken hold and was growing prolifically.

The Barnes' place was also a hide-a-way for some of the neighborhood farm children to practice mischief or try to scare each other while they prowled through the old house.

Such was the case on this afternoon as Milacent Elliot sat on the limestone rock that acted as the lone step onto the front porch.

She just lacked a few days of being fourteen years old. Dark blue eyes highlighted a pretty round face with a near prefect complexion; medium length blonde hair hung loosely on her shoulders. A smile that could melt the coldest heart was ever present. She had inherited her mother's looks, but the quiet easy going disposition was her father's trait; although at times her mother's fiery temperament would surface, usually when it was least expected.

She waited quietly and patiently for her brother Smoky and his friends Junior and Curly Bledso, knowing fully well what sort of tomfoolery they were up too.

Milacent Elliot wasn't alone, she was being watched by inquiring eyes. Eyes that had curiously studied her as the foursome walked up the trail to the old house.

The three in faded blue jeans and tattered blue chambray shirts, he did not trust. They had the faint odor of man, not the strong odor he feared, but intense enough to warn him to be extremely cautious.

It was the one on the limestone rock, wearing blue jeans, cut off at the knees, with the pink and white sleeveless blouse that had him intrigued. Mesmerized by her slender young body, still waiting for the curves of womanhood. Perhaps if he moved he could get a better look. Jumbo gingerly got to his feet, pain shot through his side—as broken ribs rubbed together. His injured shoulder hampering him as he tried to silently move around the yard, through the weeds and trees.

Her scent drifted on the breeze as he move downwind. The sweet alluring fragrance excited Jumbo as he lifted his head high drawing the ambrosial aroma deep into his nostrils. This was a sensation he had felt before but only when he was with Armella.

He pushed his way through the tangled web of green vegetation, trying to get closer, until carelessly he found himself on the trail that lead to the house.

He stood in the road captivated by the intoxicating aroma that took his mind back in time. His thoughts were of Armella as he watched the young girl stand up and slowly walk toward him, her flowing blonde hair wrapped around her attractive face by a gentle wind.

Jumbo stood fast as she moved closer. She stopped just a few feet in front of him, speaking in a enchanting voice. "Come here. Don't be afraid. I'm not going to hurt you." Her voice was soft, kind, trusting, just like Armella's.

She stepped closer. He took a step forward. "You're hurt. What in the world happened to you?" Jumbo moved to her side. She placed her hand on his back as she examined the wound on his shoulder.

Jumbo relaxed, her hands were soft, gentle and warm. He flinched as she run her hand over the broken ribs. Realizing she had touched a sore spot, she quickly pulled her hand away. "You have really taken a beating, haven't you. What in the world did you tangle with? Where did you come from? Who do you belong to?" She would be a long time waiting for the answer to these questions.

"Hey, Millie what you doin'?" A voice called from back at the house. She turned to see Smoky and the Bledso brothers standing on the front porch.

"It's a dog. He came out of the weeds. He's been hurt."

"What you goin' to do with him?" Smoky asked, as he stepped off the porch, followed by Junior and Curly.

It was a leaderless trio coming down the trail, three abreast, to check out Millie's find. Richard (Smoky) Elliot was in the middle, at five feet seven inches, he was the shortest of the threesome. His dark, almost black hair was in disarray, not an unusual occurrence; although quite manageable, combing his hair wasn't one of Smoky's priorities in life. His round face with a square jaw and ears that seemed a little large didn't make him the handsomest boy around; but with his outgoing personality and friendly smile, he made out just fine. Unlike his sister he didn't acquire his father's quiet disposition. It took very little to set him off and he was ready to fight at the slightest provocation.

Eli (Junior) Bledso flanked Smoky on the right, while his brother Luther walked on his left. They could have passed for twins, both being tall lean boys about four inches taller than Smoky. They were born in the same year, one in January and the other in December. They had red hair that was usually needing a visit to the barber shop. Junior's was straight, while his brothers was curly and for that reason he had been given the nickname Curly. Their hazel eyes set on handsome slender faces with just a few freckles to go with their red hair. They had a less than desirable home life, being raised by their grandmother, after their mother had run away when they were very small. They seemed to get in trouble here and there, sometimes it was a well thought out plan, but most of the time it was just a case of not knowing any better.

Jumbo, not feeling they could be trusted, watched them carefully as they approached. The boys were within six feet of him when he decided they were close enough. Jumbo wanted to emit a threatening bark, but from past experience, knew how much his ribs would hurt; perhaps a premonitory growl would be enough.

They stopped when they saw the hair stand up on his back and he passed off his warning.

"What's the matter with him?" Smoky took a step back, his dark eyes showing a certain amount of alarm. Junior and Curly followed Smoky's lead.

"Can't you see, he's been hurt." Millie pointed to the open wound on his shoulder.

"I can see that. I mean with this growling business?"

"Oh! I don't know. Maybe, he thinks you're going to hurt him." She run her hand across his back. "They mean you no harm."

Curly took a step closer. "He sure is an unusual color . . . almost looks like a ghost . . . I think I'll call him the Ghost Dog. Maybe you're not as bad as you act . . . huh . . . Ghost Dog." Curly stepped closer, reaching out his hand.

Jumbo snapped at his hand when he felt it was getting to close. He quickly jerked his hand back. It was only another threat but it made a believer out of Curly. "I think he might bite."

"You think he'll bite. I know he'll bite," Smoky exclaimed. "You better get away from him Millie. I think he's dangerous."

"He's alright, he likes me. Let's put him upstairs in the room with the boarded up windows."

"You're crazy Millie. Ain't no tellin' what he might do, ya lock him up there," Smoky pleaded. "Besides he might have the hydraphobie or something."

"Smoky it's hydrophobia and he don't have it. Now get, get out of my way. I'm taking him upstairs . . . I'll take care of him."

Smoky and the Bledso brothers ran ahead as she started toward the house, with Jumbo walking at her side.

Smoky turned to face Millie as he reached the porch. "I'm going to tell Daddy. He'll know how to deal with a mean dog."

"I don't want you to tell him . . . not just yet."

"I'm tellin', just as soon as I get home."

"You better not!"

"I'm tellin'," Smoky taunted.

"You're not going to tell. And you know why?"

"Why?" Smoky stuck out his jaw, as if daring her to answer.

"Because, if you do, I'm going to tell Daddy about the wine you're making upstairs." She pointed to the upper floor of the old house.

"You will not!"

Millies' face was flushed, one could almost see small sparks of fire dance from one eye to the other. "I'll tell him about that tobacco you got hid in the kitchen too, and how you tricked Big Becky into helping you get it and the sugar too, by kissing her in the back of the grocery store.

"I never kissed Becky the Behemoth." Smoky with fist clinched denied the accusation.

"You did too, Junior, Curly, you was there. Did he kiss her?"

"Well, sort of," Junior responded.

"That's right . . . sort of . . . I didn't kiss her, she kissed me." Smoky clinched his teeth.

"It don't matter, it was still kissin'. I'll tell Daddy my version, it sounds better," she smiled.

The boys stepped up on the rickety old porch floor. Jumbo's alert eyes watched them cautiously, least they make any sudden moves. He grumbled, just a little, to let them know he wasn't in the mood for any pranks.

They backed up almost to the front door. "See! I told ya . . . he's mean." Smoky moved into the doorway. "What ya gonna do with him anyway?"

"Tame him down . . . then I'll take him home and show him to Daddy."

"You don't know nothin' 'bout tamin' a dog like that . . . besides he likes you."

"I guess I'll have to get a boy to help me."

"No boy around here that dumb," Junior spoke up.

"Yeah, who you goin' to get to help you?"

"Charlie Mayfair, he'll help me."

"Charlie Mayfair don't know anything about tamin' mean dogs." Curly chimed in.

"I'll bet he does, he likes animals and they like him."

"How you goin' to get him over here anyway."

"I'll invite him to my birthday party Friday night."

"He won't come to your dumb old birthday party."

"He will too."

"Will not," Smoky shouted.

"If he won't come, you'll have to help me get him over here."

"I ain't helpin' you do nothin'."

"Yes you will, if you don't . . . I'll tell Daddy about your wine. He'll give you a whoppin' like he did when you burned down the outhouse."

"Well, ah, ah, I guess I could try to get him over here. You know, I think I might just have a better idea than your birthday party." Smoky looked up at the ramshackled porch roof. "Yes, sir, I just might have this figured out."

"What you thinkin' Smoky?" Junior looked suspiciously at him.

"Well, your dad and my dad are going to try and hunt down Ol Razor Saturday morning. Knowin' Charlie Mayfair, like I do . . . he just might like to get in on that. If his Mom would let him stay the night, he could come over Friday night and make that hog hunt Saturday morning. Millie when we get home you tell Mom how bad

19

you want Charlie to come to your birthday party. Maybe, we can get her to help us out."

"She will, she likes Charlie," Millie smiled.

"I'll call him soon as you get it squared away with Mom."

"No, we got time . . . almost a week, you write him a letter."

"I hate writin' letters."

"I don't want you talking on no party line . . . to many rubbernecks, they might figure out what's going on. Get out of my way, I'm taking him upstairs." Millie coaxed Jumbo onto the porch. The boys quickly went into the house ahead of her, slipping in the kitchen and closing the door behind themselves.

CHAPTER 4

It was early Friday afternoon when Herb Taylor turned the forty-nine Chevy pickup down the Elliot driveway. The wrinkles on his face and the slightly stooped shoulders were an indication of the hard life he had lived. Herb Taylor had been breaking and training horses since he was twenty years old; the long hours in the hot sun and the numerous bumps, bruises, falls, and broken bones had taken their toll on his body, both his arms had been broken as had his right leg. The leg gave him some problems, being stiff and not wanting to bend as it should. His quiet, modest, peaceful, demeanor had made him somewhat of a loner; even more so since his wife had passed away in the spring.

He shifted his long lean torso in the seat, as he spoke to his Grandson sitting beside him. "Charlie, I want you to be real careful, if you catch up with that old boar tomorrow morning. He's a dangerous animal. He could hurt you real bad. Hogs have been known to kill people you know. They'll eat a human body up too. People been known to get away with murder just by tossin' a body in the pig pen and leaving the hogs eat it up.

Charlie Mayfair opened his blue eyes just a bit as he listened to his Grandfathers remarks. A red ball cap set neatly on his head nearly covering his short blonde hair. He was a slender built young man, with long legs, handsome facial features, a soft spoken voice, and friendly smile, attributes that made him quite a charmer as far as the young ladies were concerned; to say nothing of the fact that their mothers felt he would certainly be acceptable as a son-in-law.

At fifteen years of age, his easy going gait and level headed thinking were traits that set him apart from the other boys his age. Charlie's interest in the fairer sex amounted to nothing more than a passing glance and a friendly, "Hi." He was more interested in going on an all day fishing trip, or taking the dogs, who were riding in the back of the pickup, on a little hunt. That is if he could pull himself away from trying to break some half wild mustang that his Grandfather thought needed a little work.

Charlie picked at a blister on his hand. "I'll be careful."

"I know you will. I doubt your mother would have let you go if I wouldn't have talked her into it. Don't let me down."

"I won't."

"Your hands pretty sore?" He asked, as two of the Elliots' hounds started up the drive to meet them.

"Sort of, back and legs hurt too."

"Well, thanks for cleaning out the horse barn for me."

"Seems like a lot of work, just to go on a hog hunt and stay over here for the weekend." .

"The barn needed cleaning and I figured that was the best way to get it done."

"You sucker punched me Gramps."

"Yeah, someday you'll grow up to be smart like me." Herb Taylor grinned as he watched the two dogs approach the truck.

"I can only hope," Charlie smiled.

Zip and Zebo the two dogs riding loose in the back of the pickup suddenly came to life, leaning over the sides of the bed barking and growling as the Elliot hounds run up beside the truck.

Zip showed a lot of Shepherd characteristics, his true ancestry was unknown, he was a tan colored dog with a black muzzle and medium length course hair. He was a good stock dog, but his favorite past time was catching rabbits, raccoons, skunks, snakes, and anything else that took his fancy at the time, including box turtles.

Zebo looked to be full hound; however, his redish-tan color wasn't true to any purebred breed. His big flat head was flanked on each side by large drooping black ears that hung loosely around his face. He stood on long straight legs that were certainly adequate to support his large body. His eyes always seemed to be open too wide, causing him to have a wild look in the eye, not a true hound trait.

"Hey, cut that out. Zip, Zebo, shut up." Charlie scolded as he stuck his head out the window. "Hope they don't get in a fight."

"They won't."

"How you know that?"

"Because Zebo won't fight and Zip's not going to fight two dogs. He's too smart."

"Zebo's got a paper heart . . . he never fights."

"What do you think our chances of catching that old boar are?" Charlie adjusted his cap.

"Slim and none." Herb Taylor braked the truck to a stop under a large oak tree that stood just a short distance from the Elliots front door.

Smoky and Millie were already waiting in the front yard.

The dogs were still making each others presence known, when a deep voice spoke up from behind the pickup. "Joker, Tess get out of here we don't need all this racket." The voice belonged to Smoky and Millie's father, John (Possum) Elliot.

Joker and Tess quieted down and backed off a short distance, keeping a close eye on the two strange canines in the back of the truck.

Zip and Zebo were still leaning over the side of the pickup, emitting sharp barks and threatening growls. "That's enough, shut up, Zip, Zebo quiet up." Herb Taylor ordered as he got out of the pickup. They quieted down but the hair was still standing up on their backs.

"Herb, lets put your dogs behind the chicken house. I think they'll be alright once they get acquainted. You can drive down there, follow me." Possum started walking in the direction of the chicken house.

Herb was getting back in the truck as Charlie was getting out his suitcase.

"Charlie, let's get your stuff upstairs, we got things to do." Smoky spoke excitedly.

They started to the house as the pickup pulled away, Joker and Little Tess followed at a safe distance.

It was a large, square built, two story house with lots of windows. The front porch was screened in and run the full length of the house. It was freshly painted white with pea green windows and screens. Not a fancy house by most standards but certainly adequate for shelter and raising a family.

"You staying all weekend?" Millie walked backwards to the front door ahead of Charlie.

"Yep, I had to clean the horse barn so I could stay. I didn't think I would ever get done, but I did. Look at my hand." He held out his right hand so she could see the blisters.

"Ouch! You poor guy. Do they hurt?" She asked sympathetically.

"They sure do. Got some on the other hand too" He switched the suitcase to his right hand so he could show her the water filled sores on his left hand.

"Maybe Mom's got something to put on those blisters...I'll ask her. Charlie, what ever you do don't say anything about the Barnes' place, or the dog, around the folks."

"I won't . . . when am I going to see this dog?"

"It won't be long, just as soon as Junior and Curly get here." Smoky whispered, as they stopped at the front door.

They entered the house and found Florence Elliot finishing up the dinner dishes. Her warm loving nature was most evident around children, it seemed she wanted to mother every child she came across and for this reason most of them called her Mom Elliot; in turn, she always called them by their given names, never using nicknames. She was a tall attractive woman, with light brown hair showing just a little gray. She wore her hair in a bun on top of her head most of the time. Her hazel-green eyes sparkled as she turned to face Charlie. She smiled while drying her hands on a blue and white apron that she was wearing around her slender waist.

"Charles! I'm glad you could make it." She gave Charlie a tender hug and stepped back to look him over. "My word you've grown. Looks like you're going to spend the weekend."

"Yes ma'am . . . spent two days cleaning the horse barn, just so I could come over here. Look at these blisters."

"Oh my word, Milacent, get me that Bag Balm out of the cupboard. You poor boy . . . pretty sore aren't they."

"Yes ma'am, sore as all get out."

Millie returned with a square green can that contained a yellow salve that was normally used on the farm to keep the milk cows teats soft and to keep them from getting chapped and sore in cold weather.

"This will help take the soreness out of your hands." Mom Elliot carefully rubbed the ointment in the palms of Charlies' hands. "Try not to get grease all over everything you touch."

"Yes ma'am."

"Now, you kids can find something to do for awhile, but be close to the house about four o'clock, I'm going to need a lot of help with this party. Milacent, show Charles where to put his stuff."

"Sure Mom," Millie replied. "Come on Charlie."

The boys followed Millie upstairs and when she reached the top, she ushered Charlie into a room that looked to be nearly square. The only furniture was an iron bed covered with a pale blue bedspread that set in one corner and a small freshly painted white dresser that sat against the opposite wall. It was a corner room with two windows surrounded by blue and white gingham curtains. The walls were covered with blue flowered wallpaper on a white background.

24

"This will be your room. Have you got anything you want t
up?" She reached in a small closet and pulled out a wire hanger.

"Naw, not really. Tell me about this dog?" Charlie sat down on tne
bed, an anxious look on his face.

Smoky closed the door before he spoke. "Me and the Bledso
brothers was makin' wine at the Barnes' place."

"Making wine!"

"Be careful, don't talk to loud," Millie warned.

"Tell me about this dog?"

Millie sat down beside Charlie on the bed. "I was outside setting
on the porch, when this big dog comes out on the trail that leads to the
house. I walked down the trail toward him, he just stood there
watching me. As I got closer, I started talking to him, it wasn't long
and he came over to me. He had a bad cut on his shoulder . . . it was
still bleeding. I petted him and he licked my hand, he seemed real
friendly."

"Yeah friendly, not to us boys."

"That's for sure, when they came down the trail, the hair stood up
on his back and he started growling. Scared me."

"Didn't scare me."

"What do you mean, didn't scare you. I didn't see you getting to
close to him."

"Not so loud," Smoky cautioned "Curly tried to put his hand on
him, almost pulled back a bloody stub."

"So what did you decide to do with him?" Charlie, stood up and
opened his suitcase.

"Well, with a little coaxing, the boys decided to help me and we
put him in one of the upstairs rooms. He's been there ever since . . .
except when I take him out for exercise."

"What's he look like?"

"He's a big dog, must weigh two hundred pounds."

Millie quickly rebuked her brothers statement. "He's not that big."

"Close to it. Got short ears and kind of a blue-grey color. Curly
calls him the Ghost Dog."

"Luther and Eli are here." Mom Elliot called, from the bottom of
the stairs.

"We'll be right there." Millie took the lead as Charlie and Smoky
followed.

Junior and Curly Bledso were standing just inside the kitchen door, both wearing old worn out cotton shirts and bib overalls that weren't much better.

Everyone exchanged "Howdy's" and quickly slipped out the kitchen door.

Mom Elliot had the final word. "Don't forget to be back by four o'clock. You hear me?"

"We hear you." Millie shouted, as the door slammed shut.

Millie once again had taken the lead as they trotted toward the barn.

The barn was only a hundred yards from the house. It was a small barn by most standards, but certainly adequate for milking the cows and shelter for livestock when it was needed.

They entered the barn single file, once inside, Millie immediately went to the back of the barn and pulled a gallon jug of milk out of some hay bales that were stacked against the wall. "Here Smoky, you carry this." She handed Smoky the milk and reached between the bales and pulled out a brown paper sack, filled with table scraps. "That should do it. Let's go."

CHAPTER 5

It was a twenty minute walk to the Barnes' place. Charlie had taken the lead as they neared the farmstead. Millie raced to keep up with him as the rest of the boys fell behind.

"Slow down, Charlie, your walking like there's no tomorrow."

"I'm sorry, I guess I'm just anxious to see this dog you been telling me about."

"Well! You don't have to run my legs off. Do you? I mean he's not going any place."

"I guess you're right." Charlie slowed his pace as they neared the trail that would lead them up to the house.

"Where did you first see him?"

"Right up there." She pointed to the spot where Jumbo had come out of the weeds.

"Where do you suppose he came from?" Charlie stopped and looked around, while digging in his pocket for a package of chewing gum.

"I don't have any idea, but I don't think he belongs to anyone around here."

"Why do you say that? Gum." He offered, as they continued to walk.

"No thanks. If someone had a dog like him around I'm sure we would have heard about it. Another thing, he's had a tough life, got scars all over his body. I think somebody really abused him and he run away."

"Hey! Wait for us," Smoky called.

"Well, hurry up poky, we're not going to wait all day for you." Millie stepped up on the unsound old porch floor.

"Yeah, hurry up poky." Charlie watched as the boys trotted up to the house.

Millie lead them through the dinning room, to a stairway that lead to the upper floor. There were five rooms upstairs, two large rooms on one side and three on the opposite side, divided by a narrow hallway. The one room was small, a storage closet.

They stopped at the first door on the right, one of the large rooms. Millie gave the door a shove, it scraped on the floor as she forcefully pushed it open.

She took the milk from Smoky and entered the room. Charlie was close behind.

The room was almost square with two windows. They contained no glass; some old boards were haphazardly nailed across them. A large bucket was setting near the door, it was half full of water. Millie had placed two old blankets in one corner for Jumbo to use as a bed. The only furniture was an old dresser, that he was using as a scent post. The smell of dog urine engulfed the room.

"Here boy, I got something for you to eat."

He was standing beside the blankets, wagging his tail and happy to see her. She was almost at his side when he spotted Charlie standing at the door. The hair stood up on his back, his lips raised to show glistening white fangs, short ears that could stand erect now lay flat on his broad head in a fighting mode, he roared his disapproval.

Charlie turned his head slightly and realized the boys had not followed him into the room. He slowly lowered his knees to the floor, hoping to make himself look less threatening.

Charlie thought for a moment about Curly calling him the Ghost Dog. His blue-grey color certainly gave him a ghost like appearance in the dimly lit room. Millie poured the milk in a pan that was sitting by his bed. He kept a close eye on Charlie as he began to lap up the milk.

Millie moved away from him and came back to the door. "Give me the food, Smoky."

Smoky handed Millie the food. She returned to his side and dumped the table scraps in the pan.

"See if you can get him to turn around. Let me see the cut on his shoulder you was telling me about."

Millie coaxed him to turn around by moving the feed pan.

"Sure looks nasty. He can lick it . . . can't he?"

"Yes, he can." Millie stood beside him with her hand on his back; flat footed he stood waist high on her.

"We could put some salve on that cut, but it wouldn't do any good, he would just lick it off." Charlie was still kneeling as Jumbo continued to cast an evil eye in his direction.

"How do you think he got that cut, Charlie? Smoky asked from the hallway.

"I don't have any idea. Got in a fight with something I'd say. You're right about one thing Smoky, he is big."

28

"What would be crazy enough to fight a dog that big?" Curly pondered.

"Something stupid," Junior replied.

"Or a critter that's as big as he is," Charlie added.

"Ain't nothing that big around here." Smoky poked his head in the door.

"Ol Razor is." Curly was quick to respond.

"I don't know why, but he might have gotten into it with that old boar. From the looks of him, he hasn't backed down from too many fights. Open that door a little more, I'm going to back out of here."

Charlie started to back out of the room. Jumbo stopped eating and intently watched his exit.

"I'm going to take him outside for some exercise as soon as he's done eating."

"You do that, but wait until we're clear of the hallway." Smoky extended his hand to help Charlie up. "What kinda dog you think he is?"

"Beats me, I've never seen a dog like that before."

"Why does he hate us so and like Millie?"

Charlie stopped to think for a moment. "For some reason he trusts her. He sure doesn't trust us."

"You think he'll ever trust us?" Curly walked ahead and turned the knob on the door across the hall.

"I don't know, maybe, it'll take some time. Any of you guys ever try to feed him?"

"No!" Smoky quickly answered. "One of us try to feed him, we might end up being dinner."

"It was just an idea." Charlie laughed, as Curly motioned him into the room.

"Not a very good one, I'd say." Smoky follow Charlie into the room.

The room was almost identical to the room they had just left, except that it was a little smaller. It was empty, the only exception, a five gallon crock container that set against the far wall. The crock was covered by a white dishtowel that had been carefully tied in place by a long piece of twine. The room had a sweet smell, the type of aroma that could only come from fermenting wine.

Smoky untied the twine and removed the dish towel.

"Where did you guys learn to make wine?" Charlie peered down into the working brew.

Smoky looked up from his squatting position. "We was in Uncle Ezra's barbershop one day, they were talking about making wine. By the time they were done talking, we had a pretty good idea on how to make wine. It's real simple all you need is some fruit, sugar, water and a little yeast.

"Where did you get the fruit?" Charlie watched as small bubbles worked their way through what looked like grapes.

"That was the easy part. We went down on Clear Creek and picked wild grapes."

"So, what was the hard part?"

"Getin' the sugar and yeast," Curly answered.

Smoky reached behind the crock and came up with a small tin cup, stuffed in a brown paper sack. He pushed some of the grapes aside and filled the cup half full of the purple potion. Everyone watched as he put the cup to his lips and took a sip. "Not bad." He smacked his lips as he handed the cup to Curly.

He took a good sized swallow. "Not bad."

"Let me try that." Junior snatched the cup from Curly's hand.

"I wouldn't drink that stuff if it was the last thing on earth to drink." Millie had entered the room. "There's worms in it."

Junior downed what was left in the cup. "There ain't no worms in this wine."

"Yes there is, I seen 'em. Little white ones."

"Now Millie, even if there was a worm or two in there, it wouldn't hurt anything. Besides, they won't drink much." Everyone laughed at Smoky's joke; except Millie.

"Ha! Ha! I hope you all get sick. Don't be looking to me for no sympathy."

"Want to try some?" Junior offered Charlie the empty cup.

"No thanks. I'll wait until it's done. How long will it take? Couple weeks."

"Oh, we're not waiting that long, maybe two or three days." Smoky grabbed the cup and fished out another small sip from the crock. He replaced the dishtowel, while still licking his lips.

"You guys about done in here? I want to take the dog outside." Millie waited at the door for an answer.

30

"Close the door and take him out we'll be down in the kitchen as soon as we're finished here." Smoky instructed, as he finished securing the dish towel. Junior and Curly watched him carefully, making sure he did it right.

"That should do it." Junior checked Smoky's knot.

Smoky stood up and strolled over to the door. He opened it a crack to see that the hallway was clear. "All clear." He pushed the door open.

They left the wine room and made their way downstairs, making a left turn at the bottom of the steps. They were in what had been the kitchen. The floor and walls still carried the scars of the fire, both being partially burnt. In the middle of the room was a table with three legs, one being broken off; a chair leaned against the wall that had the same problem.

Curly made his way to the only other furniture in the room, a small cabinet in the corner that was barely fastened to the wall. He opened the door that was only hanging on by one hinge. Reaching inside he pulled out an unopened can of Prince Albert smoking tobacco.

Junior had laid claim to the chair. He reached in his pocket and pulled out a package of cigarette papers, while trying to master the art of sitting on a three legged chair.

Curly and Smoky took a cigarette paper from Junior. They took turns pouring tobacco in the papers.

"You want to try one of these?" Junior offered Charlie.

"I think I'll pass."

"Oh, come on Charlie, it won't hurt you," Smoky added. "I'll roll one for ya."

"Might stunt my growth."

"I doubt that, you must be pushin' six foot."

"Only five-ten."

"Come on...try it. One won't hurt ya," Junior encouraged.

"No, I don't think so, Mom don't hold much with smoking and I promised her I wouldn't smoke. I try to keep my promises. Sorry."

Curly reached in his pocket and pulled out a wooden match. He struck it on the strap button of his bib overalls. The match popped like a small firecracker as it ignited. They took turns lighting their smokes.

Charlie made his way across the room to the cabinet. He carefully opened the door and found six cans of Prince Albert. "You guys have got quite a stash here. You never did tell me how you got the sugar to make that wine."

"Well, it's a long story," Junior grinned.

"Yeah, Smoky, why don't you tell Charlie how we got the sugar." Curly gave Charlie a sly wink and smiled.

"Sure I'll tell him. We helped Cedrick Miller hoe his watermelons and he paid us. We went to town and bought some sugar and yeast and made the wine." Smoky nervously paced in front of the table.

"Now wait a minute." Junior got up from his chair and stepped forward.

"Yeah, you didn't tell him all the good stuff. Charlie, let me tell you how this deal really went down." Curly was standing behind the table anxious to tell the story.

Charlie took a seat in a window that had been broken out for a long time. "Tell me."

"To begin with, we thought maybe, we would just take the sugar from Mom Elliot's pantry. We decided she would miss that much sugar and it would be hard to explain what we were going to do with it. Finally we decided we would just earn the money working for old man Miller. He gave us a job hoeing his watermelons."

"Worked us like Hebrew slaves," Junior interrupted.

"How much did he pay you?"

"Seventy-five cents a hour." Junior had sat back down on the chair.

"Let me tell my story. After we had the money, we had to buy the sugar and yeast without arousing any suspicion. We rode into town with Possum one Saturday afternoon. We still hadn't figured out how we were going to get the stuff we needed. We fooled around town for a little while. It was about two o'clock when we decided to go into Williamson's Grocery Store and look the place over. Becky Williamson was in the back of the store, she started talking to us."

Williamson's Grocery Store was set right in the middle of main street. The proprietor, Hap Williamson, had operated the store for nine years. He and his wife had one daughter and her name was Becky. She was nearly seventeen years old, not pretty and grossly over weight. Early in life, the children in town, not thinking about her feelings, had nicknamed her Becky the Behemoth. Although few were fool hearted enough to call her that to her face.

"She kinda took a liking to our boy, Smoky. She was making eyes at him and trying to run her fingers through his hair . . . you know, that lovey, lovey kinda stuff."

"Of course Smoky was trying to play hard to get." Junior took a drag on his cigarette.

Smoky was pacing back and forth, red faced, he tried to force a grin.

"Well, we saw the look in her eyes. So Junior asks her 'would she sell us some sugar and yeast.' She looked into Smokys' big brown eyes. One of them pitiful looks."

"Charlie, they was as big as silver dollars." Junior got up from his chair.

"Scared," Charlie nodded.

"Becky, she says, 'I might if Smoky would give me a little kiss'."

Smoky wasn't smiling now.

"Oh boy!" Charlie put his hands on his head in disbelief.

She had worked us into the storage area in the back of the store. She didn't give Smoky a chance to say yes or no. Just grabbed him and threw him down on a stack of flour sacks." Curly moved behind the table, leaving Smoky on the other side.

Junior took up the story. "Put a lip lock on him right there."

"He was a kickin' and makin' funny noises. His face was turnin' blue. I think she would have smothered him if we wouldn't have been there to pulled her off." Curly jumped back into the story.

Smoky had taken all he was going to take. He stood in front of the table, threw his cigarette on the floor and stomped on it with his foot. His face was beet red and the rage in his eyes was quite apparent.

Junior joined Curly behind the table. They knew he was about to go off and someone was going to get hit.

He was smaller than the other boys, but one could easily be fooled by his short stock frame. He was a handful to handle in the heat of battle. They knew that from past experience; having all tried him at different times.

Charlie remained seated in the window watching Millie and Jumbo as they played on the buffalo grass in front of the house. He was somewhat amazed at how gracefully and quickly he moved around the yard; taking into consideration his size. The affectation he showed for Millie was quite noticeable as he tried to lick her face. "Better put him up, Millie. We need to get back to the house."

"O.K.," she answered.

"Yeah, it's time to go." Junior moved toward the door, happy to be getting out of there without exchanging blows with Smoky.

"Wait 'till she gets the Ghost Dog put up."

Junior closed the door. Smoky's face was still red, but he was slowly cooling down.

Jumbo growled just a little as they passed by the kitchen door; just to let the boys know he knew they were there.

Junior opened the kitchen door when he heard the door close upstairs. "Mil, has he got plentya water?"

Millie was already coming down the steps. "Half a bucket."

"That'll hold him 'till tomorrow." Smoky took the lead as they carefully crossed the old porch floor. Silently they left the Barnes' place walking side by side, enroute back to the Elliot farm.

Charlie finally broke the silence. "Mil, who's going to be at this birthday party?"

"Some of the girls from school. I think Mrs.Williamson is coming out to help, of course that means Becky will be there."

"You mean she's going to be there?" The color was leaving Smoky's face, he had suddenly taken on a sick look.

"Of course she's coming, you know Mom and Mrs. Williamson are good friends. And besides, Becky never misses cake and ice cream."

"Damn the luck." Smoky gave an old dried up cow paddy a kick.

"Now Smoky, you know you'll be glad to see her," Junior taunted.

"Like heck, I don't care if I ever see her again."

"Oh, you don't mean that," Curly added. "Make the best of it. Maybe you can lure her down to the barn and practice your kissin'."

"But don't be expecting us to rescue you this time," Junior warned. Everyone broke into uproarious laugher, except Smoky, his face was changing colors, again.

"You know if she's going to be there . . . I might just go hide someplace."

Millie stopped and grabbed Smoky's arm, spinning him around to face her. "Don't be talking like that, you're going to be there."

"No, I ain't"

"Yes you are. Smoky if you don't like her maybe you should just tell her," Millie snapped.

"She's not going to take that to good," Junior cautioned.

"I mean it. Why don't you guys just tell her you were buttering her up, so you could use her to get your sugar and tobacco. Tell her your sorry, apologize and end it."

Smoky was facing Millie, now he glanced at Junior and Curly, shuffling his feet, he announced his decision. "Your right Mil, that's what I'm going to do."

"Now wait a minute. Let's not make any snap decisions here." Curly quickly spoke up.

"Curly's right, you better think this over."

The Bledso brothers had suddenly realized that their supply of smoking tobacco was about to go down the pipes.

"You'll break her heart," Junior pleaded.

"Better her heart than my back." Smoky turned and walked away. He turned back around to look at Charlie. "What do you think?"

Charlie hesitated a moment, he looked at Millie and than back at Smoky. "Millie's got the right idea, best to end it now. She's too old for you anyway."

"Now how do I tell her?"

"We'll think of something," Charlie answered.

CHAPTER 6

They were met at the front door by Mom Elliot when they returned to the house.

"Richard you get down to the barn and help your dad milk the cows. He's already started. Milacent you can feed the bucket calves . . . then get cleaned up. From the looks of you that's going to take awhile. Where's Luther and Eli?

"They went home. They're coming back later." Millie turned leading the way to the barn.

"I hope so. Charles, wait here, I've got a special job for you." Mom Elliot was barking orders like a drill sergeant. Charlie came to attention as she turned and went back in the house. Smoky and Millie continued their trip to the barn. Charlie waited at the front door.

Mom Elliot returned shortly, carrying a large wooden bucket ice cream freezer.

"You can start freezing this ice cream. Find yourself a comfortable place to sit under that tree." She handed Charlie the freezer and pointed at the old oak tree in the front yard.

Mom Elliot had decided the house should be built where it was, so she could have an oak tree in the front yard. It was a big tree and its long leafy branches provided ample shade for anything that went on in the Elliot farm yard. Picnics were held there quite frequently and it was Possum's favorite place to repair machinery.

Charlie had just set the freezer down when Mom Elliot returned from the house carrying a bucket of freshly crushed ice. "Here's the ice. I'll get you some salt." She spun around and returned to the house.

Charlie moved an old iron seat with legs welded on it over to the freezer. The seat had came off some old horse drawn machinery that could still be found scattered around the farmstead. Possum always liked to have a nice place to rest, and seats like these were common place around the Elliot farm.

Charlie almost had the freezer filled with ice when Mom Elliot returned with the salt. "You'll have to use quite a bit of salt with this freezer," she instructed. "Once it starts freezing, don't let it set or the dasher will freeze up." She helped fill the freezer.

Charlie started cranking the freezer as Mom Elliot returned to the house. It wasn't long before Joker and Little Tess decided to pay him

36

a visit. They soon made their presence known. Tess by trying to lick his face, while Joker had his hind leg lifted intending to relieve himself on the ice bucket. Charlie cuffed him in the ribs before he got the job done and pushed Tess away from his face.

Little Tess was Possum's favorite dog. She had a friendly disposition and her out going personality made her hard not to like. She was cherry red with four white stocking feet. Her small frame comfortably carried forth-five pounds of pure muscle; in her chest beat the heart of a true hunting hound.

She had settled down and was sitting about five feet from Charlie and the ice cream freezer. Joker was restlessly moving around, still trying to figure out how he was going to mark the ice bucket.

Joker was a big hound, nearly twice the size of Little Tess. His tan legs were long and straight. He stood proudly displaying the jet black saddle, that depicted his black and tan ancestry.

He too finally lay down just a short distance from Little Tess.

"How's the ice cream doing?" Millie walked up behind Charlie, still carrying an empty milk bucket.

"Pretty good . . . I guess. Get the calves fed?"

"Yeah."

"How many is there?"

"Nine." She picked up a bucket that was handy and moved it over beside Charlie. She sat down—ladylike.

"So you all excited about this birthday party?"

"Oh, I guess, I think Mom's getting too worked up over the whole thing."

"I need to add some more ice to this thing."

"I'll do it." She jumped up and began adding ice to the freezer.

"This party will be a lot of fun. You'll enjoy it. Besides, I bet, your going to get some real nice presents."

"Oh, I'm sure we'll all have a good time. I don't know about getting a lot of presents."

"You'll be surprised at how many presents you're going to get. I know you're going to get one."

"How you know that?"

"Because I brought it."

"Charlie did you get me a present. What did you get me?" Her attractive eyes were wide with excitement.

"Oh, I can't tell you, it would spoil the surprise," he teased.

He couldn't have told her even if he wanted too. His mother had picked up the present when she was in town, and he had never asked what she had bought.

"It won't matter. Tell me what it is?" She stood in front of Charlie begging.

"I can't."

"Yes, you can. Just tell me. I'll act surprised when I open it later." She looked at Charlie her soft blue eyes pleading.

"No, I won't tell you, but I could give it to you now. I guess I could do that. It's upstairs in my suitcase. Can you crank this ice cream?"

"Yes I can, move over." She excitedly pushed Charlie out of his seat. "Hurry up, go get it."

It was a welcome break and his walk slowed down considerably once he was out of Millie's sight. Once upstairs he sat down on the bed and began digging through his suitcase, looking for her present. What ever he had gotten her was in a small flat box, wrapped in white and pink paper with a pink bow on top.

Millie gave Charlie one of those, what took you so long looks, when he finally returned. Small beads of perspiration where starting to form on her forehead.

"Is your arm getting tired?" He tried to sound concerned.

"Yes, it is. This wasn't one of your tricks just to get me to crank this ice cream freezer . . . was it?"

"No tricks!" He showed her the present. She stood up and took it eagerly.

Charlie returned to cranking the freezer, while she carefully opened the present.

"Oh Charlie, it's beautiful!" She happily held up a little gold necklace, with a gold heart shaped locket dangling from it. "This is really nice, Charlie. I like it! Thanks!"

"You're welcome. It's just something I picked up in town," he lied.

A surprised look came over her face, when she popped the heart open. "Charlie, you even put your picture in it."

"I wh," he choked back the words for fear she might find out he didn't even know what he had brought her. "I . . . wanted you to have it. He was buying his own presents from now on, his mother must have lost her mind, he thought to himself.

38

"Charlie, I'm glad you gave me this. I'm going to wear it to the party."

"Don't get too carried away, Mil, it's just a little present," he pleaded.

"It's the best present I've ever gotten, ever." She jumped up and gave him a big hug and before he could say anything she was running for the house to show Mom Elliot.

His mother had really done it to him this time. He had found new energy and was really giving that freezer a spin when Mom Elliot come out of the house. "You don't have to crank it that fast. Here Charles, I brought you a hamburger. I'm sorry I didn't have time to make you a decent supper."

"That's fine."

"Here let me crank that, while you eat."

She handed him a plate with a hamburger and a few chips. He moved aside and she took over the crank.

"Say, this is really coming along. You are really doing a good job. That was a nice present you gave, Milacent. Did you pick it out yourself?"

"Ah . . . mother helped me pick it out."

"Well, it was very nice and she really likes it. I think she is going to wear it to the party tonight."

"I know, that's what she told me."

"What did you kids do this afternoon?"

"Nothing much, just went for a walk. Here let me crank that thing," Mom Elliot was asking too many questions.

"No, finish eating your hamburger. I'm not in that biga hurry."

Charlie silently finished eating his burger and chips, when he had finished, Mom Elliot got up and wiped her hands on the red and white apron she was wearing. "Keep up the good work, Charles. You should be done in thirty minutes or so."

"I'll try, I hope it doesn't take any longer than that."

Charlie was sore from the barn cleaning incident, and bending over the ice cream freezer wasn't helping one bit.

Mom Elliot returned to the house, leaving him alone with Little Tess and Joker for company. "How's she doin', Charlie?" Possum had quietly strolled up behind Charlie.

"Pretty good . . . I think."

Lon D. Haden

He moved over another homemade seat, and sat down beside Charlie. Possum wasn't particularly handsome and easily carried an extra twenty-five pounds on his five foot ten inch frame. The extra weight a compliment to Mom Elliot's good cooking.

He was well respected in the community and many times his advice was sought before people made major decisions. Everyone knew of his honesty and his integrity was unquestionable. It wasn't unusual for someone to tell Possum something that they had never told anyone else. He knew a lot about everybody but he seldom told anyone, and if he did, it was someone he was sure he could trust.

Everything Possum owned he had earned through hard work and his own ingenuity.

****

He was in his early teens when his father was rendering lard, in a large cast iron kettle. It was a cold miserable day and had snowed some the night before. The snow had covered up a frozen dirt clod, no bigger than a grapefruit, but this would become an instrument of death. His father was adding more wood to the fire, when he stumbled over the frozen dirt clod and plunged head first into the boiling lard. He was in a deplorable condition when help arrived. He died a short time later.

Possum was the man of the family and, somehow, he had to figure out a way, to help support his mother and two younger sisters. The whole country was in an uncompromising depression. Kansas and many other states were in a severe drought, which brought about the era known as the Dirty Thirties. The picture was not a pretty one, for the Elliot's or many of the other families in the area.

Possum or John as he was known in his early years, liked to read. Somewhere, he had found a book entitled, THE ART OF TRAPPING MINK. He read and studied the book every chance he had.

He knew there were some traps hanging on the wall of the old shed behind the house. The Smoky Hill River would surely be a likely spot to find mink. Upon further investigation, he found that rich ladies had a taste for the beautiful coats, that the mink's luxurious and elegant fur could produce. He also discovered that even during these hard times, when men were working for a dollar a day, the mink's fur was a valuable commodity.

40

He scrubbed and cleaned up the old traps, as best he could. The traps were then boiled in walnut husk to destroy any scent that might be left on them.

Winter was beginning to set in when he took off for the river, hoping to catch just one mink. Loaded down with his traps and whatever equipment the book said he might need, John (Possum) Elliot, made the long walk to the river.

He cautiously walked the river, trying to find the perfect spot to place every trap, painstakingly he made every set, just like the book instructed, until he had covered nearly a mile and a half of river.

He returned home in time to help his mother and sisters milk the cows and do the evening chores. Possum was exhausted and forced himself to eat some supper. He went to bed early.

Morning came too soon. Possum rolled out of bed just in time to help do the chores. He wanted to check his trap line, but this was Monday, a school day. He was afraid to ask his mother if he could skip school. He was already anticipating what her answer would be, considering he was two years behind most of the children his age.

The next morning he woke up bright and early. He was well rested and full of energy. The family was eating breakfast when Possum worked up enough nerve to ask his mother if he could skip school and check his trap line.

Her answer was a stern, "No."

He went to school, but his mind certainly wasn't on his studies. He returned home that evening with his mind made up. The next day he was going to check his traps.

Possum didn't wait until breakfast to start working on his mother. He started the minute his feet hit the cold floor. He was relentless and by breakfast she had given in to his wishes. She knew her son too well, his mind was made up, even if she said no, he would sneak off from school and head for the river. He had pulled that trick on her before.

It turned out to be a bright, sunny day and unusually warm for that time of the year. Possum made it to the river in record time and before the day would end, Possum would make a startling revelation. He could out think, out smart, and capture one of the wiliest little critters that God had ever turned loose on the Kansas prairie.

He returned home with two large buck mink and a small female, certainly a respectable catch for even a seasoned trapper.

The winter passed quickly, as time usually does when your luck is running on the good side. The days started getting longer and Possum knew it was time to pull his traps, spring was just around the corner.

During the winter, word had gotten around that Possum was running a trap line on the river. Possum's mother was a secretive type person and had warned him not to go around bragging about his good luck. He took his mother's words to heart and anytime he was asked if he was catching anything, he would always answer, "Just a few Possums." His answer satisfied everyone, as that was what most of the young boys caught on their trap lines.

On a Saturday morning, Mrs. Elliot and Possum loaded the winters catch and headed for Ellsworth to visit the local fur buyer.

They arrived at the fur buyers about mid-morning. Possum carried in the two gunny sacks, that contained his furs. Jimmy Schwerdtfeger, the fur buyer, came out of his office as Possum dropped the gunny sacks on the floor.

Several of the local loafers, soothsayers, and cob rollers had gathered around to take a look at Possum's catch. They all had a shocked look on their faces when this fourteen year old boy dumped two sacks of mink pelts on the grading table.

Schwerdtfeger looked in awe, "My word, son, you've got a pile of money here. I expected you had possums in them sack, you know what I mean. How'd you catch all these mink?"

"Just luck, I guess."

"Luck my foot, I ain't ever seen anyone bring in that many mink, if you know what I mean. I didn't know there was that many mink in the country. What kinda set you use to catch 'em?"

"Jist grade da boys firs, ver kinda in ah hurry," Possums mother intervened.

Schwerdtfeger began sorting the furs into three piles. When he had finished, he turned to face Mrs. Elliot, "Ma'am, if you and the boy will come into my office I'll give you a check."

"Din't vant naw check, vant cash money."

"Ma'am, the check will be good. I guarantee it."

"Mayba, so, but I'm ah vantin' cash money."

"Mrs. Elliot, I'm going to have to go to the bank and get some money, you know what I mean. I just don't keep that kinda money around here." He stood at the door, looking out the window, watching so no one took any of the valuable merchandise, lying on the table.

"Vell, how much ah money ve talkin' 'bout?" Possum's mother stood beside the fur buyer looking out the window.

"I haven't figured it out yet. Several hundred dollars, I guess."

"Yoa, yoa, kiddin'." She turned and looked at Possum.

"No, I'm not, this boy made more money this winter than most of the men around here made working. Ma'am, I'm not trying to tell you how to do your business, but I think you should come with me to the bank. My advice would be to put that money right into a checking account, if you know what I mean."

"I din't trust banks!" She was quick to reply.

"Well, you could put it in a safe deposit box. Then you could take it out a little at a time, as you needed it, you know what I mean."

"I guess ve could do dat."

"Believe me, that's the thing to do. There's some desperate people around here. They would do most anything for that kinda money. I'll make it known that you left the money in the bank."

They left town that day, with money in the bank, something they hadn't been able to do for a long time. They could buy seed for spring planting, and Mrs. Elliot could replace her aging flock of laying hens.

Everyone around tried to get Possum, to tell them how he trapped the mink, but he never would tell. Pretty soon, he was known as the Little Possum, because of his tight-lipped, secretive nature.

****

"How long does it usually take to get this ice cream hard, Possum?"

Possum, had pulled a pouch of tobacco out of his shirt pocket and was filling his pipe. "You just keep cranking . . . until you can't go no more. Then you open it up . . . if it's hard . . . you eat it." He lit his pipe.

"What if it's not hard?"

"I usually get a cup and drink it." He smiled, showing off the two teeth he had worn down holding his pipe.

"If I have to crank this much longer we might just have to get two cups."

Possum's belly quivered as he let out a loud chuckle. "Tell ya what Charlie . . . let me crank that thing for a little while. I put some milk in the wash house for your dogs . . . why don't you go feed 'em." Possum reached over and took charge of the ice cream.

Little Tess and Joker followed Charlie as he went to the wash house to get the milk. Zip and Zebo saw him coming and let out several yips and bawls.

Charlie slipped into the pen, making sure to keep Joker and Little Tess out. There was only one pan, he poured half the milk in it. Zebo claimed the pan, while Zip ate from the bucket. Joker crowded the fence. Zip pulled his head out of the bucket and complained, signifying he wasn't in a sharing mood.

Charlie waited for them to finish eating before returning to Possum and the ice cream freezer. Coming up on Possum's back side, he couldn't help noticing his salt and pepper hair sticking out from under a well used straw hat. Possum's stocky arms and broad shoulders had the ice cream freezer under complete control.

"Possum, do you think we have a chance of catchin' that old boar?" Charlie moved a seat over beside Possum.

"Maybe . . . but it won't be easy."

"Why do you say that?"

"Well, for one thing, we don't know where to start. I'm sure he's staying down there on the river . . . but. . . there's a lot of river and a lot of cover." He was still holding his pipe in his mouth; it had been out for sometime.

"I've heard he's been seen several miles off the river."

"That's true. . . but believe me . . . he always goes back to the river." Possum stood up. "I think this ice cream is done."

"So, we're going to hunt down on the river?"

"Unless someone makes a sighting tonight or early in the morning. Eli Bledso has put out the word . . . if anyone sees him . . . they're to let us know. If that doesn't work we'll hunt down around Cedrick Miller's place. He's been seen around there more than anyplace else . . . as far as I can tell anyway."

"It should be fun, even if we don't catch him."

"Son, this is not going to be a fun trip. That old boar is a dangerous animal and if we get lucky and catch him . . . you stay plenty far away. Because he could hurt you bad . . . maybe even kill ya." Possum had poured the water and dumped what ice was left in the freezer.

"Really! So you think Ol Razor is the most dangerous animal we ever had in this part of the country?"

"Most dangerous four legged animal."

"What you mean by that?"

"Man is the most dangerous animal."

"I never did think of man as an animal."

"Believe me Charlie . . . man is the most dangerous animal. He may walk on two legs, but that doesn't make him any less dangerous. You see man can reason, and he'll lie, cheat, deceive . . . all for his own personal gain. Ol Razor . . . he's just trying to survive in his own way. He doesn't want anything but food to eat, a place to rest, and to be left alone. The problem is he's interfering with man's well-being. He's destroying crops, people's property, and certainly capable of hurting someone . . . and he will someday."

"Why, do you say that?" Charlie scratched his head, as he tried to comprehend what Possum was saying.

"Because he was raised by man. He's been humanized . . . he doesn't fear man like a true wild animal. A wild animal always tries to stay away from people. Razor . . . he was fed and cared for by someone . . . so he doesn't necessarily try to get away when he sees a human. He's more daring and, therefore, more dangerous. It's a shame but the best thing to do . . . is destroy him."

"Maybe, we should just try to catch him, and pen him up, like other hogs."

"Too risky, he's got a mouth full of teeth that are sharp as razors. No telling, how many people or dogs might get hurt before we get that pulled off. Remember Charlie, stay away from him . . . because he sure could hurt ya."

"I'll be careful."

"I'm going to set this ice cream in the wash house. You go in the house and rest for awhile."

Charlie took Possum's advice.

CHAPTER 7

"Charlie wake up." The voice was loud, urgent, and onerous.

"Ah, what's the matter?" Charlie rolled over facing Smoky.

"You need to get up. The party has started, everybody is here, except Junior and Curly. I been lookin' all over for ya."

Charlie rubbed his eyes as he sat up on the side of the bed. "I, ah . . . must have dozed off."

"Charlie, before we go downstairs, we need to talk."

"About what?"

"About Becky, you told me you would help me figure out a way to get her off my back."

"Oh! Yeah, I did. Let's see." He reached for one of his shoes and began pulling it on.

"Come on, you said you would help me," Smoky pleaded..

"Well, be quiet and let me think." He finished tying his shoes, stood up, sat back down, untied his shoes and kicked them off.

"Now what you doin'?" Smoky gave Charlie an inquisitive look.

"I forgot, I brought clean clothes for the party." He reached in the suitcase and brought out a nearly new pair of jeans.

"Too bad you didn't bring some clean shoes, these don't smell so good."

"I did." Charlie reached in the suitcase and produced a pair of black loafers. "See."

"Good deal. Now what have you figured out?"

"I'm still thinking."

"Well, you better think of something pretty quick, or everybody is going to wonder where we're at." Smoky was pacing nervously at the foot of the bed. "I guess she is quite a bit older than you, maybe, some how, we could make her feel guilty about that."

"Like how?" A bewildered look appeared on his face.

"How about, sometime this evening, I'll bring up the difference in your ages. We'll talk about that and I'll try to get someone else involved in the conversation. Like Millie. When the time is right, you say something like, 'I'm not really interested in being anyone's boy friend.' Maybe we can work something out from there."

"I guess we could try that." A note of uncertainty in his voice.

Charlie wasn't real comfortable with the plan; but on short notice it was the best he could come up with.

He finished dressing and they made their way downstairs. There was a knock at the kitchen door as they neared the bottom of the stairs. Mom Elliot answered the door and welcomed Junior and Curly to the party. They hadn't gone to much trouble getting ready for the shindig, wearing the same clothes they had on that afternoon. The boys strolled into the living room where the festivities seem to be running in high gear.

Millie was setting at a round oak table, surrounded by five girls that were in her class at school. She was wearing a pink and white cotton dress with a pleated skirt. Her hair was down, draping freely on her shoulders. She smiled as Charlie entered the room, her eyes sparkled as she stroked the necklace and locket he had given her.

Charlie shyly smiled back, hoping no one would notice how smitten he was by her beauty, he quickly looked away.

Becky Williamson was sitting across the table from Millie, she turned to look at Smoky, who immediately looked down at the floor, trying to act as if he hadn't noticed her.

The girls were all wearing colored blouses and pleated skirts. Except Rosie Lopez who was wearing a red tight fitting dress, and Sandi Hendershot had chosen a white blouse and a tight fitting black skirt.

Sandi, a pretty, petite, dark-eyed brunette, stood beside Millie. She smiled at Smoky from across the table.

Smoky smiled back.

Becky didn't miss Sandi's flirtations, giving her a dirty look, through dark threatening eyes.

"Milacent, you better start opening your presents." Mom Elliot coaxed from the doorway. Five chairs set around the table and they were quickly filled by excited, happy, chattering girls. Sandi and Trinie Thompson were left standing. Sandi moved around the table until she was directly across from Smoky, who was standing with his back against the wall.

Millie began to open her presents. Becky continued to keep a close eye on Sandi.

Millie cautiously opened every present, being careful not to tear the paper or disturb any of the bows. By the time she had finished,

47

there was an assortment of jewelry, stationary, perfume and Mom Elliot had given her a fancy pink blouse.

"I want to thank you all. This is the best birthday I've ever had."

"Milacent, why don't you tell everyone where the locket came from?" Mom Elliot coaxed as Mrs.Williamson entered the dining room from the kitchen.

"Charlie gave it to me." Millie took the locket in her hand and held it out for everyone to see. "Look here!" She excitedly popped open the locket to show everyone the picture that was inside.

Everyone turned to look at Charlie standing with his back to the wall. His face had turned beet red. He was speechless, wishing he could find a place to hide.

Sandi came to his rescue. "I wish some boy would give me a locket with his picture in it." She gave Smoky a wide-eyed look.

Smoky fidgeted and looked down at the floor, blushing as he nervously shuffled his feet.

Becky saw what was happening and her face was flushed, but not from being embarrassed. She was hot.

"Let's eat." Mom Elliot interrupted, sensing the tension in the air. "You boys can eat in the kitchen."

The suggestion was welcomed and Smoky quickly took the lead as the boys moved to the kitchen. They sat down around the kitchen table, patiently waiting for the cake and ice cream.

Mrs. Williamson, who had been silent all evening, spoke in the living room. "Girls we haven't sang Happy Birthday to Millie. Let's do that."

The girls began to warble the Happy Birthday tune. Mrs.Williamson took the lead with a high pitched screeching voice that would send a cold chill down the back of the mightiest of men.

They hadn't finished their singing before an extra guest arrived in the kitchen. Becky the Behemoth moved a chair beside Smoky, squeezing her oversized torso between Smoky and Curly.

The birthday cake, which had been patiently waiting on the kitchen counter, was moved to the living room by Mom Elliot.

The silence was nearly deafening in the kitchen, as everyone waited to see what was going to happen next. The living room was more lively with the endless pandemonium of girl chatter as the candles were lit on the cake. The smell of burnt wax engulfed the house.

"Make a wish and blow out the candles." Mrs. Williamson coaxed from across the room. There was considerable hoopla as Millie blew out the candles on the first try.

Trinie Thompson a tall, slender built, dark eyed, quiet speaking girl, whispered in Millie's ear. "Did you make a wish?"

"I sure did." Millie looked back over her shoulder at Trinie.

Sandi was standing close enough to overhear Trinie's question. "What did you wish for?"

"Oh, I couldn't tell, it might not come true."

"I bet it had something to do with that locket." Sandi's remark, caused Charlie to fidget nervously in the kitchen.

Becky was giving Smoky her undivided attention fearing what the little vixen in the other room might be up to. Everyone watched as she made cow-eyes at Smoky; who in turn nonchalantly looked away, a move that wasn't taken lightly by Becky.

"You girls cut the cake and put a nice piece on five saucers for those that are eating in the kitchen." Mom Elliot returned to the kitchen and opened the ice cream freezer. "Charles, cranked the ice cream freezer and it certainly looks like he did a good job." She began dipping ice cream into some dishes that set beside the sink.

"It's about time he did something right," Junior quipped.

Charlie ignored his remark, while Curly and Smoky forced a weak laugh.

The cake and ice cream shuffle began, as the girls paraded in with the cake. Millie set a nice sized piece in front of Charlie. He politely thanked her. "Thank you."

As Charlie looked around the table it became quite apparent that Sandi had placed a hunk of cake in front of Smoky that was twice the size of anyone else's. Closer scrutiny reveled that somehow Becky had come up on the short end of the stick, when it came to passing out the cake. The dissatisfied look on her face was quite apparent as she took note of the situation.

Sandi, who was developing a little faster than the other girls her age, seemed to have a noticeable sway in her hips, which was being very poorly hidden by the tight black skirt she was wearing.

Smoky was keeping a close eye on every move as she picked up her ice cream. Everyone watched as she returned to the dining room, ice cream in hand.

Becky gave her a hostile look as she passed by; once out of sight, Smoky and the rest got the same look. Her face was red and under that short black hair, her ears had turned purple.

Mom Elliot could feel the tension building in the kitchen. She set a big bowl of ice cream in front of Becky, hoping to cool her off.

Everyone was uneasy as they ate their ice cream and kept their mouths shut.

Charlie had put his plan on hold, it looked as if a new romance was in the making. All that was needed now was for Sweet Sandi to swing and sway her way through the kitchen, one more time.

Mom Elliot, Mrs. Williamson, and the other girls were in the living room visiting, talking, giggling, and enjoying the festive occasion.

"Could I have a little more ice cream, Mrs. Elliot." Sandi asked, in a polite sounding voice.

"Sure, go help yourself."

Sandi appeared at the door, dish in hand.

"Right on cue." Charlie said, under his breath.

Everyone noticed the extra hip action as she moved through the kitchen to the ice cream freezer.

Smoky's infatuation was quite apparent as he watched her irrepressibly. Becky was about to explode as she looked at Smoky and then back at Sandi.

She whispered in Smoky's ear. "You like that."

"Looks nice."

"I'll show you nice . . . after all I've done for you." She pushed her chair back from the table, stood up, and carried her bowl to the ice cream freezer. "Give me some of that ice cream!" She demanded, as she pushed Sandi aside.

Sandi stepped back, surprised by her aggressive action. She watched Becky as she dipped out two huge spoonfuls of ice cream nearly filling the bowl and topping it off with chocolate syrup and strawberries. Becky gave Sandi a dirty look, as she returned to the table, stopping behind Smoky.

She took the ice cream bowl in both hands, turning it upside down on Smoky's head. Not satisfied, she lifted the bowl up and banged it down hard a second time. Smoky was feeling the wrath of a woman scorned, he gritted his teeth, too dumbfounded to speak. Becky the Behemoth was going ballistic. She turned to face Sandi, who was transfixed at the sink. "Now I'm going to take care of you, you little witch." She lunged at Sandi, grabbing two hands full of long brunette hair.

Sandi, came to life in a hurry, retaliating she snatched up a couple of hands full of hair herself. They were both screaming obscenities at each other while Becky was tossing Sandi around like a rag doll. Sandi was way over matched, giving up well over a hundred pounds to the much larger Becky, who was no longer holding Sandi by the hair, but had her in a death grip bear hug.

Sandi had managed to keep her right arm free, in desperation, she delivered a hard fist to the tip of Becky's nose. Blood began to drip freely from both nostrils. Becky hung on with the tenacity of a Pit Bull, slowly squeezing the air out of Sandi's lungs. In desperation she drew her fist back and with all the power she could muster delivered a sledgehammer blow to the bridge of Becky's nose. The pain from a broken nose was excruciating. Becky released her grip. Sandi fell to the floor gasping for air.

Charlie was trying to get up, when Mrs. Williamson rushed by and knocked him back in his chair.

"What have you done to my baby?" She screamed hysterically.

"She broke my nose." Becky was hanging onto the table with one hand and her nose with the other.

Sandi had drawn in a couple breaths and was slowly getting to her feet.

Mrs. Williamson, a heavy weight herself, grabbed Sandi from behind, capturing her in a bear hug for the second time.

Becky, seeing Sandi in a helpless predicament, drew her fist back prepared to deliver the coup de grace.

The rest of the girls had rushed into the kitchen followed by Mom Elliot. Realizing the trouble their little friend was in, they piled on Becky before she could deliver the fatal blow. Becky staggered backward as the girls hit her. She slipped and went down, taking out two chairs plus Junior and Curly, who weren't quick enough to get out of the way.

The girls were trying to get Becky under control. Sandi, somehow, broke loose from Mrs. Williamson's death grip. She jumped right in the middle of the fracas. Sandi was searching for Becky through a pile of human flesh; she was going for the jugular.

Mom Elliot and Mrs.Williamson were caught up in the middle of the battle, as they tried to restore some order to the situation.

Charlie hesitated to jump in the brawl, for fear he might end up like Junior and Curly, who were still trapped under the flailing mass of tangled arms, legs, and torsos. He was seeing sights he had never seen before and a couple, he hoped, he would never see again. The girls continued to use some very unladylike language, along with a considerable amount of hollering and screaming.

Mom Elliot, realizing the hopelessness of the predicament, looked at Smoky, who was still setting at the table, chocolate syrup and ice cream running down his face as a large strawberry hung precariously on the tip of his nose. He was in shock and couldn't move.

"Charles, go get John."

Charlie ran out the door to find Possum, who was just coming out of the barn, oblivious to the siege that had befallen Mom Elliot's kitchen.

"There's a fight. We need your help."

"A fight. Where?" He closed the corral gate, quickening his pace as he closed the distance between himself and Charlie.

"In the kitchen."

"Who's Smoky fighting with?"

"Not Smoky. The girls."

"What." Suddenly Possum understood the urgency of the situation. He broke into a trot as he raced for the front door.

Charlie was close behind.

Possum jerked open the door to get a first hand look at the battle, that had turned Mom Elliot's kitchen into a disaster area.

Mom Elliot and Mrs.Williamson were trying to keep Becky under control. Rosie Lopez and Julie Crabtree were trying to hold Sandi, while the rest of the girls had made a half moon around them, just in case the Behemoth got loose. Junior and Curly had finally gotten off the floor and had positioned themselves with the girls. Smoky had disappeared.

Possum moved toward Becky. "Let's try to get her out of here, you kids stay where you're at." He waved his hand at the group surrounding Sandi.

Possum, Mom Elliot, and Mrs.Williamson pushed, pulled and dragged Becky toward the door. She was still hurling obscenities at Sandi, who was sending them right back.

Becky set her feet at the door and refused to leave the war zone.

"Charlie. Help us." Possum begged, as Becky put a death grip on the door frame.

Mom Elliot and Mrs. Williamson were trying to dislodge her hands while Possum pushed on her back. Charlie put a shoulder in the small of her back and grabbed hold of the door frame for leverage. Her grip weakened as they forced her through the doorway.

She seemed to be wearing down a little as they guided her to the waiting automobile. She bulked as they tried to push her in the car.

"Get this car started and when we get her loaded, get out of here as fast as you can," Possum ordered Mrs. Williamson.

It took a considerable amount of pushing, prodding and brute force, but at last the oversized mad woman was loaded. Possum forced the door shut. Mrs. Williamson threw the Studebaker Champion in gear and sped down the driveway. Becky's head was hanging out the window, throwing some colorful language back in the direction of the group that had just loaded her.

"What was that all about?" Possum wiped his brow with his shirt sleeve.

Possum and Mom Elliot both looked at Charlie, waiting for an answer.

He tried to tell them what had transpired, leaving out some of the more pertinent details, feeling it wouldn't be in Smoky's best interest for them not to know how Becky had helped Smoky and the Bledso brothers get their smoking tobacco and the sugar for the wine. Charlie wasn't sure they bought his story, but when he finished, Possum just shook his head. Mom Elliot had a blank look on her face, still trying to figure out how so much could go wrong so fast.

"Well, Florence, let's go in and access the damage. I don't know, we've got a fifteen year old boy and he's already got the girls fighting over him. I got a feeling the next few years are going to be a real test."

They returned to the disaster area; it could be cleaned up, except for the two chairs that were beyond repair.

The girls all had scars from the battle. Their beautiful clothes were ruined, covered with blood and ice cream, to say nothing of the numerous rips and tears they all carried.

Millie had taken a punch in her right eye and it was already starting to swell shut and change colors.

Smoky returned to the kitchen. He didn't look too good, but he had cleaned the ice cream out of his hair.

The kitchen got real quiet as Mom Elliot prepared to speak. "John, take these girls home. I'll be talking to all your mothers tomorrow. So you might as well tell the truth when you get home."

Junior and Curly were already out the door before Mom Elliot finished her speech.

"And you three, clean up and go to bed." Mom Elliot had spoken.

CHAPTER 8

It was well before daylight when Possum came upstairs to wake Smoky and Charlie.

"Boys, if you want to make this hunt you better get up. We need to start early before it gets to hot."

"What time is it?" Smoky grumbled.

"Almost five o'clock. You better hurry up, breakfast is just about ready." Possum turned and left the bedroom, switching on the light as a parting gesture. The boys rubbed their eyes, begrudgingly, they got up and silently got dressed.

Mom Elliot had breakfast on the table by the time they made their way downstairs. The kitchen was completely cleaned up. No one would have ever guessed the mayhem and destruction that had taken place the night before. Bacon and eggs where already sitting on the table.

"Set down and eat Charlie." Possum motioned to a chair that was setting at his side.

Charlie filled his plate and passed the bacon and eggs to Smoky. Mom Elliot tossed them each a slices of toast, just as the phone rang in the living room. Possum answered the phone that was hanging on the wall.

"Hello."

Charlie watched Possum from where he was setting in the kitchen. His jaw dropped and a serious look appeared on his face. "No kidding!" He almost sounded excited.

It was Eli Bledso on the other end of the line and he certainly had Possums attention, he was doing way more listening than he was talking. "We'll be over in a little bit." He hung up the phone.

Possum, returned to the kitchen, a big grin on his face. "Boys, we're in luck, Ol Razor hit Grandma Bledso's garden this morning. Eli says she's madder than a hive of hornets. I guess she got a couplea shots at him with her shotgun."

"Did she hit him?" Smoky asked, through a mouth full of bacon.

"Yeah, I guess, but all she hit him with was bird shot," Possum laughed. "Tough hided as he is, that didn't do any more than send him on his way."

"John, be careful, there's no telling what that crazy old woman might do," Mom Elliot warned. She had sat down at the table, still in her house coat.

"We will . . . boys go out and load them dogs. I'll be right out."

Smoky pushed his chair back from the table, Charlie followed suit. They left half their breakfast on their plates and Mom Elliot was telling them about it as they cleared the kitchen door. "You boys finish your breakfast. John those boys haven't even finished their breakfast."

Possum's fifty-two Chevrolet Thriftmaster pickup was under the oak tree, with a poor excuse for a dog box already loaded.

Charlie ran down behind the chicken house to get Zip and Zebo. In the mean time, Smoky was calling for Little Tess and Joker. Before he got his dogs caught up, Smoky had their's loaded. Charlie had found some rope and made it into a lead. Zip and Zebo were dragging him to the pickup, eager to get the hunt started. Smoky helped load them in one side of the two compartment dog box. They secured the door and jumped in the pickup, waiting for Possum.

It was a short wait, shortly Possum emerged from the house, carrying a thirty-ought six bolt action rifle. He also had a twenty-two revolver, in a leather holster, strapped around his waist. Wearing bib overalls, a faded blue shirt with work shoes that were old and worn to the point of needing to be replaced, he slipped under the steering wheel, turned on the switch and hit the starter with his foot. The starter turned over the engine half a dozen times before it took hold and the motor started. The dogs began to bark and bawl, there was a sense of excitement in the air as Possum pushed the gear shift into low gear, snapped out the clutch and threw gravel as they left the yard.

The Bledso farm had been established by Luther Bledso in the early nineteen hundreds. The farmstead was well laid out, highlighted by a beautiful house, that in its prime, was the envy of everyone in the area. The house was certainly a sight to behold, but one couldn't help being attracted to the huge barn that set on top of a hill, some distance from the house. A large headhouse set in the middle of the roof. It was a known fact that if you climbed into the headhouse, you could see for miles. There was a reason for that, some of Luther Bledso's enterprises were not exactly on the up and up. Bledso was an unsavory individual with just a few immoral characteristics.

It was rumored that during prohibition he was one of the largest bootleggers in the state. Not only did he market his spirits locally, but a large part of it went to Kansas City. The people he dealt with there were even more unscrupulous than Luther.

Numerous stories surfaced from time to time as too how the operation was run. One was that the liquor was transported to Kansas City in a hearse complete with a coffin.

Another story was that Luther Bledso had laid some hard cash in the hands of several influential politicians, and that the local law enforcement people turned their backs on his operation. Luther Bledso was never caught doing any of his illegal activities, his liquor making facilities were never found and if there really was a hearse, no one knew where it had gone.

He died in August of 1942. His secrets went to his grave with him.

There was one person who knew more about Luther Bledso and his illicit affairs than anyone else. His wife was still alive and everyone figured she knew everything that went on at the Bledso farm. She was known as Grandma Bledso and she was the most cantankerous, sharp-tongued, ill-tempered, coldhearted old woman anyone would ever hope to meet.

Everyone was afraid of her, and she had very few friends. At times stories circulated around the area that she was into witchcraft or devil worship, but no one had any proof and most people figured she was just a little odd.

Grandma Bledso had one son by Luther Bledso and that was Eli. Eli took care of the farm, but everyone knew that Grandma made most of the decisions.

Eli was a tall, unusually handsome man with broad shoulders and a friendly smile, with all these fine attributes it comes as no surprise that he was quite popular with the ladies. To a fault, perhaps, because it was a known fact that some of his lady friends weren't exactly available.

He had married once and from that union came two sons. Eli Jr. and Luther or as most people called them Junior and Curly.

The marriage was a mistake. Grandma Bledso didn't take kindly to having a second woman in her son's life. Nancy Bledso left one night, leaving behind her two small sons.

No one knew where she had gone and her sudden disappearance led many to believe that she had met with foul play. The authorities launched an investigation. The inquiry was short lived when the sheriff reported that Nancy Bledso had been found and she was safe.

Grandma Bledso had taken on the chore of raising her grandsons. Everyone felt that this was what she had in mind all along. The challenge was almost more than the old woman could handle. The boys always needed haircuts, and their clothes were usually old, dirty, and torn. Eli did the best he could to help the boys get along, but they certainly missed the nurturing only a mother can provide.

Possum and the boys arrived at the Bledso's to find Grandma Bledso standing in what was left of her garden; still carrying a double barrel twelve gauge shotgun that was almost as long as she was tall. The upper front teeth she was missing were quite noticeable as she stormed across the garden, wearing a red checkered flour sack dress that looked like it hadn't seen a wash machine in a month of Sundays. The teeth had been missing for a long time. Her face was badly wrinkled and her nose was a little crooked from being broken. Her eyes were full of fire as she stopped in front of the pickup. "About damn time you was gettin' here."

Possum was getting out of the truck as she continued the conversation. "Some day this has started out to be. First thing I see when I walk out on the porch is that big ugly hog wreckin' my garden. Look at this." Grandma picked up what was left of a tomato plant and shook it in Possum's face.

"Old Mathusula and me would have killed his sorry ass if Eli would have had him loaded with buckshot. Double ought buckshot that's what we needed." She gave the poor excuse for a tomato plant a sling almost dropping the old cannon. "Bird shot, bird shot that's what he had my gun loaded with. How you gonea kill a sorry assed son-of-a-bitch like that with bird shot."

Smoky and Charlie slipped out the passenger side door and quickly stepped behind the pickup, hoping to stay out of harms way.

Eli Bledso and his boys walked up leading a pair of their dogs. One was a black and white spotted dog he called Truman, reputed by most hunters to be a top notch hunting hound. The other dog was Shag, a full blooded Airedale; he was a fighter, a quality that would surely be needed before this day was over.

Grandma Bledso had just picked up another tomato plant, she gave it a distasteful look, and threw it back on the ground, jumped up and down on the poor thing, leaving out a list of profanities that would have made a mule skinners ears burn.

"What you think, Eli?" Possum asked quietly.

"I think you need to get them sorry potlickers on that old boar's trail, that's what I think. I got something special for him the next time we meet. He's going to find out what pain and suffering is all about." Smoky and Charlie looked at one another wide-eyed, there was no doubt in their minds that Grandma knew all about causing pain and suffering.

"Where did he leave the garden when you dusted him, Grandma?" Possum inquired, as he stood in front of the truck with his hands intertwined in the bib of his overalls.

"Right over in that corner, headed for the river in high gear." She pointed south toward the river.

"Possum, let's have Charlie take Zebo down there and see if he'll take that track. He's our best chance since we know he'll trail almost anything." Eli Bledso had never spoken truer words, anything was fair game to Zebo.

Charlie, Smoky and Possum unloaded Zebo while trying to keep Zip in the box. Zip clawed at the door, still trying to get out, while Charlie lead Zebo away. The other dogs voiced their displeasure at being locked up.

Possum followed as Charlie lead Zebo to the area of the garden, where Ol Razor had left for the river.

Razor's tracks were everywhere, he had methodically destroyed the entire garden; leaving it looking as if it had been freshly plowed. He had started on one end of a row of beets and with his powerful neck and callused nose, had left a twelve inch furrow that took out every beet in the row.

"Here Charlie, lead him over these tracks and coax him a little." Possum pointed at Razor's fresh tracks in the soft dirt.

Charlie lead Zebo over the tracks, the coaxing was not going to be necessary. He put his nose to the ground and took a good whiff of Ol Razor's spore, a short bawl followed. Zebo drug Charlie as he tried to run the track, he let out another longer bawl.

"He's gonna take it." Possum shouted back to the group at the other end of the garden. "Turn him loose, Charlie."

Charlie quickly unsnapped the lead rope just as Truman and Shag came racing across the garden eager to get their share of the track.

"Might as well turn the rest of 'em loose," Possum ordered.

Zip, Joker, and Little Tess hit the ground on the run, not knowing what they were getting into, but happy to be there just the same.

The dogs had worked the track across a small open field and into the prairie grass that stretched to the river. Possum and Charlie returned to the pickup.

"Somebody better follow them dogs on foot or we'll loose track of 'em." Possum leaned his back against the pickup filling his pipe.

"He's goin' to the river to soak his burnin' hide. Lets go!" Grandma Bledso was already climbing into the truck.

Eli looked at Possum and then the kids. "You boys follow the dogs on foot, we'll meet you somewhere around the Ferris caves. We should be able to keep track of 'em that way."

"I guess that should work." Possum spoke through a cloud of smoke as he lit his pipe.

"Mom, you might as well stay home, you're not going to be able to get around down there on the river," Eli suggested.

"Like hell! I'm goin' along. I got a score to settle, I'm shootin' first and talkin' later."

"You boys get started, before them dogs get out of hearing," Possum motioned with his hands toward the river.

The boys crossed the garden, hoping they could keep up with the bawling pack of hounds. Eli and Grandma Bledso were still arguing. Grandma was already in the pickup and nothing short of TNT was going to get her unseated.

The boys had traveled nearly a half mile toward the river when the dogs picked up the pace as the scent became stronger.

Bawls, chops, and yips told them that Zebo was still leading the pack. Little Tess was running nearly silent, still trying to figure out if Ol Razor was something she should really be chasing.

They were running at a trot, trying to keep up with the fast moving pack. It was already hot and the humidity was high. Smoky started taking off his shirt as they run. Charlie liked the idea and removed his as well. They were both wearing blue jeans and it was no trick to remove their shirts on the run as they tried to keep the dogs in hearing.

Curly and Junior were wearing overalls, making it impossible for them to remove their shirts on the run. They stopped to catch their breath and listen for the dogs as they neared the river. The Bledso brothers seized the opportunity to remove their shirts.

Smoky took a deep breath and spoke in a weak voice. "You know . . . I'm wondering." He stopped to suck in more air. "I think we got sent after these dogs to get us out of the way."

No one bothered to answer. Smoky was right, but they all felt it was safer following the dogs, than riding around in the pickup with Grandma Bledso and that shotgun.

The dogs had tracked Ol Razor to the river and were going west, up stream. The air was dead still making it easy to hear the dogs. The boys were hot and sweating profusely, a little breeze would have been welcome.

Charlie wondered if they might not be getting themselves in a lot of trouble, as he tied his shirt through the belt of his jeans..

Two bridges crossed the Smoky Hill River in this area, within a mile of each other. The Old Iron Bridge or Hummel Bridge as it was more commonly called, was constructed in 1936 and named after the Hummel family that lived nearby. The bridge was constructed of steel beams and trusses and the floor was made from four by twelve wooden planks. Some of the planks were always loose and they would bang, clang and make a lot of noise, anytime someone drove over the bridge. This morning the bridge was silent. Possum and Eli Bledso should have already crossed the bridge. Even if they drove down to the Ferris Caves, they should have heard the dogs and doubled back and crossed the bridge.

West of the Hummel Bridge was the Grubb Bridge that was more modern, constructed of concrete and steel. From the Grubb Bridge the river ran north, made a horseshoe loop that circled back to the south and the Old Iron Bridge. The dogs were quickly working their way into the bottom of the loop that connected the two bridges.

Charlie, Smoky and the Bledso brothers continued to follow the dogs, jogging along the edge of the timber. The dogs were running at top speed now, the track was hot and Little Tess had taken the lead. Her short bawls had turned to screams, an indication that they were closing in on Ol Razor.

The troops had been slowed down considerable as they tried to make their way through a cane field that was over head high and so thick they could barely force their way through it on foot.

"Let's get in the timber," Junior suggested. The going was still tough but they were making better time than in the cane.

Charlie held up his hand, a signal for everyone to stop. They needed to catch their breath and while doing this listened for the dogs. They were all breathing so hard, no one could hear anything, except their own lungs crying for more air.

"They must be." Smoky gasped for air. "A half mile ahead of us."

"At least." Charlie managed to answer.

Junior had moved away from the rest of the army. He spun around. "I think I heard a hog squeal." His voice sounded weak, but it put new life in their tired legs and aching lungs, they pushed on.

Junior had taken the lead, climbing over logs, circling trees, picking their way through weeds, brush, and dodging low hanging tree limbs, was taking a real toll on everyone's body. To make matters worse they had run into a patch of stinging nettles which had left burning red welts every place they touched bare skin.

"We'll never get to them dogs at this rate." Junior remarked, when they found themselves in a tangle of vines that had slowed them down to a crawl.

"Let's get down in the river," Charlie suggested.

"I'm for that, at least we can cool off in the water." Curly was already making his way to the stream

Smoky wiped his face with his shirt. "Look, I'm bleeding." He reported as he looked at his blood stained shirt. The blood was coming from a scratch on his left cheek. The wound was bleeding, but didn't look serious.

"It's just a little scratch, you'll live," Charlie interjected. Charlie was bleeding himself, someplace he had acquired a puncture wound in his right hand; blood was dripping off his fingers. He pulled a large red bandanna handkerchief out of his hip pocket and wrapped it around the wound. Junior helped him tie it off.

They walked some distance before finding a place to get down in the river. Once in the water they wet themselves down. The river was low, only running two feet of water in many places. They were working against the current, but by hop-scotching from sandbar to sandbar were only in the water half the time. The dogs sounded as if they were no longer moving, they had caught up with Ol Razor.

Charlie was beginning to worry. Possum and Eli should have crossed the Old Iron Bridge by now, but he had not heard a thing.

They could have easily driven down to the river and gotten within two hundred yards of where the dogs had Ol Razor bayed up. He was sure something must have happened.

"What's that?" Curly pointed a stubby finger at something floating down the river.

"It looks like a dog." Junior charged into the water as the rest followed. "I'm going to get me a better look."

"It is a dog." Curly grabbed a leather collar, as it passed by in the slow moving current. "It's Truman!"

Charlie reached down and grabbed a hind leg. The body rolled over exposing a ten inch gash in his abdomen. His intestines began to string out of the body cavity, caught up by the current they floated downstream.

"What happened to him?" Smoky's face was pale, he swallowed hard trying to keep down his breakfast.

"He got to close to that old boar." Charlie grabbed the other hind leg.

"A hog can do that?" Smoky stared at the open wound.

"Yep, let's drag him over here to the sandbar." Curly took one of the hind legs as he helped Charlie drag Truman out of the water.

"What we gonna do."

"Smoky, I think we better catch up to them dogs, and hope we don't find anymore dead ones." Charlie adjusted his ball cap.

"What about Truman?" Curly wiped a tear from his cheek with the back of his hand.

"I guess we'll have to leave him here, not much we can do for him." Charlie took the lead.

Much of the color had left the Bledso brothers' faces; as they trudged up the river.

They were moving at a snail's pace, leg weary and tired, fighting the current and afraid of what would be found when they reached their destination.

Ol Razor and the dogs were still in the river when the hunting party finally arrived at the scene. Shag was not there. Little Tess lay on a sandbar a short distance from where Ol Razor had taken refuge in the river. She had a gaping rip in her right side and lay motionless, unable to move. She looked up at the boys as they approached. She whimpered as Smoky knelt down and tenderly stroked her head. Tears began to run down his cheeks.

The whole situation had run amuck. Ol Razor had taken refuge behind a tree that had fallen in the river when a large piece of the river bank had broken loose and it too had tumbled into the water. The dislodged tree was a good place for him to make his stand. His backside was well protected when he backed up to the tree. Also, the dogs would be forced to fight the current if they wanted to move in on him.

The tree didn't have many limbs on it and Zip had taken up a position on the lower part of the tree. He was really giving Razor an ear full, who didn't seem to be too impressed, only giving Zip an occasional glare. It was Joker who was getting his undivided attention. He was standing in a little over a foot of water about twelve feet in front of the killer boar not saying much only an occasional bawl.

Razor was a scary and dangerous looking sight standing in the water. His big head was impressive, frightening, alarming, with razor sharp tusks sticking out of his lower jaw. He watched Joker with deep set black calculating eyes, waiting for a chance to rip him open and send him floating down the river just like Truman.

Zebo was still standing on the sandbar, giving out long bawls, making sure he didn't get to close to the action, giving orders like a General, while being careful not to spill any of his own blood.

"Anyone got any ideas, what we should do?" Charlie inquired.

No one answered, just shook their heads from side to side. Indicating they didn't have any ideas.

Razor charged out from his sanctuary at Joker, who quickly retreated and managed to stay away from Razor's lethal tusks. Razor returned to the safety of his wooden fortress, realizing he had missed his chance.

"I'm gettin' Joker out of there before he gets killed, too." Smoky stepped in the water.

Charlie grabbed him by the arm to spin him around. He faced Charlie with clinched fist.

"Don't do it, Smoky." He released his arm.

"What you want to do, Charlie, just stand here and let him kill the rest of the dogs? Tess is hurt . . . maybe dyin'. Truman's dead and Shag might be dead. We better do somethin'." He looked at Little Tess lying in a pool of blood.

64

"Get hold of yourself, Smoky. You get too close to that old boar and he'll take you just like one of them dogs. They're a lot quicker than you. We don't need you gettin' hurt, too."

"We need to get 'em caught up and get out of here. Maybe, we can call 'em off." Junior paced nervously at the edge of the sandbar.

"Let's try that." Charlie didn't think the plan would work, the dogs were too intense on the quarry they had bayed up.

They spread out and began calling the dogs by name, trying to coax them to the sandbar. It became obvious after awhile, that the plan was not going to work.

Suddenly, Razor made another run at Joker. This time it was a longer and harder challenge than his earlier charge. In an effort to avoid those dangerous and lethal tusk, Joker darted onto the sandbar. Razor, not wanting to leave the water, stopped short of coming onto the sandbar. Joker was only a few feet from the boys when Razor halted his attack. He backed up wanting deeper water.

"Spread out around him before he gets back in the water." Charlie shouted, wanting to seize the opportunity while Joker was on the sandbar.

They formed a half circle around him before he realized what they were doing.

"Smoky, pick up a couple of those little sandstones and hit him, not hard. Everybody get ready to grab him if Smoky can distract him. Charlie had managed to get himself between Razor and Joker who was still standing at the water's edge. Joker was facing Charlie, wanting to get back in the water to harass Ol Razor.

Smoky tossed a small stone at Joker. It fell short. Smoky made his second attempt count, the small stone struck Joker square in the ribs. He jumped and spun around to see what had hit him. Curly and Charlie rushed him while he was distracted. Curly latched onto a hind leg, while Charlie grabbed his collar.

Razor had nestled in behind his tree, once again feeling secure.

Curly ran a rope through Joker's collar. "Smoky, hang on to this dog." He handed Smoky the rope. "And watch so he doesn't chew that rope up and get loose."

Zebo was staying his distance, far back from the action, bawling and still trying to play General. Zip was still standing on the fallen tree, trying to get up enough courage to work his way closer to the old boar.

Razor was giving Zip a lot of attention now that Joker was out of the way.

The boys gathered on the sandbar to figure out a way to get Zip out of his tree stand.

"Any ideas?" Junior looked at Charlie.

"Maybe, we could come up on the back side of that tree and get hold of him. I believe it's too high for Razor to jump. I hope."

"How about Smoky taking Joker down there on the sandbar and distracting him a little bit?" Junior pointed down the sandbar.

"Good idea, Smoky take him down there. Be careful . . . don't get too close."

Smoky made his way down the sandbar as Charlie, Junior, and Curly went upstream and entered the river above Ol Razor.

Curly and Junior flanked Charlie on either side, as they slowly moved closer to Ol Razor, Zip and the fallen tree. Hopefully, the tree would provide protection from Ol Razor's wrath.

Razor peered over the tree, watching them move closer. He would open and shut his mouth, making a popping sound, as he snapped his jaws together. He showed no fear, but the hate in his eyes was obvious. He wasn't afraid of the boys or the dogs. They were like flies at a picnic; just a little irritation. He would take care of them all, one by one, given enough time.

They were within a few feet of Zip, when suddenly, Razor rose up on his hind legs, coming down with his front feet in the tree. He grunted loudly and began to throw his head from side to side; while giving out a deep hog like squeal.

This unpredictable move startled Zip. He jumped back, and lost his footing and slipped into the water. Hanging on to the tree bark with his front feet, he tried to pull himself back into the tree.

He would never make it. Junior, who was the closest, saw his chance and quickly grabbed his collar. He drug the struggling hound to the sandbar. Curly and Charlie were close behind.

Charlie went to the end of the sandbar and ran a rope through Zebo's collar, while Junior and Curly gave Zip the same treatment. Zebo was still making a lot of noise, trying to encourage an army that had given up the fight.

Ol Razor was the winner. He watched as they gathered up their shirts and made their way out of the river. As the boys climbed the river bank, Razor walked up the river as if nothing had ever happened.

They left Little Tess lying on the sandbar. For now, they had their hands full with three unruly dogs. They would come back for her later.

They drug the dogs up the river bank; it was steep, slick and hard to climb.

They were exhausted by the time they reached the summit and were in the timber. Tired legs carried them through the tangled vines, weeds, and brush. To make matters worse, the dogs were continuously getting their lead ropes wrapped around trees or anything else that would slow them down. They were almost ready to collapse.

They stopped to catch their breath, when they got out of the timber and into an open field. Curly and Junior dropped to their knees, Smoky and Charlie quickly joined them. The slight breeze that had come up out of the south felt good but they were still in the sun. Perspiration was dripping out of every pore in their bodies; parched throats begged for water. The burning from the stinging nettles had eased quite a bit, but the red welts were still quite visible.

Over a mile away they could hear a vehicle crossing the Old Iron Bridge. Shortly Eli Bledso's blue Ford truck would appear on the county road that ran parallel to the river and between the two bridges. They had changed vehicles. Making a right turn off the road the truck was coming down a well traveled trail that would end a couple hundred yards from where the boys were resting.

They struggled to their feet. The dogs were extremely hot and they too had laid down. The boys coaxed them to their feet.

Everyone's legs had started to stiffen up. They forced themselves to walk across the open field. Eli brought the truck to a stop before they were half way across the field.

Possum immediately jumped out and started toward the exhausted troops. Eli soon followed.

"Truman's dead Pa, that old boar killed him, we found him dead in the river." Curly hollered to his father.

"We ain't seen Shag either . . . I think he's dead too," Junior added.

No one spoke for a short time as they closed the distance between them.

"Where's Tess?" Possum drew in a deep breath as they met.

No one wanted to tell him. Charlie finally answered, "She's down there on the sandbar." He pointed toward the river. "She's hurt real bad."

"Eli take these boys up to the truck . . . make sure they get some water, and put 'em in the shade. I'm going to get Tess."

Possum walked to the river, as Eli and the boys trudged to the pickup. By the time they arrived, Grandma Bledso had gotten out and was awaiting their arrival.

"Did they catch 'im?" She was quick to ask.

"They caught him, Grandma. He killed Truman," Junior answered.

"Killed Truman! What about Shag?"

"We ain't seen him." Junior reach for a jug of water in the pickup bed.

"Did you see 'im? The old boar, did you see 'im?"

"These dogs had him bayed up in the river." Junior passed the water jug to his brother.

"So why didn't you wait for us? Me and old Mathusula would have took care of 'im."

"We didn't know if you would ever find us. Besides, it was only a matter of time before he would have gotten them, too." Charlie tied Zebo to the bumper of the pickup.

Smoky handed him the water jug. He took a drink and set it in the back of the pickup, beside Grandma's shotgun which was laying among some shovels and other tools.

"Them's just dogs. They could a been replaced. Damn! I would a liked to laid my sights on 'im." She stomped around the truck.

Eli, who had been silent, spoke in a quiet orderly voice. "You boys go over there and sit down in the shade. You need to get out of the sun." He pointed to a hedgerow just off the trail. The boys didn't need any coaxing to get out of the sun. The dogs had crawled under the truck, looking for relief from the heat.

"You boys are lucky we found you. We might still be looking for you, if Uncle Ezra wouldn't have been fishing off the bridge. He heard the dogs and gave us some idea where ya was."

A pistol shot from the river caught everyone's attention. The boys looked toward the river and than one another, no one spoke, but they all knew Little Tess had made her last hunt.. Charlie turned away from everyone as his lower lip began to quiver. He composed himself and turned around to face everyone. Tears were running down

Smoky's cheeks, Charlie walked over and patted him on the back, hoping to say something, but no words would come out. No one had came through the morning unscathed. The scratch on Smoky's cheek had quit bleeding, but certainly needed some attention. He had lost his cap somewhere and as usual his hair was in disarray. Junior had the worst injury, an L shaped laceration on his upper left arm, it would require some medical attention. Curly was by far in the best shape, coming through the whole ordeal with only a small scrap on his chin.

Charlie studied his wound as he peeked under the handkerchief he had wrapped around his hand. It was sore, he grimaced as he began to unwrap the blood soaked bandanna.

Everyone else was lying on their backs, with their eyes closed, as Possum walked up. "You boy's goin' to be alright?"

Smoky was the first to open his eyes and speak. "Did you have to kill her."

"I put her out of her misery, son. Her back was broke and she had nearly bleed to death anyway." He spoke quietly, his voice sounded weak. "What did you run into?" Possum took a close look at Smoky's face.

"Tree limb I guess, I'm not sure," Smoky answered.

"I don't think it's too bad . . . needs to be cleaned up."

He turned toward Junior, who was still lying on the ground. "Eli, this boy is going to need some medical attention."

"I'll take care of him." Grandma stepped forward an insensitive look on her face.

"Yeah . . . I'll bet." He filled his pipe.

"Eli, I'm going to bury Tess under that big cottonwood." He motioned to a large tree that stood above any other in the area.

"I'll stay here with the boys," Eli volunteered.

"We ain't got time to bury no damn dog. I wanta get home." Grandma stood with her hands on her hips, hoping to intimidate Possum.

Possum squared up in front of Grandma Bledso and spoke in a voice that anyone could tell meant business. "Now listen to me woman, most of what has happened here is your fault. You're the one that was fooling around with that damn shotgun and blew the tire off my pickup. I think what you need to do is set yourself down, shut-up and wait until I'm done." Possum struck a match on the button of his bib overalls and lit his pipe.

Grandma Bledso looked shell shocked.

Possum turned to Eli. "If that's not all right with you . . . get her out of here. I'll walk home."

"We'll wait for you, go ahead." Eli had a funny little grin on his face.

Grandma stomped back to the truck. She sat down in the seat, stone faced and sober.

Possum reached in the pickup bed and pulled out a round nosed shovel. His face was red and he was blowing smoke out of that pipe the likes of which no one had never seen before. He walked toward the river, as if, he was in a hurry to burn up some energy on the end of that shovel.

Eli sat down in the shade with the boys. "Tell me what happened down there?"

Junior started telling his dad the story of the Smoky Hill River bloodbath. It was a story Charlie didn't care to hear; having lived through it. He thought about Possum down on the river, by himself, burying his dog. He remembered seeing a spade in the back of Eli's truck.

"I think Possum might need that sharpshooter that's in your truck, Eli."

"You can take it down to him if you want too. Take that axe along, he might run into some tree roots," Eli suggested.

Possum had already started digging the grave by the time Charlie got there. He had taken his gun belt off; and hung it on a nearby tree limb.

"I thought you might need these." Charlie leaned the well used tools against the cottonwood tree.

"Yeah . . . I might. You hurt, too?" He looked down at Charlie's hand.

"A little, run something in the palm of my hand."

"Let me see that." Possum untied the handkerchief. "That's going to get pretty sore. Florence will clean it up when we get home." He rewrapped his hand with the blood soiled handkerchief.

"Possum, I'm sorry about what happened. I wish I could have done more. I was so scared, I didn't know what to do."

"Ah, Charlie, I think you did the best anyone could expect of you. It wasn't your fault. Don't blame yourself." Possum returned too digging the grave.

Possum had already carried Little Tess up to the grave site. Charlie positioned himself so his back was to her, not wanting to look at her.

"I never knew a person could be so scared," Charlie admitted.

"There's no shame in being afraid, the shame is not being able to face your fears. I'm afraid right now, I've got to ride home with Grandma Bledso. After the way I talked to her . . . it's not going to be a easy trip." He straighten up, shaking his head, he struck a match on the shovel to relight his pipe. "Charlie, she blew the tire off my pickup."

"How did that happen?"

"Well, we got to the crossroads over there east of Cedrick Millers. We stopped to see if we could hear the dogs. Of course, Grandma had to get out too . . . with her shotgun. Eli and me was listening for the dogs. She's fiddling around with that double barrel . . . sets the damn thing off. Blew a hole in the front tire you could stick your head in. Then the spare was flat, that's why we were so slow getting here. We still wouldn't be here if some stranger hadn't came along and gave Eli a ride back to his place . . . to get his pickup."

Possum returned to his grave digging chore. The damp and sandy ground made his task somewhat easier.

"Has she always been so hateful?"

"Yep, she's worked at it for years. Luther, he could handle her. He's the only one that could do anything with her. He would put up with that sharp tongue for awhile, but eventually he'd work her over."

"You mean he beat her."

"Didn't no dentist take out them front teeth . . . she wasn't born with that crooked nose."

"I know, but I never figured he did that to her."

"Well . . . he did. Luther felt bad about them two teeth, told her she should go to a dentist and get something done. She wouldn't go, said she was going to make him look at her like that the rest of his life. They tell me when he was about to die, the last thing she did was put her face real close to his and smile, so he would get one last good look."

"You're kiddin'!" Charlie backed up a couple steps, a shocked look on his face.

"Nope, that's what I was told by a pretty reliable source."

"I kinda feel sorry for Junior and Curly."

Possum stopped digging. "Why you feel that way? Give me that axe, I need to cut this tree root."

He handed Possum the axe. "Oh, you know, Grandma being the way she is and then their Mom running off when they were so little."

"Let me tell you something, Junior and Curly's mother loves them boys just as much as your mother loves you."

"How can a mother love her children and just up and leave them, like she did?"

"Charlie, a lot of people have told me things about themselves, that they never told anyone else. I never repeated any of their secrets, but I don't know what happened . . . the night Nancy Bledso ran out on them boys."

"Seems kinda strange doesn't it."

"There must have been something pretty bad went on in that house. Mothers don't give up their children without a fight. A good mother will crawl through hell for her kids. I knew Nancy Bledso. She was a good mother. Even a sorry mother doesn't want someone else raising her children. Now I'll tell you something else . . . but you have to promise me you'll never tell anyone." He had finished cutting the tree root.

"I can keep a secret, if that's what you mean."

"Promise?" He looked Charlie in the eye.

"Yes, I promise."

"Nancy Bledso writes them boys a letter nearly every week."

"How you know that?"

"Because, the letters comes to our mail box. They're addressed to Florence and she gives them to the boys.

"Well, I'll be! So Grandma doesn't know about that?"

"She sure doesn't and we don't want her findin' out either."

"So, do they answer her letters?"

"Oh, yeah! I know, because Florence mails them for the boys. Nancy and Florence were pretty good friends. They write each other every once in a while."

"So, where's she at?"

"I'm not sure. Florence knows . . . I've never asked. She never did remarry. Fact is, I'm not sure her and Eli ever got divorced. Florence says, she's still in love with him."

"You think she will ever come back?"

"I doubt it . . . not as long as Grandma's alive, anyway. I think that's deep enough."

Possum tossed the shovel aside and stepped out of the three foot deep hole.

"Charlie, give me a hand with her. Take her hind legs."

This wasn't a job Charlie really wanted to do, but he knew Possum needed help. They carried her the short distance to the grave and laid her gently in the ground.

Possum walked over to the tree where his pistol was hanging, he removed it from the holster. Standing over Little Tess he removed the bullets from the cylinder. He pushed the five live rounds in the pocket of his overalls and tossed the empty revolver in the grave beside her. "Why you doin' that?" Charlie asked curiously.

"Oh, that old gun don't work real good. It's a good time to get rid of it. Besides it'll only bring back bad memories for me. You want it? You can have it."

"No, I don't think so. Mom don't hold much with having guns around."

Silently Possum shoveled dirt in the grave.

"I guess we've done the best we could for her." His voice sounded weak and quivered a little bit. Possum handed Charlie the spade. "If you can carry that I'll bring the rest of this stuff."

When they returned to the pickup, Grandma was still sitting in the front seat. She didn't look as if she had moved a muscle and the expression on her face hadn't changed. She looked, as if, she had turned to stone. The boys loaded the dogs in the back of the truck and then climbed in themselves. Possum took a good look at Grandma Bledso and climbed in the back of the pickup with the boys.

CHAPTER 9

The sun was high when Eli Bledso's pickup turned down the Elliot's driveway. They had made two stops on the way home. The first one was on the Old Iron Bridge, where Uncle Ezra was still fishing. Eli asked him to stop by the house on his way home.

Uncle Ezra was the local barber; a real piece of work. No one knew why he was called Uncle Ezra, everyone knew he wasn't anyone's uncle. He was an only child and had never married, making it impossible for him to be a blood Uncle to anyone. He was a small man, with a sanguine complexion, gray hair, and dark brown eyes. A thin weasel like face supported a long gray mustache that drooped at the ends.

Uncle Ezra had graduated from college and after graduation he went to medical school with high aspirations of becoming a fine doctor. His plans were interrupted when the United States declared war on Germany. The war effort was badly in need of people with medical training and Uncle Ezra got caught up in the war.

He returned home when the war ended, with no desire to finish medical school or become a doctor. He never talked about the war, but his life had changed forever. It wasn't unusual for people to seek his advise for simple medical problems, but that was as close as he cared to get to the medical profession.

Uncle Ezra was a heavy drinker and it wasn't unusual for him to be drinking a beer while giving someone a haircut. He would belch in his customers' ear from time to time, just to make sure they stayed awake to hear his stories.

Uncle Ezra's barbershop was an interesting place to get a haircut. Everyone tolerated his disgusting habits, after all, he was the only barber in town.

The second stop was to pick up Possum's spare tire. The tire on the front of the pickup was certainly beyond repair. Grandma and Old Mathusula had done a fine piece of work.

They had barely gotten into the yard, when Millie came running out the door. The after effects of the free for all the night before were plain to see. She certainly didn't look to lady like, showing off a black eye that a prize fighter would have been proud to boast about.

It wasn't bothering her much, she was smiling and happy as she approached.

Smoky wiped the smile off her face. "Little Tess got killed."

"How?"

"The boar killed her," he answered.

"Killed Truman too, and maybe Shag, we haven't seen him," Curly added.

Millie ran back to the house, tears streaming down her face.

The dogs were just unloaded when Mom Elliot burst out of the kitchen door. She was about to speak, when she got a good look at the boys. "God have mercy! What happened to you boys?" She cast an evil eye in Possum's direction.

Possum could see he was in trouble. He tried to make a case for himself. "Florence, we had just a little bit of trouble. It's nothing to get excited about."

"Nothing to get excited about, what you mean a little bit of trouble? Look at these children, they look like they came out of a war zone."

"Florence, relax and let me tell you what happened," Possum pleaded.

"I haven't got time for one of your lamebrained stories."

Possum turned to face Eli, who had a funny little smile on his face. "I'll get that tire fixed this afternoon. Could you stop by this evening and give me a lift, so I can get my truck home."

"Sure, about eight o'clock." Eli was already in the truck and starting the engine.

Mom Elliot had taken charge of the situation. "Richard, you get in the house and take a quick bath. Then I'll clean that cut up. Charles, soon as he's done, you get in that tub." She turned her attention to Eli. "That boys arm needs to be taken care of." She gave Junior's arm a quick look and shook her head in disbelief.

"Uncle Ezra is going to come by and take a look at it." Eli answered, in his defense.

"Somebody better take care of it, before he gets gangrene and loses his whole arm."

Junior turned pale at the thought of losing his arm.

Charlie looked down at his hand, wondering if he might not get the gangrene as well. He wasn't sure what gangrene was, but sure didn't want any part of it if it meant loosing body parts. "I'm going to run these dogs down to the pen."

"Well, be quick about it," Mom Elliot snapped.

He rushed Zip and Zebo down to the pen, quickly pushing them inside. His hand was really starting to hurt; no doubt in his mind, the gangrene was setting in.

The Bledso's were pulling out of the yard as Charlie rounded the corner of the chicken house. Junior and Curly waved, Charlie waved back.

Mom Elliot spotted him as he tried to slip in the kitchen door. "Let me see that hand." She took Charlie's hand and unwrapped the makeshift bandage he had made. She studied the wound for a moment. "As soon as Richard gets out of the tub, you get in. Have you got clean clothes?"

"Yes, ma'am."

"Go get them."

Charlie's legs were sore and climbing stairs didn't make them feel any better. He finally reached the top of the stairs and slipped into the bedroom, gathering up his last clean clothes.

Millie met him in the hall as he came out of the bedroom. Her eyes were red from crying. She spoke in an unsteady voice. "How's . . . your hand?"

"Hurts some. Hope I don't get the gangrene."

"Don't worry about that . . . Moms been using that line forever. She always tells us that so we wouldn't complain when she's trying to play nurse."

"Does your eye hurt?" Charlie asked sympathetically, as he studied the black and blue bruise that run from her eyebrow to her cheekbone.

"Yes, I can't see out of it very good, either. I look terrible, don't I?" She tried to wipe the tears from her eyes with the back of her hand.

"Oh, I guess I've seen you look a lot better." Charlie tried not to hurt her feeling. She had almost stopped crying.

"There's something I want you to know."

"What?"

"Well, last night during the fight, something terrible happened." She held out her hand and opened it up for Charlie to see. "I lost the locket you gave me and someone stepped on it. I'm sorry . . . it's ruined."

She was right, the locket looked as if it had been run over by a train, or Becky the Behemoth.

"You're not mad at me . . . are you?" She looked as if she was about to start crying again.

"I'm not mad at you. Please don't start crying again."

"I won't, come here, I got the picture out."

She grabbed Charlie by the hand and half drug him into her bedroom. Her room was a little more showy than Smoky's or the one Charlie was using. The bed was made and covered by a bright colored pink bedspread. Several pictures hung on the wall above and around a large chest of drawers. A dresser with a large mirror set along the opposite wall. The whole room was clean and tidy with everything in its place.

She led Charlie over to the dresser. "See, I found a place for your picture."

The picture was right there in the middle of the dresser mirror, glued down, forever. Charlie's mouth dropped open, his heart fluttered, perspiration began to form on his forehead. He was hoping the boys at school never found out about this. There was no doubt in his mind, this was going to haunt him the rest of his life.

"I better get downstairs and let your mother doctor my hand."

"You don't like it." Her eyes began to fill with tears.

"No, it's fine, I like it. It's just that . . . my hand hurts."

Charlie bolted for the door. Millie was right behind him as he started down the stairs.

Smoky was just coming out of the bathroom with only a towel wrapped around his waist, as they entered the kitchen.

"Richard, get some clothes on and get down here so I can clean up that cut. Charles your next." Mom Elliot pointed toward the bathroom.

Charlie did as Mom Elliot instructed. Smoky took his time finding clean clothes, fearing what Mom Elliot's next course of action might be.

Charlie was just coming out of the bathroom as Smoky returned to the kitchen. Charlie took a seat at the far end of the long wooden kitchen table, flanked on either side by Millie and Smoky. He watched intently as Mom Elliot cleaned Smoky's wound with soap and water. She finished the cleaning process by dabbing on some peroxide with a clean wash cloth. The peroxide bubbled and a white foam formed on the cut.

Mom Elliot stepped back a little bit and looked over her handy work. "That don't look too bad."

The cut was about three inches long, but had just barely gone through Smoky's tender skin.

Mom Elliot carefully wiped Smoky's face, cleaning off the peroxide that was running down his cheek. She pulled a bottle of Mercurochrome out of her apron pocket.

"You're not goin' to use any of that stuff on me. . . are you?" Smoky asked nervously.

"Yes, I am. Now just sit still and lean your head over to the side."

"Mom, that stuff burns like fire."

"I know. We don't want you getting infection and end up with a big doctor bill."

"Or you might get gangrene and we would have to cut your head off," Millie added.

Charlie chuckled a little, and a grin came across Mom Elliot's face, as she grabbed Smoky by the hair and pushed his face down on the table so the cut was facing up.

"Very funny, Millie."

Those were Smoky's last words before Mom Elliot started putting on the Mercurochrome with a small piece of cotton.

"Damn that burns." Smoky complained while banging his clenched fist on the table.

"Don't be using that kinda language in this house, young man," Mom Elliot warned.

"Hells bells, my face feels like it's on fire," Smoky screamed.

"Richard, I told you not to talk like that." Before Smoky could say any more Mom Elliot grabbed the bottle of Mercurochrom and splashed it on Smoky's face, covering the cut and half of one side of his face.

Smoky jumped up, let out a blood curdling scream and began dancing around the kitchen table.

Millie was trying to keep from laughing, but it was a losing battle. Finally, a little chuckle escaped.

Charlie wasn't laughing, Mom Elliot was looking at him now. He was next in line for the Mercurochrome treatment.

"Charles, I want you to tell me everything that happened this morning." She started cleaning up his hand as he began telling her about the adventure that had taken place that morning. She worked slowly and carefully, using soap, water, and peroxide, while listening silently to his story. She started taking more interest when he got to the part where they found Little Tess and Ol Razor.

"Charles, are you telling me that you boys are there all alone, facing that old boar?"

"Well, ah, yeah, I guess."

"Where was John and Eli?"

"They hadn't got there yet."

"Well, why not? They stop and visit along the way?" A disgusted look came over her face.

"No, but they had some other trouble."

"Sounds to me like you boys was the ones in trouble. What kinda trouble did they have?"

"Ah-hum!" Charlie cleared his throat. "Grandma Bledso blew a hole in Possum's pickup tire with her shotgun."

"Oh, my word! You can't be serious . . . are you?" She crossed her hands on her chest.

"There was a hole big enough, you could stick your head in it." Smoky answered for Charlie. He had sat down at the table, having completed his dance. The right side of his face orange from the Mercurochrome bath his mother had given him.

"I guess that explains why Eli Bledso brought you home. Let's get that hand finished up." She pushed her chair back and stood up.

"It looks pretty good to me, doesn't even hurt," Charlie lied.

Millie who had been unusually quiet, spoke, as she leaned over and looked at the hole in his hand. "Needs a little Mercurochrome, Mom."

"You shut up, what makes you think you know so much about medical problems?" While Charlie was trying to get Millie straightened out, Mom Elliot was already pouring liquid fire on his wounded hand. "Wheeee, does that stuff burn." He jumped up, shaking his hand back and forth, up and down as he danced around the kitchen table. Orange drops were beginning to show up all over the kitchen as the Mercurochrome dripped off his hand. Mom Elliot quickly wrapped a clean rag around his hand as he continued to dance.

Smoky had a big grin on his face and Millie was giggling. The pain was intense, Charlie gritted his teeth to keep from using those words that didn't meet with Mom Elliots approval.

Mom Elliot spun him around. "Charles, now hold still and let me put some of this salve on that hand."

"It's not going to hurt, is it?"

"No, it should make it feel better."

"What is it?" Trying to make sure he wasn't falling for that old, "this isn't going to hurt line."

Mom Elliot showed him the square green can that contained the Bag Balm she had used on his hand the day before.

Charlie offered her his hand. She cautiously rubbed the yellow ointment over the wound. He watched as she gently wrapped his hand with gauze. She was deep in thought as she finished tying on the bandage. Upset about the mornings activities, she had made up her mind Possum was going to get a tongue lashing.

"How's that feel?" She finished wrapping tape around Charlie's hand to keep everything in place.

"Feels pretty good." He opened and closed his hand.

"Milacent, peel some potatoes," Mom Elliot ordered. "I'm going outside to talk to your father."

She stalked out of the house, on the hunt for poor Possum.

Smoky and Charlie remained seated at the table as they watched Millie peel the potatoes.

"What's for dinner?" Charlie asked.

"Potatoes." Millie laughed a little and smiled at Charlie.

"You're just a real comedian this morning, aren't you?" Charlie smiled back.

"Maybe." She was still smiling. "I think there might be some fried chicken to go with these potatoes."

If there was one thing Charlie was looking forward too, it was some of Mom Elliot's fried chicken; perhaps, there was going to be a bright spot to this tragic morning after all. The large cast iron skillet was already setting on the stove, waiting to be put to work. He could already taste one of those golden brown chicken breasts, the likes of which he hadn't tasted since the last time his feet were under Mom Elliot's table.

Smoky had gotten very quite, his face red; tears running down his cheeks.

Charlie took notice. "Been a tough morning hasn't it, Smoky? Anything you want to talk about?"

"I don't know, Little Tess is dead, we're never going to see her again, and we sit here talkin' about eatin' like nothing ever happened. Truman's dead, Shag is more than likely dead, and we sit here laughing, makin' jokes. It don't make sense.

"Gramps told me when Grandma died, death is something you never get used too, but as you get older, you toughen to it. Everyone faces death, most of the time you do the buryin' but some day you'll be the buried, some die young, some die old, some know when, most don't, so you best always be ready."

"Do you think Tess knew she was going to die?" Smoky wiped tears away with his hand as they run down his cheeks.

"I doubt it. Animals don't understand death like we do. They don't realize how final it is." Charlie paused a second. "Now I'll tell you something else. Little Tess was a huntin' dog, she lived to hunt; she would have never been happy lying around waiting to die. If she could, she would have thanked your dad for putting her out of her misery. I'm going upstairs and rest for a little while. Call me when dinner's ready." Charlie slowly got up from the table. He was sore, it even hurt to breathe.

"I'll call you," Millie promised.

"Wait up, Charlie, I'm going with you." Smoky moaned as he got up. He was starting to stiffen up too. "My legs hurt." He complained as they reached the top of the stairs.

"Your legs hurt, I hurt all over."

Smoky followed Charlie in the bedroom and sat down on the bed. "Charlie, I'm worried."

"You worry, that'll be the day." Charlie sat down on the bed beside him.

"This is serious."

"O.K., what's got you so worried?"

"Well, ya know, last night that whole mess with Becky." He was speaking quietly, softly, as if he was afraid someone might hear.

"Wasn't that something, all those girls fighting, rolling around on the floor. I never saw anything like it," Charlie laughed.

"There's nothing funny about this, I'm telling you we're in trouble."

"What do you mean we're in trouble?"

81

"Becky knows all about the wine and where we made it and everything."

"You told her?"

"It just kinda slipped out when we were trying to get her to give us the sugar. I'm afraid she might tell and get us all in trouble."

"You better believe she's going to tell. It's only a matter of time."

"What we gonna do?" Smoky got up and nervously began pacing the floor.

"I guess." Charlie rubbed his chin. "You might just dump that wine. Get rid of the evidence."

"I don't know if I can do that. Junior and Curly would get mad at me."

"They're the ones that came up with this wine making idea, aren't they?"

"Well, yeah, how did you know?" He turned to face Charlie.

"I know you, and you wouldn't think up something like making wine on your own. I'll tell you one thing, you want to think about some of their hair-brained ideas before you get to involved."

"What you mean?" He took a step toward Charlie.

"I mean Junior and Curly could get a guy in a lot of trouble with some of their crazy ideas."

"I guess your right." Smoky walked over to the window that overlooked the front yard.

He became interested in something that was going on outside. Charlie strolled over to see what had drawn his attention. He pulled the plain white curtain aside and gazed out the window.

Mom Elliot had caught up with Possum under the old oak tree. Her mouth was running at full speed. Possum couldn't get a word in edgewise.

"Seems like your dad is in hot water with your mother."

"She's a little upset, for sure," Smoky agreed.

"I think we better help him out."

"How?" Smoky asked curiously.

"Come on." They hurried down the stairs and out the front door, with Charlie in the lead. Mom Elliot was still doing the talking. "You should have better sense than to let a crazy old woman have a shotgun anyway. Why didn't you take that gun away from her?" She stopped to catch her breath, waiting for an answer.

"Florence, it's not the simplest thing in the world to take a shotgun away from a woman that's a little touched in the head. My word, someone might get shot."

Mom Elliot couldn't help noticing the boys as they took a position at Possum's side.

"You two go back to the house. I'm not done with this discussion," she ordered. "Did Milacent get the potatoes peeled?"

"Yes, she did," Charlie answered. "But I think she's burning the chicken."

"What, she better not burn that chicken." She double timed it back to the house.

"Thanks boys. I think we better disappear for awhile. Give her a chance to cool down." Possum took the lead as they walked to the barn. They would lay low there, as they waited to see if the dinner bell would ring.

CHAPTER 10

Mom Elliot was busy fixing supper as Charlie entered the kitchen. "Finally decided to get up, I see."

Charlie glanced at the battery operated clock hanging on the wall above the sink. "My word, I slept all afternoon, it's almost seven o'clock."

"Feeling any better?"

"Not really. I still hurt all over." He pulled a chair from under the table and sat down.

Mom Elliot was busily stirring a cast iron skillet of freshly pealed potatoes that were frying on the stove. "You was pretty tired, almost fell asleep eating dinner.

"I did. I did not. I remember how good that chicken tasted."

"It must have been pretty good, you ate half a chicken yourself." She smiled then laughed.

"I guess I made a pig of myself."

"Don't you be ashamed of being hungry. I made it for you to eat. I'm a little surprised you ate it, since Milacent burnt it. Why did you tell me that?"

"Ah, well, ah, I thought Possum needed a little help."

"You men all stick together. That man is old enough to take care of himself. He doesn't need your help."

"Charlie, I want to thank you for what you did this morning." She sat down in a chair beside Charlie, still wearing the blue and white checkered dress she had on at dinner.

"What do you mean?"

"Richard told me how you kept him from taking any chances with that old boar. He says, if it wouldn't have been for you, someone most likely would have gotten hurt."

"I don't know, I was pretty scared myself."

"I'm sure you were. Nonetheless, you did good and we're all proud of you."

She patted Charlie on the arm and as she got up. "You need to move around a little and limber up. John and Richard are out doing the chores, more than likely you'll find them down at the barn."

Charlie moaned a little as he slowly got up. "I'm not sure I'll ever be normal again. Maybe, I'm getting polio."

Mom Elliot shook her head. "I don't think so, you would be in a lot worse shape if you had polio."

"What do you feel like when you get gangrene?"

"Oh, in your case, your hand would swell up and get all sorts of funny colors. You would most likely start running a high fever, and then in order to save your life, we would have to chop it off."

Charlie decided he didn't want to hear any more about the gangrene. He could just see Possum laying his hand on that old tree stump that he used to chop chickens' heads off and whooping off his hand and throwing it to Joker like it was a chicken head.

"Where's Millie?" He changed the subject.

"I'm not sure where she went."

"I guess I'll hunt Possum and Smoky up."

"That's a good idea, but don't let them trick you into milking cows. I don't want you to get that bandage dirty," she warned.

Charlie was thinking about Millie as he left the house. He was sure she had gone over to the Barnes' place to take care of the dog. He wished she would have taken him along, his desire was to make friends with this oversized hound. He would like to feed him; perhaps, that would be one way to win his trust.

It was still hot outside, but there was a nice southerly breeze that made the heat somewhat bearable. Possum and Smoky were almost done with the chores by the time Charlie found them behind the barn feeding the bucket calves.

Possum gave Charlie some skim milk to feed his dogs. They were tired and didn't really seem to care if they ate or not.

From the dog pen, he could see across the pasture land that lead to the Barnes' place. A small form was taking shape in the distance as it moved in his direction.

It was Millie, just as he had suspected, she had gone over to visit the mysterious dog that had chosen her to be his friend.

Charlie walked out to meet her. As they narrowed the distance between them, she quickened her pace.

They met on the summit of a small knoll, her hair blowing freely around her face in the wind. "Hi, Charlie. How you feeling?" She brushed the hair from her face.

"Sore as all get out. I'm not sure that nap was such a good idea. I wish you would have woke me up. It would have been nice to see him again. How's he doin'?"

"Alright, I guess. I'm wondering how long we'll be able to keep him there?"

"Certainly not forever. His disposition being what it is, certainly could create some problems, too."

"I'm sure you're right. I don't think Dad will let me keep a dog that wants to growl and maybe even bite every man he sees."

"Yeah, and I don't think he'll get along with other dogs either. That's certainly not going to set good with your dad."

She stopped walking and turned to face Charlie, once again pushing the hair from her face. "Why do you say that?"

"Well, he's got all them scars and I'll bet most of them came from fights of one kind or another."

"You think he was a fightin' dog."

"I don't know, maybe."

They continued their walk back to the Elliot farm; both thinking, neither one speaking.

Millie broke the silence. "Maybe I should just turn him loose."

"Might not be a bad idea," Charlie agreed. "There's another problem that needs to be dealt with."

"What's that?"

"Smoky told me that Becky knows all about the wine they're making and even where it's at."

Millie stopped placing her hands on her hips. "She's going to tell."

"Most likely already has."

"What are we going to do?"

"Smoky talked to me about the situation, he doesn't know what to do. He asked me. I told him to dump the wine before anyone found it."

"What did he say?"

"He doesn't want to do that, because he thinks Junior and Curly will be mad at him."

"So, what if they get caught? Smoky's the one that's going to take the heat. They'll say it was Smoky's idea." Millie spoke with a discussed look on her face.

"I know, I done told him that."

"I think you're right, Charlie. I'll talk to him, first chance I get."

CHAPTER 11

Charlie, Smoky and Millie were playing Monopoly at the dinning room table. The game had started shortly after supper.

Eli Bledso had came by just before dark to pick Possum up, so they could get Possum's tire changed while they still had some daylight. They had been gone over two hours. The Monopoly game was about to be declared a stalemate, when Possum's truck pulled in the yard. The pickup door slammed shut with a certain amount of authority. It would be several minutes before he would come in the house.

"What in the world happened to you?" Mom Elliot exclaimed, as Possum entered the kitchen.

"Ohhhh! Let me sit down."

Possum was shuffling to a nearby chair, as everyone rushed into the kitchen. His face and arms had numerous cuts, scrapes, and abrasions, the knees of his overalls were bloody and badly torn. He looked like he had been in a fight with a wildcat. One sleeve of his blue chambray shirt was missing and the other one was barely hanging on. He moaned as he gently sat down on a kitchen chair. "My back hurts."

"John, did you wreck the truck?" Mom Elliot inquired.

"No . . . worse." He looked toward Millie. "Get me a drink, Hon."

Millie grabbed a water glass that was setting by the sink. She quickly filled it with water. "Here Dad, now tell us what happened?"

"It's a long story." He gulped down half the water. "It's a long story."

"He must have hit his head. He's repeating himself." Mom Elliot felt his forehead.

"I'm alright, except my back hurts and I might bleed to death."

"Do you need a doctor?" Mom Elliot asked.

"Let's wait a day or two. See if I'm still alive."

"I'm going to start cleaning you up. Now, while I'm doing that, you tell us what happened," Mom Elliot pleaded. She was already heating water on the stove. "Was there an explosion?"

"Worse. Have you kids been making wine over at the Barnes' place?"

"Making wine! I know you got hit in the head," Mom Elliot exclaimed. "Why did you ask a question like that?"

"Because, when Eli came over and picked me up. He told me that Becky Williamson was telling around town, that his boys and Smoky was making wine at the old Barnes' place." Possum looked at Smoky.

"We wasn't making no wine," Smoky spontaneously answered.

"Becky's mad at Smoky. She might say anything," Millie added.

"John, you still haven't told us what happened?" Mom Elliot helped Possum take off his shirt. She had assembled the same assortment of supplies she had used earlier in the day, including Mercurochrome.

"Well, Eli and me decided after we changed the tire, we would go over there and see for ourselves if there was any wine being made. It was dark as a tomb by the time we got there and all we had for light was a two cell flashlight.

"So you went in the house?" Smoky asked nervously.

"How else was we going to find out if there was any wine over there? Of course we went in the house. We started downstairs, didn't find anything. Then we went upstairs. Eli had the flashlight, he took the lead. He opened the first door we came too, at the top of the stairs. Eli shined the light around the room. All of a sudden there was two big balls of fire charging at us. I'm not sure what it was, but I think it was a giant dog. We ran back into the hall. Eli rushed by, spinning me around. I guess I got a little confused in the dark, because I ran down the hall, away from the stairs. That hall is a dead end except for a broken out window at the end of the hallway. Eli runs down the stairs. He slams the door shut, saving his hide."

"Here I am, no light, nothing to protect myself, trapped with this oversized demon. I can hear him breathing as he comes closer, stalking me." Possum's voice quivered. "I can hear his toe nails as they scrape against the floor. He stops, only a few feet in front of me. I can still hear his breathing. I know he's getting ready to jump on me, like a cat pounces on a mouse." Possum stopped to catch his breath.

"What did you do?" Mom Elliot, asked anxiously.

"What did I do? The only thing I could do." Possum raised his voice. "I jumped out the window, on the porch roof."

"Thank God," she uttered.

"Thank God . . . my foot. I fell through the porch roof and the floor of the porch too."

"Oh, for heavens sake. It's a wonder you weren't killed."

"I may have been, I just haven't died . . . yet."

Mom Elliot had pulled a chair around so she was setting in front of Possum. She patted his hands. "You go on with your story, dear. I'm going to start cleaning you up."

"There's not much more to tell. I scrambled out of that porch floor and run for the truck. Eli already had it running, in fact, he was starting down the driveway, but I caught up with him and jumped in the back of the truck. We was gettin' out of there as fast as we could. The last thing I heard was that oversized hound let out a mournful howl, like he was warning us not to come back."

"Dad did you really run down the truck?" Millie asked.

"John, you haven't run in years." Mom Elliot remarked, as she began to clean up Possums injuries.

"Well, I run tonight. Like a watermelon thief racin' buckshot. You kids know anything about that dog?" He looked at Millie then Smoky, a scowl on his face.

Millie shyly stepped forward. "Dad, I've got a confession to make. I found that dog. I been hiding him over there at the Barnes' place."

"Land sakes child, it's a wonder you wasn't eaten alive." Mom Elliot glanced over at Millie.

"He likes me, I can do anything with him."

"You should have told me. How longs he been over there?" There was a note of concerned in Possum's voice.

"About two weeks. I wanted to tell you but he's got a little problem."

"What's that?" Possum asked.

"He don't like the boys." Millie moved closer to the table. "I don't think he likes men either."

"I can believe that. I'm living proof. You boys tried to mess with him?"

"He won't let us get close to him. He just barks and growls at us," Smoky spoke up.

"That's strange isn't it. Doesn't trust men. Huh! Interesting isn't it, Florence?"

"Oh, I don't know. Sounds like a pretty smart dog to me," she taunted.

"You would. What did you kids figure on doin' with him?"

"We was hoping we could get him tamed down and like us. Then we was going to bring him home." Millie sat down across the table from Possum. "We took Charlie over to see him. He's got a way with animals, but he couldn't do anything with him."

Possum closed his eyes a second, he opened them and blinked a couple of times. "I got a feeling there's a past behind him, that we may never understand. What do you think, Charlie?"

"I'm not sure what I think. He looks like he's had a pretty tough life. He's got a lot of scars, all over his body—maybe—he was abused by someone, most likely a man.

Mom Elliot was slowly getting Possum cleaned up. The cuts and scrapes were small and not too deep. He was looking a lot better after the dried blood and dirt was cleaned off. She had begun to dab Peroxide on his wounds.

"What's he look like?" Possum inquired.

"He's big, must weigh a hundred-fifty pounds. Kind of a blue-grey color. Short hair, short ears, big flat head," Charlie answered.

"I'm sure he's big, sounded like a cow running up the hallway after me. You know, I think I'll go back over there in the daylight, as soon as I'm feeling better. Eli shut the stairway door as he was gettin' out of there. He might be trapped upstairs. We might have to destroy him before he hurts someone. He sounds a little dangerous to me."

"I don't think he'll hurt anyone, Dad." Millie was getting ready to plead her case.

"He might." Possum cut her off. "We'll talk about it later. You kids better go to bed. I'm not feeling so hot."

Charlie, Millie, and Smoky weren't ready for bed. Truth was, they wanted to see how Possum took the Mercurochrome treatment. Finally, they decided that wasn't such a good idea. They went to bed.

CHAPTER 12

It was a warm still morning and the sun was just coming up, a beautiful redish-orange sunrise with just a few small clouds floating around on the horizon.

Herb Taylor held his Grandson by the arm, leading him from the house to an area behind the chicken coop. Charlie's hand had swollen to the point it looked grotesque. All sorts of colors blue, green, red and even a little yellow. The pain was unbearable, there was no doubt, his hand had become infected with gangrene. The decision had been made, if he was going to live, the hand had to come off.

They rounded the corner of the chicken coop. The old chopping block was waiting. The same one that had been used to turn the lights out for more spring fryers than anyone would care to count.

Charlie's mother and Mom Elliot were both there, crying in huge dishtowels.

A large fire helped the rising sun light up the area to the right of the chopping block, a freshly sharpened axe lay in the edge of the flame, its twelve inch blade slowly turning a fiery red. Perspiration poured from Charlie's fever racked body, his legs so heavy he could barely lift them. He pulled back, but his Grandfather only gripped his arms tighter.

"Maybe, we should wait until tomorrow. I think my hand looks better," he pleaded.

Possum was standing by the fire, smoking his pipe. He came over to help Herb Taylor drag Charlie over to the chopping block. He was screaming now, begging them to stop.

Suddenly Grandma Bledso appeared by the fire, pitching on more wood. She was laughing, cackling, enjoying herself.

They strapped his hand to the chopping block.

"Do you have to heat up the ax?" He asked, trying to stall off the inevitable.

"We have to sear the cut, so you won't bleed to death," Possum answered.

Zip had taken up a spot in front of the chopping block, waiting for Charlie's hand, so he could take his prize and bury it. He would leave it in the ground, until it was tender and smelled just right for a fine feast.

"No, No, don't chop off my hand," Charlie screamed.

Possum stood beside him, putting on heavy leather gloves. He lifted the red hot, steel handled ax from the fire.

"It has to be done, Charlie." His voice quivered as he spoke softly.

Grandma Bledso knelt down beside Charlie, putting her wrinkled, ugly face so close to his that all he could see was her crooked nose and missing teeth. Her breath smelling like garlic and dead carp.

"The hand's coming off," she screeched.

"No, no, please don't," he begged

"Charlie, Charlie wake up." He felt a soft hand touch his bare arm. "Charlie, wake up."

Opening his eyes, he realized he was setting up in bed, his body drenched in sweat. "Where am I?"

"You're at our place, Charlie. The Elliot's, remember."

His head began to clear. Millie was sitting on the bed beside him.

"You must have been having a terrible dream." She spoke in a whisper.

"You can say that again." He held up his sore hand, just to be sure it was still there.

"You was talking and making all kinds of noises in here. What was you dreaming about?"

"I don't want to talk about it."

"Well, anyway, me and Smoky are going over to the Barnes' place. I talked to Smoky, he's agreed to dump the wine."

"What about the dog?" Charlie rubbed his eyes, trying to wake up.

"I'm going to turn him loose. If he's still there. Before someone hurts him."

"What time is it, anyway?"

"I don't know, late. We'll go downstairs one at a time. We can slip out the back door. If Mom or Dad says anything, tell them you're going to the bathroom."

"We'll, need a light."

"I got one. Get your clothes on and meet us at the barn." She stood up and left the bedroom.

Charlie quickly pulled on his blue jeans; cautiously, he slipped down the stairs and out the back door.

Millie and Smoky were already waiting at the barn. Millie flashed a two cell flashlight at him as he entered the barn.

"Did they hear you?" Millie switched off the light.

92

"No, I don't think so. Nothing was said . . . anyway."

"Good, let's get going." She led them out the side door of the barn. Once clear of the yard, she turned off the light.

The moon was full, the sky filled with stars. It was a quiet night, with only a slight breeze out of the east. They walked side by side, Charlie in the middle, enjoying the peacefulness of the night.

A coyote let out a long howl from the river to the right. It was answered by a poor excuse for a howl and then another and another.

"What's all that about?" Smoky looked toward the river as the howls, wails, and yawls continued.

"Sounds to me like a bitch coyote made a kill and she's calling her pups to feed."

"How you know that?" Millie asked.

"I don't know, but I think that's what it's all about."

"You sure know a lot about animals, and they seem to trust you. How you explain that, Charlie?"

"I can't, Millie . . . they're eating now."

They continued the trip silently, each with their own thoughts. Charlie's were of the dream he had earlier. He certainly wasn't looking forward to going back to sleep. He wondered about the mysterious dog. Where had he come from? What had driven him to the point that he didn't trust, even hated, every man or boy that got near him? Even more intriguing, what mystical control did this petite, wisp of a girl, walking beside him, have over this otherwise savage beast?

They were questions he doubted would ever be answered. Charlie was sure they would never see him again, once given his freedom.

The Barnes' house began to take shape as they neared the yard. It looked eerie and spooky in the moonlight. A dark shadow that looked like a cottontail scurried across the path.

"Did you see that? What was it?" Smoky stopped short.

"It's just a rabbit. Don't be so jumpy," Millie quickly answered.

"Turn that light on. What are we doing walking around in the dark when we got a light."

"Oh. O.K.! What you so afraid of, anyway?"

"Who knows what might be out there lurking in the dark." Smoky grabbed the flashlight from Millie's hand. "Let me have that thing." He shined the light around the yard and then the house.

"See Smoky, there's nothing to be afraid of." Millie watched the beam of light as it circled the yard.

93

"Maybe not, but this place is giving me the willies."

They had reached the front step while Smoky and Millie bickered back and forth. They stopped, waiting for someone to volunteer to take the lead.

"Let's go, you got the light, Smoky." Charlie nudged Smoky with his elbow.

"I'm not going in there first. Not with that dog running loose."

"Give me the light. He might eat you two up." Millie took back the flashlight.

The porch floor creaked as they carefully followed Millie to the front door. Once inside they made their way to the steps that lead to the upper floor. The door was still closed.

"I'll bet he's still up there. Millie you better start talking to him, so we don't startle him like Possum and Eli did," Charlie warned.

She pushed the door open, it made a scratchy sound as it drug across the floor. Speaking softly she entered the stairway, shining the light up the stairs. Moving forward—they started up the steps. "Here boy, it's just me. Where you at?" There was no response, only silence.

Reaching the top floor, Millie, spoke again as she entered the room he had been calling home. "It's just me, come here boy."

Smoky and Charlie waited in the hallway.

"He's not in here." Millie spoke from inside the room.

"Check the other rooms," Charlie suggested.

She worked her way up the hall, checking each room. She stopped at the partially opened door of the wine room, the last room to check. "Didn't you guys close this door?"

"We closed it," Smoky answered nervously.

"You in here boy?" She slipped through the door. "Here he is, lying on the floor. I think he's dead."

Charlie and Smoky rushed in behind her. The oversized hound was lying in the middle of the room on his side, stretched out, not moving.

Charlie knelt down beside him, and placed his hand on his chest. "He's still breathing,"

"What's the matter with him?" Smoky moved closer.

"I don't know." Charlie ran his hand over Jumbo's massive head. He responded with a weak moan.

Smoky, took a step back. Millie joined Charlie at Jumbo's side.

"Let me see the light, Millie." Charlie took the light from her hand and shined it around the room.

The wine container was still setting in the corner. However, the dishtowel was ripped off and lay in a heap on the floor. Together they rush over and peered into the near empty crock container.

"He's been drinking the wine!" Millie exclaimed.

"Dog's don't drink wine. Do they, Charlie?" Smoky looked on in disbelief.

"This one does, we got a drunk dog," Charlie concluded.

"Boy, you can really pick 'em Millie, found a wino dog." Smoky ran his hand through his already ruffled hair.

"I didn't know he would drink wine. I wonder if he's going to die? What should we do with him?" She looked at Charlie.

"He should make it. I don't know how long it takes an intoxicated dog to sober up. He's carrying quite a load. Smoky, let's get that crock out of here."

They picked up the crock and carried it downstairs. Millie followed with the flashlight. It was carefully slid across the rickety old porch floor, safely off the porch, it was again picked up and carried to the edge of the buffalo grass where they dumped what was left of the brew in the weeds.

"Where we going to put this thing?"

"Well, Smoky, I think I saw an old shed over there, that might be as good a place as any for right now." Charlie pointed to the west.

They made their way through the weeds to a small broken down wooden shed a short distance from the house. Charlie and Smoky carefully set the crock in one corner, as Millie held the flashlight.

"Let me see that light." Charlie extended his hand toward Millie, as they returned to the house. He shined the light at the porch roof. "I want to see where your Dad fell through the roof. Should be right over here." He took a few steps to the right. The hole wasn't hard to find, it was right under the hallway window, just as Possum had stated. It was a jagged, roughhewn hole that appeared to be just the right size for Possum to fit through. His missing shirt sleeve was hanging limply on a splintered two by four.

"It's a wonder he didn't break his legs," Millie remarked.

"That's for sure, must be a ten foot drop." Charlie continued to study the hole.

"What are we going to do with the dog?" Smoky changed the subject.

"I think we'll leave him where he's at. When he sobers up, he can go on his merry way."

"Charlie, do you think he'll be sober by morning?"

"I don't know. I've never seen anyone passed out drunk, let alone a dog."

"I bet he's going to be in a bad mood when he sobers up," Smoky speculated.

"Why you say that?" Charlie asked.

"Because, Junior and Curly claim their dad is always in a bad mood after he's been drinking."

"Let's go back up there . . . I've got some unfinished business with that big boy."

"What you mean?" Smoky and Millie follow Charlie back into the house.

"You'll see, Smoky."

They climbed the steps to the upper floor. Jumbo hadn't moved he was still lying in the same place. Millie knelt down beside him and stroked his head. He remained motionless and emitted a low moan.

Charlie reached in the hip pocket of his jeans and pulled out the bandanna handkerchief, used to wrap his hand the day before.

"What you doin'?" He had awoken Smoky's curiosity.

"I'm going to leave him a little present." He kneeled down across from Millie and wrapped the handkerchief around Jumbo's neck. His neck was big and there was just enough cloth left to tie a knot. Charlie was having trouble tying the knot, with his bandaged hand.

"Here let me help you, Charlie," Millie offered.

Working together they finished the job. Charlie ran his hand over his powerful, well-muscled body; his hair was short and soft, almost like silk.

"Why did you tie your handkerchief around his neck?" Smoky asked, as he too cautiously ran his hand over his sleek body.

"I want him to know what I smell like . . . just in case we ever meet again. Also, maybe, he'll understand that we don't mean him no harm."

Smoky stood up. "Let's go home, I'm tired."

"Me too." Millie turned and shined the light toward the door.

"Give me that light." Smoky spoke at the bottom of the stairs. "I want to get our tobacco."

"Your tobacco, don't be trying to drag us in on your schemes." Millie handed Smoky the flashlight.

CHAPTER 13

Ol Razor visited the snow covered corn field again, the fourth time in as many days. He searched under the snow for an ear of corn that the harvest crew had missed. It was useless, the field had been gleaned clean. Hungry and disgusted, he left the field and returned to the river. The winter had been hard on Razor, food was scarce and what little food there was had been covered up by the snow. He had turned to feeding with domestic hogs when the opportunity arose. This usually meant a fight, even they didn't want to give up their grub. He had crippled several herd boars, making them useless for breeding purposes.

Once he had been caught by farm dogs as he raided their masters feed room. It was a fatal mistake, one dog was killed and two others badly injured. Razor went about his business as usual, still free and causing havoc as he chose.

The winter was equally hard on Jumbo, not only did he have to find food, usually he had to catch it after he found it, many times he failed. He hunted the river and searched the prairie, but adequate food for his large body was always in short supply.

He would sleep where he could find shelter; a warm bed was just as big a challenge. He found a cave at Murphy's Grove that was quite comfortable, except when mother nature sent a cold wind from the North. The cave faced the north and the cold air would whip through the entrance, causing it to feel like an ice box. The area around the cave provided some food, but there was more game on the river.

He spent the nights at abandoned farmsteads from time to time. The cottontail rabbit liked to live around the old deserted buildings, as winter wore on the rabbits were getting harder to find. Sometimes he would find food at the Barnes' place, left in the upstairs room where he had stayed. He knew who was leaving it there; the odor of the young girl was always around.

In his travels he found a straw stack some distance off the river. This would become his favorite place to spend the night. He could burrow deep in the straw, curl up in a ball, nose tucked under his tail. Finding warmth here, he could find no other place. The smell of the fresh clean straw brought back memories of the house of straw bales that Armella had built for him. He had dreams of her warm soft hands stroking his velvet like coat or a tender hug as she left for school. Jumbo would wake up yearning to hear her gentle voice.

The antisocial life he was leading and the loneliness of the cold nights would become more than Jumbo could bear at times. He would leave his warm bed and walk to the highest hill where he would begin a wailing ululation that would sometimes last until dawn.

The vociferation attracted the attention of all the night creatures. The little wolverine of the plains, the precarious Silver Tipped Badger, pound for pound the most ferocious animal on the prairie, digging for a gopher in the alfalfa field, rested his long sharp claws, his quest for food interrupted by this wretched howl in the night.

The mother raccoon and her nearly grown kittens listened inquisitively to this eerie bay, as they searched for freeze dried fruit in an old hackberry tree.

The crafty coyote, quieted his stentor caterwaul, as he heeded this painful solo that carried across the frozen prairie like a train whistle on a still morning.

The Great Horned Owl with wings spread, glided silently over the graveyard. He stopped to rest on Luther Bledso's black granite tombstone, the tallest in the cemetery. He understood this mournful melody, as did all the creatures of the night. This was not just a lamenting cry of loneliness, this was a foreboding call, carried by an icy wind, a warning—of impending misfortune.

CHAPTER 14

Jumbo sat at the edge of a plum thicket on a warm May morning in nineteen fifty-four. He had been watching the boy ever since he crested the hill that over looked Murphy's Grove. First appearing as a tiny figure on the hill top, but now as he drew closer, Jumbo thought perhaps this was the boy he had seen in the upstairs room of the old Barnes' house.

Murphy's Grove was one of Charlie Mayfair's favorite places to fish. He had packed a lunch and planned to spend the day, fishing and doing whatever took his fancy at the time. The large spring feed pond with crystal clear water was well stocked with fish, everything from bullheads to large mouth bass. It was surrounded by over five acres of woods that abounded with song birds and wildlife; certainly, an appealing place for a young man to spend the day. A pair of squirrels were playing tag in an oak tree just off the shore line. A bluejay scolded Charlie from his perch in a large willow as he invaded his territory.

Charlie found a comfortable looking spot below the dam and kneeled down to bait one of the two poles he had brought along. Slowly he weaved a worm on the hook, and set the cork about three feet above the bait. His cast settled the cork a short distance off the shore line near a large log that lay in the water.

Charlie's mother had bought him new shoes for the summer. They hurt his feet, so he slipped them off as he watched the bobber sitting quietly on the still water. He removed a lure from his tackle box and carefully tied it on the line of the second pole he had brought along.

Jumbo had stayed in the timber as he circled the pond. Now he stood behind the dam. A light southerly breeze lifted Charlie's scent over the dam. Jumbo took notice as his nostrils sucked in a familiar aroma. It was the same odor that had been around his neck for over a month last fall.

The scent aroused Jumbo's curiosity, slowly, quietly, he worked his way up the steep bank, and peeked over the top.

Charlie raised the rod over his head as he prepared to flip the off white lure in the water. The hair stood up on the back of his neck as he got the feeling he was being watched. He turned his head slightly to the right and saw nothing, a look to the left provided the same outcome. A cold chill ran down his spine, causing the rest of his body to quiver. Then he realized something was on the pond dam behind him. The whole area had gotten very quiet except for the panting sound behind his back.

He turned slowly, cautiously, fearfully to see what had brought about the eerie silence that had subdued the woods.

He saw the large blue-grey silhouette, out of the corner of his eye, outlined against a backdrop of willows and cottonwood trees. He turned slowly, still on his knees.

He understood now what had hushed the area. The King of the Woods was watching him from the top of the pond dam.

He spoke in a quiet voice. "Nice to see you again. Did you spend the winter here?"

He turned his head to one side as if trying to understand what was being said. His dark leering eyes following Charlie's every move.

"Come here, boy," Charlie coaxed.

Jumbo stood his ground, not moving.

"It's alright, I'm not going to hurt you." He took a small step forward.

His ears rose up a little, he wagged his tail once—twice. He carefully inched forward.

"You can trust me . . . I'm your friend."

Charlie's heart was pounding in his chest as he realized this might be his only chance to make up with the big hound. His lunch was setting within arms reach, carefully he picked it up. "Are you hungry?" He pulled a bologna sandwich from the brown paper sack.

Jumbo's ears perked up a little more as he moved a step closer. Charlie held out the sandwich, hoping he would accept his offering.

"Here, boy, take it. I hope you like mustard . . . that's all we got."

He took another step. Charlie took a step toward him. He dropped his ears so they lay flat on his head, a caution flag—he was still in control. Charlie's heart was in his throat as he kneeled back down on the ground. Jumbo's ears lifted as he took another step closer. They were almost within reach of each other. Charlie extended his hand, laying the bologna sandwich on the ground. Jumbo moved forward, cautiously he smelled Charlie's gift. Satisfied he picked it up and wolfed it down.

"You liked that, didn't you. I got another one here." Charlie pulled a second sandwich from the brown paper bag.

He watched Charlie, running his tongue over his lips. "Now big boy, you have to come and get this one and let me put my hands on you." He extended his hand toward Jumbo who stood back for a few seconds and finally took a step forward. His ears were standing up again as his keen eyes followed the sandwich, as Charlie moved it from side to side. He moved toward Charlie, stopping just short of his hand. Charlie pulled his hand back, almost to his waist, forcing Jumbo to take another step forward. Finally his powerful jaws grasp the mouthful of food Charlie held. He placed his left hand gently on Jumbo's head as he grasp the sandwich. He pulled his head back slightly and looked up at Charlie's hand. Satisfied that Charlie meant him no harm, he took the food from his hand as Charlie stroked his head.

He finished the sandwich in one swallow. Slowly Charlie ran his hand from Jumbo's head to his back as he examined the numerous scars that covered his body. Most of them looked as if they had come from rips or tears that had been left to heal themselves. Charlie wondered what could have inflicted this much damage on a dog this big. Jumbo began to lick his hand.

"So you're going to make up with me. Boy, you sure have been abused sometime in your life. Looks like your shoulder healed up real nice, unusual scar . . . looks like an upside down cross."

He rubbed his head against Charlie's leg, as he playfully scratched him behind the ears. Jumbo liked the attention and stood calmly by his side. Charlie accidentally turned his right ear over exposing the underside to the bright sunlight; something caught his eye, a closer examination revealed what looked like a tattoo.

"What you got here, big fellow?" He pulled his head away but not before Charlie made out the five letters that had been stamped in his ear for life. He ran the letters through his mind S-H-A-N-K. "Did someone named Shank own you, boy? I never have heard of nobody named Shank around here." He looked up at Charlie as if he recognized the name.

Charlie noticed movement as the bobber began to do a dance on the water.

"We got a fish." He quickly raced down to the pole, setting the hook as the bobber disappeared under the water.

Jumbo followed Charlie to the edge of the water, watching as he reeled in the fish. Charlie was disappointed when it turned out to be

102

only a small bullhead. He took the hook out of its mouth and tossed it on the bank. Jumbo stood over Charlie's catch, watching as it flopped around in the grass. Charlie was digging another worm from the can when he realized Jumbo was disappearing over the pond dam with his catch.

"Hey! Come back here with my fish." Charlie grabbed his shoes and rushed to the top of the dam. Jumbo was just below the dam, standing still, facing him; the fish still in his mouth. Charlie quickly pulled on his shoes. "Bring my fish back here, you thief," he ordered. Jumbo moved away as Charlie ran down the pond dam, following Jumbo into the timber. Jumbo stayed well ahead, but turned to face Charlie from time to time, checking to see if he was still coming.

Slowly he was leading Charlie to the west side of the woods. They came to an area where a rocky bluff blended into the landscape. Jumbo waited for Charlie at an opening in the rock wall, he vanished into the wall of sandstone as Charlie got closer.

The opening was narrow, but certainly large enough for the mysterious hound to slip through with ease. When Charlie reached the entrance, Jumbo met him, preventing him from entering. He was no longer carrying the bullhead, but had a piece of cloth dangling from his mouth. Charlie quickly recognized it as part of the bandanna handkerchief he had tied around his neck at the Barnes' house. Charlie took it in his hand, Jumbo released his grip and gave it to him.

"Is this suppose to be some kind of a trade, you take my fish and give me back my own handkerchief . . . or what's left of it. You're a real horse trader, you are." Charlie stuffed the rag in his hip pocket.

Jumbo moved to the side of the entrance. Charlie wondered if that was a sign that he could enter. Charlie tested him by moving toward his lair. He let him in, following close behind, Charlie knew now that he had accepted him and he had won his trust.

The cave was rather small, Jumbo could stand up but that was about all. There was very little light, Charlie's eyes slowly adjusted to the darkness. He couldn't help noticing that Jumbo had picked up several toys that were lying around the cave; everything, from the leg bone of a cow to a rusty old hammer. Charlie didn't see his fish, it was most likely buried in the loose sand that covered the floor of the cave.

Jumbo lay down beside Charlie, resting his head on his leg. Charlie stroked his silky hair as they bonded their friendship. They both fell asleep.

Charlie didn't know how long they slept, but when he crawled out of the cave, the sun had disappeared and dark clouds covered the sky.

"Rain clouds." Charlie said, to Jumbo. "Maybe I better get home."

Jumbo was standing beside him. "I'm headin' for the house. You better stay here, boy. I'll bring you some food the first chance I get." He licked his hand as thunder rumbled in the west.

Jumbo followed as Charlie moved around the pond to pick up his fishing poles. It was starting to sprinkle as he gathered his fishing equipment. He hurried for home, hoping he could make it before the rain really started coming down. The rain was coming down in torrents by the time he reached the front door.

It rained off and on all afternoon. The rain continued through the night and into the next day. It was well into the next afternoon when the clouds finally cleared, and the sun began to warm the water saturated ground. The creeks and river were running bank full.

CHAPTER 15

Herb Taylor got up from the breakfast table as the phone hanging on the kitchen wall rang for the third time. He answered it with his usual, "Howdy." He smiled as he listened to the voice on the other end of the line. "Yeah, he's here. It's for you Charlie. Smoky."

Charlie moved his chair over to the phone as his Grandfather handed him the receiver. "Hi! What's up?"

"The river," Smoky answered. "The catfish are biting like crazy. Cedrick Miller pulled out a whole gunny sack full yesterday. Any chance you could get over here."

"I don't know. Let me call you back. I'll see what's going on around here."

"Alright, but try to get over here."

"I will." He hung up the phone. "Smoky wants me to come over and go fishing. I guess they're really biting. Cedrick Miller caught a sack full yesterday."

"I guess you can, but I don't have time to take you over there." He stopped at the door as he broke off a small piece of chewing tobacco from a plug he carried in his shirt pocket.

"How about riding that black filly we been breaking? She rides pretty good and she needs the work." Charlie had his Grandfather figured out, it always looked better if you were doing something worthwhile.

"That's not a bad idea. She needs riding. See what your mother says?"

Charlie turned to face his mother. "Is it O.K. Mother?"

Anna Mayfair looked over the table at her son. She was a tall, slender, attractive woman with dark brown eyes that matched her short curly hair. She left home to attend college where she met and married Charlie's father. They were married only a short time when her husband was called into the service of his country. He would never return, giving his life at Normandy Beach. She grieved her loss and when it became more than she could bear alone, she returned home, with her infant son, to live with her parents. She had never remarried; content to raise her son alone. She was a gentle likable woman who seldom raised her voice, if she did, everyone took notice.

She loved hard work and took on every task with the tenacity of a whirlwind.

"I guess, but you be real careful, that river can be pretty dangerous when it's running bank full." She wiped her hands on the dark red apron she was wearing around her slender waist.

Charlie was already dialing the phone.

"Did you hear what I said, Charlie?" She raised her voice just a bit.

"Yes, Mother, I heard you?" Charlie respectfully answered, while he finished dialing the number.

****

Everyone was waiting for Charlie's arrival as he reined in the little black filly in front of Smoky, Junior, Curly and Millie. He had barely dismounted, when Curly and Junior began too unsaddled her, leading her to the barn after they finished.

They were just about to leave when Mom Elliot shouted in a demanding voice. "You kids come here, I want to talk to you."

They walked up to the house, knowing what to expect.

"Now I want you kids to be careful. Don't fall in the river. I don't want you to do any horsing around, when you're around that river . . . understand."

They all nodded their heads indicating they understood.

"Charles, how are you this morning?" She looked at Charlie and smiled.

"I'm just fine, ma'am" He smiled back at her.

"I fixed you kids something to eat." She held out a brown paper sack. Junior was quick to take charge of the food. "Does anyone have a watch?"

"I do." Charlie reached in his pocket and held up an old pocket watch for all to see.

"Good, Charles you're the timekeeper. I want you all home, here, by five o'clock." She pointed her finger toward the ground.

They turned to leave, hoping the lecture was over.

"Charles, I want to speak with you for a minute." Mom Elliot spoke with a certain amount of authority.

He stopped, wondering what he had done.

"You kids go ahead, Charles will catch up."

Charlie followed her into the kitchen. She stopped just inside the kitchen door. "Charles, I want you to do me a favor."

"Re, really?" He stammered, hands in his pockets.

"Would you please keep an eye on Milacent? I know Richard won't and Eli and Luther could care less. She has certainly been a handful lately. In trouble of one kind or another all the time. Moody, rebellious, I guess she's just growing up. Can you do that for me, Charles?"

"Well, I'll try."

"I know you will." She patted Charlie on the shoulder as she guided him toward the door.

"Bye, ma'am." Charlie quickly stepped out the door.

"Thanks, Charles," she concluded.

He ran to catch up with the gang.

"What did she want?" Smoky asked, as he approached.

"She just wanted to know how my folks were getting along?" He lied, fearing he might hurt someone's feelings.

Smoky handed Charlie two fishing poles and a tackle box. The boys were all loaded down with fishing tackle, bait and a milk jug filled with water. Junior was still in charge of the food.

Millie wasn't carrying anything. She was full of energy, running at times to check flowers, bugs, or anything else that aroused her curiosity. She raced ahead, wearing a pair of faded blue jeans and a pink sleeveless blouse with shoes that had seen better days, but were certainly good enough for this outing.

With the rain came high humidity. Everyone was sweating profusely as they neared the river. Smoky and Junior's shirts had already been tied around their waist, half covering worn out jeans. Curly's bib overalls were full of holes, allowing for plenty of ventilation. Charlie's jeans were in a little better shape, but his shirt was certainly down to its final trip.

"Where we going to fish?" Charlie wiped the sweat off his brow with an old handkerchief.

"There's a good place just north of the Farris Caves," Junior replied.

"I think I've fished there before, that is a good place." Charlie set the cap back on his head.

Everyone was anxious to get to the river, anticipating a large catch, because the fishing was always good when the Smoky Hill

River was running bank full. In nineteen forty-six the Kanopolis Lake was completed and it was only a few miles downstream. The fish would come out of the lake, swimming for miles upstream, feeding on worms, birds or anything else that got caught up in the flood waters.

They looked in awe when they finally arrived at the river; it was a sight to behold. Millions of gallons of cold, fresh rain water cascaded downstream to an unknown destination, carrying with it tons of precious top soil, trees, trash and anything else it could pick up on its rambunctious journey to the lake.

The troops had chosen to fish off a high steep dirt bank on the east side of the river. A good stand of weeds had grown up on the bank. They began pulling them up and tossing them in the river. It didn't take long and a small area was cleared, now they had a place to sit, bait their hooks and rest while they waited for the catfish to come to dinner.

Smoky reached in a burlap gunny sack and pulled out a quart jar filled with a pink looking liquid, with chunks of what looked like meat floating at the top.

"What in the world is that, Smoky?" Charlie inquired, being careful not too get to close.

"This, my friend, is Smoky's Genuine Smoky River Catfish Bait. Guaranteed to catch fish when all else fails." Smoky held his head high as he kneeled down beside his prized bait.

"Where did you get it?" Charlie took another step back.

"I made it." Smoky threw out his chest swelling up a bit.

"Out of what?" Millie stepped back from the concoction.

The lid was dome shaped and the whole thing looked as if it could explode at any time.

"I took a road killed jackrabbit, skinned it and cut the meat in nice sized chunks. Then I put it in this jar and added some spring water. It's been setting in the sun for three days, now if that's not catfish bait, I'll eat my hat." Smoky hovered proudly over his prize winning recipe.

Junior and Curly moved closer to examine Smoky's miracle catfish bait.

"You're really going to open that stuff up and put it on a hook?" Charlie took another step back.

"You damn betcha." Smoky got a good grip on the lid and gave it a quick turn.

Charlie stepped behind a tree, fearing what the consequences might be for such reckless action. Millie quickly joined him.

The ugly liquid run down the side of the jar as it began to gurgle and fizz, the smell so bad it would have gagged a maggot.

The odor took Junior and Curly's breath away as they made a quick exit, stepping back a good ten yards.

Smoky wasn't giving up, slowly he finished unscrewing the lid. The smell of decaying flesh was atrocious. He stepped back and turned away to catch his breath. He had a reputation for having a weak stomach, but his honor was at stake now. He swallowed hard trying to keep down his breakfast. "Millie give me a pole."

"I'm as close to that foul smelling junk as I'm going to get." She clearly announced. "Get your own pole."

"Coward." He taunted as he walked over and picked up one of the nearby fishing poles. He returned to his prize winning recipe and knelt down to bait his hook.

"You're not going to touch that stuff with your hands, are you?" Millie shouted, a disgusted look on her face.

"I don't know any other way to get it on a hook, do you?" Smoky gagged, but still managed to keep down his breakfast.

"Well! You're not touching any of our food." Millie proclaimed, as she raced out from behind the tree and grabbed the sack containing their lunch.

Smoky had picked up two small sticks and was trying to fish out a chunk of the pungent bait without putting his hand in the nasty smelling liquid. He was holding his breath, and finally had to turn away to draw in some air. He returned to the task at hand and painstakingly got one of the delicate morsels out of the jar and on the ground. He quickly screwed the lid back on the jar. The color had left his face as he stood up and walked a few feet away to catch his breath.

They all watched in awe, as he threaded the sharp smelling bait on the hook. Smoky didn't look too good, but he still managed to cast the baited hook twenty feet out into the river. The swift running current picked it up and rapidly brought it in to the riverbank downstream. He left out some more line, when he was satisfied with its placement, he set the drag. Placing the pole in a forked stick, he sat down on a nearby log, downwind from everyone else.

"I think I'll stick to worms." Junior conceded, as he dug for a worm in a coffee can.

"I'm with you, Junior, give me one of them worms." Junior handed Charlie the worms.

In the meantime, Curly was reaching in the bib pocket of his overalls. He pulled out a large leopard frog. "Now here we have the best catfish bait known to mankind." Curly held the frog up by the legs for all to see. "And I am sure the biggest fish in the river is waiting for this baby to hit the water."

With their baited hooks in the fast moving current they all found comfortable places to rest, while they waited for something to happen. Millie was sitting on a log behind the boys, still protecting the lunch. The trees that lined the river bank offered shade, from the noon day sun.

They were all nearly asleep when someone's casting reel began to click. Charlie looked up as the clicks became more rapid. "Somebody's got a bite!"

Smoky was already setting the hook as he spoke. "I got 'im! I got 'im!" Smoky was holding the pole high in the air, the line was taunt as a fiddle string, his pole nearly bent into a horseshoe. He held the line tight as the fish continued to pull.

"Give him some line, if you have to, or he'll break it," Junior advised.

Everyone had gathered around Smoky, hoping to be of some help.

"Maybe, we should get these other lines out of the water, so they don't get all tangled up," Junior suggested. They quickly took his idea to heart and reeled in their poles.

Smoky continued to play the fish, who was now heading downstream. It was a big fish and Smoky had his hands full. Line was spinning off the casting reel at a record pace. "If he doesn't turn, I'm going to run out of line!"

"Put a little pressure on that line, maybe he'll turn," Curly suggested.

"I told you guys I had the best catfish bait there ever was," Smoky bragged.

"Oh! Don't be so cocky. Any fish that would eat something that rotten, can't be too bright." Millie snapped back.

The big fish turned coming upstream along the riverbank. Smoky was cranking line back on the reel so fast his hand was only a blur as the fish went past on his trip upstream.

Smoky continued to play the big fish and was slowly winning the battle. His runs up and down the river were getting shorter and slower. Smoky lured him closer to the bank with every pass.

Pandemonium broke loose as he surfaced, rolling over, exposing his snow white belly. The fish was even bigger than anyone expected, certainly a near record channel cat. Everyone began to holler and jump up and down as they realized what Smoky had on the end of his line.

There was a problem looming ahead. The sides of the river were very steep, and somehow they had to lift this monster from the water and onto the bank. The water was only two to three feet from going over the bank, but Smoky certainly couldn't lift this big fish with his pole and line. The line would break for sure.

Charlie brought the problem to everyone's attention. "Anybody got any idea how we're going to get him out of the water and onto the bank?"

"We need a net," Curly replied.

"Forget that idea, we don't have a net." Millie answered, as she peered over the bank.

"Don't get too close to the edge of that bank," Charlie warned.

She stepped back.

"I'll lay down on my belly and reach down and grab him," Junior volunteered.

"He'll drag you right in the river." Charlie quickly responded. "Well, maybe if you lay down and I grab onto your legs and Curly holds onto me, we could make a human chain and horse him out of there."

"Yeah, I think that'll work," Junior agreed. "Charlie, you should be on the back, you're the biggest."

Smoky had worked his catch to within six feet of the bank.

"Let's get ready, boys." Junior lay down on the river bank.

Curly took Juniors leg's and clamped his ankles against his ribs with his upper arms. Charlie in turn wrapped his arms around Curly's waist. All they needed now was to get the fish close enough for Junior to grab.

Millie was keeping a keen eye on the fish as she tried to give Smoky directions. "Bring him in, this way." She pointed up river.

Junior was doing his best, but the big catfish was staying out of his reach. Smoky was getting tired, but he wasn't giving up, he knew if he landed this monster he would be the talk of the town for weeks.

"Let me down a little bit more!" Junior hollered.

They edged forward a few inches.

"Just a little closer," Junior coached. "I got him!"

Junior had reached in the fish's mouth and grabbed his lower jaw with both hands. "Pull, pull you guys! He's chewing the hell out of my hands!"

They set their feet and pulled as hard as they could.

Millie was at the edge of the bank She grabbed onto Juniors belt to help pull. "He's coming, keep pulling!" She screamed.

Smoky had laid down his pole and grabbed onto Charlie to help pull. The riverbank was slick from the rain and it was hard to get much leverage. At last the big fish began to clear the water. He panicked realizing he was coming out of the water. He threw the lower half of his body from side to side, splashing water all over, in one last desperate effort to break Junior's grip.

"Get him up, I'm loosing my grip!" Junior hollered.

Just as they were bringing him up onto the bank, he gave one last powerful lunge. The boys began to slip on the slick ground. Junior slid part way down the bank.

Millie was still hanging onto his belt. She lost her footing and pitched head first into the river, barely getting out a short scream before she hit the cold water.

Junior lost his grip and the fish was gone.

As fear set in, they found new strength, with one mighty pull Junior was jerked onto the riverbank.

They scrambled to the river's edge to help Millie. She had already been pulled away from the bank and was rapidly being taken down stream by the strong current.

"Swim to shore, Millie!" Smoky screamed.

Millie was not a good swimmer. Just staying afloat in the cold water was going to be a struggle for the frightened girl.

The boys ran along the riverbank, hoping to catch up, and help her in some way. The riverbank was too slick to make good time and she was quickly disappearing down the river as they dodged trees, trash and vines, trying to catch up.

Everyone realized the urgency of the situation and the tragedy that was taking place right before their eyes. They had always gone to the river to play and have a good time. Now suddenly, they saw the dark side of the river. The truth was, the river could be cold, dangerous and certainly unforgiving.

Charlie had a knot in his stomach and tears in his eyes, as he still hoped to catch up with the panic stricken girl. He thought about how Mom Elliot had asked him to watch out for her. How was he ever going to face her; if worse came to worse and Millie drowned? She was out of sight. "God help her." He prayed, tears running down his face.

He could think of only one thing that might save her. They were close to the Old Iron Bridge. If she could just make it to the bridge, maybe, she could grab hold of the steel trusses or stringers and pull herself out of the water, until they could get help.

They arrived at the bridge, out of breath, scared and pale. Millie wasn't there. They stood on the bridge, looking at each other, afraid to think about her limp, lifeless body floating at the bottom of the river.

Smoky was on his knees, sobbing uncontrollably.

Curly was halfway across the bridge, he turned and shouted, "I hear someone talking."

Everyone raced to his side. They too, could hear voices coming from the other side of the river. They ran across the bridge. Uncle Ezra's green Dodge pickup was parked at the west end of the bridge. The voices seemed to be coming from the pickup. The boys crossed the bridge and soon realized it was only the noon news on the radio.

"Who's up there?" A voice called from under the bridge.

They rushed to the bridge railing and peered over the side—seeing nothing. "It's Charlie Mayfair. Is that you Uncle Ezra?"

"Yeah. You with the Elliot girl?"

"Yes sir. Have you seen her." Charlie answered, hoping to hear some good news.

"She's down here with me, nearly drown. I may need some help. There's a blanket on the seat of my pickup, bring it down."

"I'll get it," Curly volunteered.

"We'll be right down." Charlie, Smoky, and Junior hurried to the west end of the bridge, leaping over the side when there was only about a four foot drop. They found Uncle Ezra twenty feet up the riverbank, under the bridge, with Millie lying face down in the sand. Uncle Ezra was working frantically on the motionless girl, systematically pushing on her ribs and back. She was wet, pale, cold, seeing nothing out of half open eyes, coughing up river water as Uncle Ezra pushed on her back.

Smoky dropped to his knees beside her, tears still running down his cheeks. "Millie, Millie!" He shook her shoulder with both hands. "You alright? Answer me—please!"

"Take it easy son, leave me work on her. Where's that blanket."

"Here it is." Curly answered, as he arrived at the scene.

"Let's get her on this blanket." Uncle Ezra took the blanket and spread it out beside Millie. "Charlie, grab her legs and help me lift her over here." They carefully lifted her up and laid her face down on the blanket.

Everyone watched quietly as Uncle Ezra continued to try and revive the limp body on the blanket. "You boys ever see a big dog around here?"

The boys looked at one another, as Smoky paced nervously back and forth.

"Why do you ask?" Charlie broke the silence.

"Boy's...a big blue-grey colored dog drug her to shore down there. If it wouldn't have been for that dog, she would still be floating down the river."

"There's been a dog seen around here that looks like that." Charlie finally answered after a moments hesitation.

"Well, this girl is certainly lucky he was around today . . . or she'd be a goner fer sure."

Millie coughed a couple of times, gagged and spit up more river water. Her eyes fluttered as she coughed again. Her eyes opened as she rolled over on her back.

"Take it easy, don't try to get up." Uncle Ezra cautioned as he wrapped the blanket around her.

"How did she fall in the river?"

The boys took turns telling Uncle Ezra about the big fish and how Millie had fallen in the river. By the time they had finished, Millie was starting to get some color back in her face. She spoke, her first words since she had fallen in the river, "What happened to the dog?"

"He took off when I started coming down to help you. How did that dog come to help you?" Uncle Ezra helped her set up.

"I don't really know," Millie answered. "I remember thinking I was going to drown." She spoke slowly as if trying to understand what had happened. "Then he swam up beside me. I put my arms around his neck. That's the last thing I remember."

"Well, he drug you to shore by the arm." Uncle Ezra reached down and lifted Millie's right arm. Teeth marks were still quite visible on her arm. There was no doubt in anyone's mind, that they had been made by a large dog.

"Help me up, Charlie." Millie reached out her hand.

"Not so fast. You just sit there and rest a minute young lady. I think she's going to be alright." Uncle Ezra stood up and readjusted a worn out straw hat that was setting to one side of his head. "But, I think I better give her a ride home. You boys want a ride home?"

The color was coming back to Smoky's face and everyone was starting to feel better as they helped Millie to her feet. She wasn't to steady, but she was certainly looking better.

"We better get our poles and stuff," Junior replied.

"Yeah, we'll walk," Smoky spoke up.

The walking idea was appealing, no one was going to be anxious to see Mom Elliot after she found out about this ordeal.

Charlie helped Uncle Ezra load Millie in the pickup while Junior and Curly gathered up his fishing equipment.

The boys were almost across the bridge when the hair stood up on the back of Charlie Mayfair's neck and a cold chill ran down his spine. The same feeling he had felt just a few days earlier at Murphy's Grove. He looked around, not seeing anything, but he knew Jumbo was watching.

CHAPTER 16

Millie Elliot's near fatal drowning caused considerable excitement in the area and the newspapers had made the adventure front page material. The wire service picked the incident up as well and the story appeared in newspapers all over the country. A month had passed and everything had returned to normal or as normal as it gets in a small town.

Herb Taylor eased his pickup in a parking place in front of the grocery store. He looked over at his passenger as he shut off the switch. "Charlie, I've got some things I need to pick up here for your mother. You go over and get yourself a haircut. Here's some money." He fished a dollar bill out of his wallet and handed it to his Grandson. "You can get yourself a soda or something with what's left. I'm going over to the blacksmiths after I'm done here. Stick around main street, so I can find ya."

"Slow as things go in that barbershop on a Saturday morning, I'll still be waiting in line." Charlie opened the car door and slowly eased his long legs out onto the blacktop street. He stood up, stretched, and adjusted his ball cap.

"I know what you mean. Just be around, I'll find ya."

Charlie crossed the street to Uncle Ezra's Barbershop. The door was propped open with two red clay bricks, stacked one on top the other. The morning sun shined in the door, brightening up the otherwise drab decor. The barbershop was in a long narrow building with a large window that overlooked the street. A wall had been put up about a third of the way back to separate the barbershop from the rest of the building. Uncle Ezra lived in the back of the building.

Charlie casually stepped through the door, taking a seat in one of a dozen old wooden chairs that lined the walls of the barbershop. Two Saturday morning loafers had their noses buried in a couple of three day old newspapers that they had picked up off a small round table in the corner. A large ceiling fan hung in the middle of the room. It turned slowly and created the only air movement in the room.

Uncle Ezra was removing the barbers apron from the only paying customer in the shop.

"Your next, Charlie." Uncle Ezra took a half dollar from his customer and put it in the cash register. "There's been a fellow in town, asking about you. Says he wants to talk to you." Uncle Ezra took a sip from a nearby bottle of beer.

"What's he want to talk to me about?"

"I think he wants to talk to you about that dog." He belched. "I told him what I knew."

"Who is he? Where's he from?" Charlie sat down in the barbers chair.

"Oklahoma. He's an Indian."

Uncle Ezra had just finished pinning the apron around Charlie's neck, when a stranger stepped in the open door. He looked around the room from habit; finally his eyes settled on Charlie Mayfair.

He was a medium sized man, wearing faded blue jeans and a blue chambray shirt. His long black hair was woven together in one long braid that ran down his back nearly to his waist. He walked with a slight limp on his right leg. The barbershop was silent except for the walking heel on his black cowboy boots, causing the old barbershop floor to creak as he walked across it. He wasn't a real handsome man, but he had a friendly smile on his cherry-bronze face. He stopped in front of the barber's chair. "You Charlie Mayfair?"

Possum Elliot slipped in the door and took a seat in the nearest chair.

"Yes." Charlie had his feet planted solidly on the foot rest, ready to make a quick exit if necessary.

"I figured you were, someone told me to look for a tall, good looking boy, that looked like he needed a haircut." He smiled as he extended a large callused hand.

Charlie reached a boyish hand out from under the apron. He soon realized his hold was no match for the strangers powerful grip. "What is it you want with me?"

"My name's Billy Hawks, I came down here from Oklahoma." He released Charlie's hand and took a step back, resting his body weight on his good leg.

"What part of Oklahoma?" Uncle Ezra popped the lid off a bottle of beer, he had cooling in a bucket of ice setting on the floor.

"Down around Oklahoma City. I can wait until you finish your haircut, if you like."

"Go ahead and ask your questions. I'm kinda interested in what you want with the boy." Possum leaned back in the chair as he filled his pipe.

Hawks turned to face Possum. "Who might you be sir?" He took a couple steps toward Possum extending his hand.

Possum stood up and took a step toward Hawks. "John Elliot, most folks call me Possum." They shook hands in the middle of the barbershop, both standing straight and tall, looking each other straight in the eye. They were the same height, but Possum was the heavier of the two.

"Nice to meet you Mr. Elliot." Hawks released Possum's hand and turned back toward Charlie. "What I wanted to talk to you about, Mr. Mayfair."

"Call me, Charlie."

"O.K., Charlie, what can you tell me about this big dog, that pulled the girl out of the river?"

"How did you hear about that clear in Oklahoma?" Possum struck a match on the floor.

"I can't really answer that. The people I work for told me to come down here and check the story out. I don't know how they got wind of it."

"Well, ah, who are these people?" Possum drew the flame into the bowl of his pipe.

"The lady's name is Lois Shank." Hawks sat down, a couple of chairs to the left of Possum.

Charlie looked away from Hawks when he mentioned the name Shank.

"So exactly why are these people so interested in this dog?" Possum gave Hawks a hard look.

"Mr. Elliot, from what I've been told, this dog looks like he could be the dog that killed a man in Oklahoma."

"Who did he kill?" Uncle Ezra shut off his clippers and took another sip from his beer.

"Mrs. Shank's husband, Orie." Hawks leaned forward in his chair. "Now it's my understanding that you kids were keeping this dog at an old abandoned house at one time?"

"Yes, that's true." Charlie answered, wondering, how he had found that out.

"So how many times did you see him?"

"Only a couple," Charlie replied.

"Tell me what he looks like?" Hawks slid back in his chair crossing his legs.

"He's a big dog, might weigh hundred fifty pounds. Blue-grey color, big wide flat head, with short ears." Charlie volunteered information he figured Hawks already knew.

"Did he have any white on his chest?" He inquired.

"I don't recall."

"You didn't happen to get a chance to look in his ears, did you?"

"No." A knot formed in Charlie's stomach as he lied.

"Mr. Hawks, tell us a little about this murder that dog is suspected of committing?" Possum interrupted the interrogation.

"My understanding is that Orie Shank had that dog for about two years. He got him as a pup. No one seems to know where he came from. Shank was into dog fighting and that's what he figured on doing with the pup. He bought him thinking he was a pure breed Pit Bull, which is what his mother was. Shank came to realize as the pup got older, that he wasn't sired by no Pit Bull. He just kept growing and eventually got so big that Shank had trouble handling him. Charlie, did the dog you saw have a lot of scars?"

"Some, I guess, it was pretty dark where I saw him."

"Shank put most of them scars on him."

"Sounds like Shank treated him pretty bad?" Possum took his pipe out of his mouth as he spoke.

"He did, and that dog hated old man Shank, don't think he didn't. Shank was afraid of that dog too, of course he never did anything but abuse him. Eventually he would have had to destroy him, but Shank was no dummy about dogs. He had a granddaughter and she took care of him and played with him when he was a pup. My understanding is she could do about anything with him."

"How old was the girl?" Possum leaned forward striking a match on the floor, relighting his pipe.

"I'm not sure, I think around ten or eleven. Maybe a little older." Hawks rubbed his chin.

Uncle Ezra was sitting on his stool listening to Hawks tell his story. "You know Possum, if Shank had a young girl around there that took care of the dog, that might explain why he took up with Millie." Uncle Ezra belched in Charlie's ear as he took a sip from a half empty bottle of beer.

"Maybe, if it's the same dog," Possum offered.

"Did he have a name?" Charlie looked across the room at Hawks.

"They called him Jumbo."

"Tell us about the murder." Uncle Ezra encouraged Hawks to continue, as he started using a pair of scissors to finish up Charlie's haircut.

"There's not that much to tell. Mrs. Shank came home one afternoon. She found the granddaughter unconscious in front of the dog pen with Jumbo standing over her. Orie Shank was dead, hanging on a limb that stuck out on the corner post of the dog pen. The girl didn't regain consciousness for ten days, and she had no recollection of what had happened when she did."

"Sounds like it might have been an accident," Possum surmised.

"Maybe." Hawks stood up.

Uncle Ezra belched in Charlie's ear, again. It was a loud, nasty bleach that smelled like stale beer and garlic. "Just exactly what is it the Shank family wants you to do?"

"Well, my orders are to bring the dog back to Oklahoma dead or alive." Hawks turned and looked out the window.

"They're paying you to do this." Uncle Ezra laid his scissors on the counter.

"That's right."

"You might be here a long time looking for that dog, you know what I mean, might run into quite a bit of money."

"Yes that's true, but Mrs. Shank is a rich woman. That's interesting too, Orie Shanks parents were quite wealthy, but when they died, it didn't take long for Orie to go through the family fortune. His parents fearing that might happen, took out a large life insurance policy on Orie . . . making his wife and any blood relative from that union the beneficiaries.

"Are you going to try and catch Jumbo or just kill him?" Charlie asked, while Uncle Ezra removed the barbers apron.

"I don't know." Hawks turned away from the window and looked over Uncle Ezra at Charlie. "I know which one would be the easiest, but I want to be sure I got the right dog. Where do you think he's staying, Charlie?"

"The river, I guess."

"Maybe we could work together. I'd give you five hundred dollars if you would help me get him. Hawks took a couple steps toward Charlie.

Uncle Ezra choked on the drink of beer he had just taken.

Possum got out of his chair. "It was my daughter that dog pulled out of the river. I doubt that you'll be getting much help from us, Mr. Hawks."

Hawks became uneasy when he realized who he had been talking to. "I'm sorry, Mr. Elliot, I should have recognized the name."

"I should have told you right away," Possum apologized.

"There's a good chance that it's not the same dog. I wish I could get a good look at him." Hawks was working his way toward the door. He extended his hand, they shook hands as they passed.

Hawks stopped at the door and looked back at Charlie. "I've got a camp set up down on the river, North of the Iron Bridge, west side of the river. Charlie, if your ever down that way, stop in and see me."

"Hawks, beings your down there on the river, there's a old rough boar running loose in that part of the country. He's been doing a lot of damage around here. He's cost some people a lot of money. If you get a chance, kill him, you would be doing us all a favor."

"What's he look like?"

"Oh, he'd weigh four-fifty to five hundred pounds. Red in color. There's no mistaking him."

"I'll keep an eye out for him."

"Be careful down there on the river." Possum warned, as Hawks disappeared out the door.

Charlie reached in his pocket and handed Uncle Ezra the dollar bill his Grandfather had given him.

"Thanks, Charlie." He dropped the money in the cash register and handed Charlie his change.

"I don't know Charlie, that Indian could be trouble. He's got the eyes of a hunter and carries himself like a tracker." Possum watched Hawks through the open door. "See how he walks with his head up, but his eyes are looking at the ground." Charlie looked out the door with Possum. "He's done so much tracking he's looking for tracks in the street."

Uncle Ezra looked out the window. "I used to walk like that, when I was a kid, walking barefoot in the corral."

They all laughed, as Uncle Ezra downed what was left of his beer.

Charlie had change jingling in his pocket and was anxious to spend it. "Possum, I better get going."

"Take care of yourself." Possum patted him on the back as he stepped out the door.

CHAPTER 17

Charlie had been left alone for the day. His mother and grandfather had gone to a farm sale some twenty miles west near Wilson, Kansas. He had warmed up some ham and beans for lunch, leftovers from the day before. The phone rang as he finished his meal. "Hello."

"Charlie, is that you?"

"Yeah, it's me. What you doin'?" He recognized Millie Elliot's voice.

"Boy, I'm glad I got you." Her voice sounded strange, as if she had been crying.

"Something wrong?"

"Plenty's wrong. He's back at the old house."

"Who's back?"

"Jumbo, he's hurt, hurt bad," she sobbed.

"What happened to him?"

"I don't know . . . he's all cut up . . . looks like he's been in a fight. He's laying in the house . . . by the stairs . . . in a pool, pool of blood. We have to do something . . . or he's, he's going to die." She was crying now, making it almost impossible for her to talk.

"Are you sure he's in that bad a shape?"

"Yes . . . he, he can't move . . . he's so weak he can't even lift his head." There was a note of urgency in her voice as she continued to cry. "We, we have to do something. Charlie, he'll die."

"I'm not sure there's anything I can do."

"You have to get over here and help me," she pleaded.

"I don't have a way to get there. I'm here by myself."

"Don't you have a horse you could ride or something," she suggested.

"Not really, the only horse around here is Diablo. I'm not sure I could stay on him. We moved the rest of the horses to the north pasture, so he wouldn't be messing with them."

"Charlie, . . . help me . . . please," she begged.

"I want to, but I'm not sure how."

"Please, please meet me at the house . . . see what you think."

"O.K! O.K! I'll be there, soon as I can." Charlie weakened as the flow of tears continued.

"You're sure?"

"I'm sure, I'm sure."

"I'll meet you over there. You'll be there for sure? Won't you, Charlie?"

"Yes, Yes, I'll be there."

"Hurry! Bye!" She hung up the phone.

Charlie fretted about Jumbo as he walked out of the house. There was no doubt in his mind that he was in trouble, not only was he hurt, but Billy Hawks was scouring the country looking for him.

Diablo, the paint stallion, was acting up at the corral. He held his head high, tossing it from side to side, as he pranced back and forth. Strong, powerful muscles rippled under his hide as he reared up on his hind legs, his white coat with three large red spots glistening in the midday sun, as he gave out a deep stud horse whinny.

Diablo had the typical stallion temperament, high spirited and hard to handle. Herb Taylor didn't like breaking stallions, feeling they were too unpredictable and seldom made good riding horses. They had been working with him for three months, and he was still far from broke.

Charlie walked slowly toward the barn. He had to get over to the Barnes' place; the only solution he could come up with, short of walking, was to put a saddle on Diablo and take his chances. Charlie shuttered at the thought, for he certainly couldn't be considered a reliable mount.

He watched Charlie walk from the house to the corral nickering as he approached, a deep, loud, threatening warning.

Diablo pawed the ground as Charlie open the corral gate. He walked into the barn, Diablo watched as he opened the feed box. Diablo had a weakness—his stomach. He liked the grain and protein mix Herb Taylor had made for the horses.

Charlie stirred the feed in a galvanized bucket as he walk out the barn door, hoping to get his attention. "Come here, Diablo, I got something for you." He reached in the bucket and picked up a handful of the grain, holding it up and leaving it trickle through his fingers back into the bucket. Diablo threw his head in the air and came toward Charlie at a trot, wanting what he had to offer. He followed Charlie into the barn, trying to get at the grain while they walked. Charlie dumped the grain into the manger and quickly snapped a stud chain to his halter, securing him to the manger. He seemed gentle enough, standing there munching on his lunch.

Charlie went to the tack room and grabbed an old Longhorn saddle, now was the time to saddle him, while he was thinking about filling his belly.

Diablo watched Charlie out of the corner of his eye as he approached. He stopped eating as Charlie ran his hand over his back, speaking too him in a quiet voice. "Easy does it big fellow. I got some work to do today and you're going to help me. Yeah, you are."

He stuck his head back in the feed trough. He jumped to the side and pulled the stud chain taunt as Charlie set the saddle on his back. "Easy does it, it's O.K., just take it easy."

When he settled down, Charlie cautiously reached under his belly for the girth strap, pulling it tight just behind his front legs. He followed the same procedure with the belly strap as Diablo fidgeted and danced around the stall.

Charlie was jittery as he went back to the tack room to get a bridle. From past experience he knew Diablo wasn't going to like him messing around his head.

He returned, laying the bridle on the manger for him to smell. He ran his hand over his shoulder, to his neck, then stroked his head and face. He tried to pull his head away as Charlie touched his ears, an action that came as no surprise.

"Now big boy we're going to put this bit in your mouth." Charlie picked up the bridle, trying to work the bit into his mouth as he held the bridle in the other hand was turning into quite a chore. Diablo tried to turn his head away and succeeded. He wasn't cooperating and when Charlie was about to give up, he took the bit. Charlie quickly slipped the bridle over his ears. He was agitated, tossing his head from side to side, pulling back on the chain that confined him to the manger. Charlie stepped out of the stall while he waited for Diablo to settle down.

He walked back to the house to get a drink of water. It was a warm afternoon and when he returned to the barn, Diablo had broken into a nervous sweat.

He snapped a six foot bull rope to his halter and unsnapped the chain. Diablo was alert to his new found freedom and hastily left the stall, dragging Charlie with him. Once outside Charlie set his feet, as he slowed down, the bull rope was quickly wrapped and snapped around one of the post that supported the wooden corral fence. Charlie stepped back trying to muster enough courage to climb in the saddle. He moved slowly to Diablo's side, putting his left foot in the stirrup, Diablo tried to move away until he trapped himself against the corral fence. Charlie grabbed the pummel and threw his right leg over the saddle. Diablo moved around some but didn't act as if he was going to buck. Charlie dismounted and remounted until Diablo stood still for him to get into the saddle.

Diablo watched as Charlie unlatched the corral gate. The gate hung on a pair of rusty old hinges; it took a little effort to push it open. The gate was still closed, only a bluff now that it was unlatched. Charlie hoped if he got bucked off, Diablo would stay in the corral.

Charlie's stomach was tied in a knot, his heart pounding in his chest, his under arms soaked with perspiration. Diablo gave Charlie a inquisitive look as he unsnapped the bull rope. The rope was hung on the saddle horn with one hand while Charlie held the reins in the other.

Charlie talked as he slipped his foot in the stirrup. "Easy does it, Diablo. Don't get crazy on me." The big stallion fidgeted a little and tried to spin away as Charlie pulled himself up in the saddle. Realizing he was free, Diablo trotted across the corral while Charlie searched for the right stirrup with his foot. He found it, just as they reached the fence. Diablo turned quickly and repeated his trip across the corral, trotting toward the gate.

He bumped the gate with his rump as he made another sharp turn. The gate opened, Diablo spied the hole as they made a circle around the corral. Sensing his chance to be loose, he rushed for the crack that would set him free. He escaped through the gate into the yard.

Charlie was hanging on to the saddle horn with one hand while pulling back on the reins with the other, hoping to keep this half broke mustang under control, as he danced down the driveway on his hind legs. There was no turning back now, Charlie had to stay in the saddle, if he became dislodged, the results could be disastrous. He placed both hands on the saddle horn. Zip was lying under the hay wagon and as they passed, he decided to get in on the excitement. He ran up behind Diablo and gave out a loud bark and then another. Diablo came down on four feet as they neared the end of the driveway. Trying to avoid this savage banshee that was hot on his heels.

Charlie managed to get him headed in the right direction as they cleared the driveway. He was in a hurry and gave him a free rein, hoping he would have himself worn out by the time they arrived at the Barnes' place. His cap had already been dislodged and was laying just outside the driveway in the road. He had no intention of going back for it. If he got off Diablo now, it was doubtful that he would ever get back on him. Charlie wasn't sure he would ever get him stopped, at least not with Zip in hot pursuit.

Charlie pulled hard on the right rein to turn him south toward the river. Reluctantly, Diablo made the turn, so far he hadn't offered to buck or try to unseat his rider, but he certainly was out of control.

Diablo was lathered up by the time they got to the Barnes' place. He had run at a hard gallop all the way, even after Zip had given up the chase a couple miles from home. He was actually responding as Charlie worked the reins. He pulled back hard, slowing him down as they entered the yard. He went another twenty-five feet before he slowed down enough for Charlie to dismount. He followed as Charlie lead him to a nearby tree, where he was tied with the bull rope.

"Millie, Millie where you at?"

"In here." An answer came from inside the house.

Charlie walked toward the house as Millie appeared at the front door. She gave him a hurry up wave as he approached.

Dried blood was quite visible on the old porch floor. Charlie carefully crossed the porch as he made his way to the door. Millie grabbed his hand and lead him to the bottom of the stairs.

"I found him here this morning, about eleven o'clock."

Jumbo was lying at the foot of the stairs, with his back against the bottom step, in a pool of nearly dried blood He looked to be near death's door, breathing very shallow, eyes closed.

Numerous cuts covered his body, most of them had quit bleeding. The worst was on the left side of his neck, a deep gash that was nearly four inches long, still dripping crimson that ran down his neck, creating a pool of fresh blood on the dirty floor.

"He doesn't look too good, does he?" Millie sobbed, as she wiped reddened eyes with the back of her hand.

"No he doesn't, if he doesn't get some help, I'm afraid he's going to die." Charlie leaned over and stroked his head. His eyes remained closed, he gave no indication of knowing they were there.

"What do you think happened to him, Charlie?"

"I don't know, those cuts look just like the ones our dogs got when they were fighting with Ol Razor."

"Why would he be fightin' with that old boar?"

"That, I just don't know. I just don't know. We need to get him out of here. He really needs a vet." He rubbed his back and hips, as he pondered the situation.

They walked in the kitchen. Charlie sat down in the window. Millie had stopped crying, she stood beside him, her back leaning against the wall.

Looking out the window, Charlie saw foot prints in the soft dirt around the house. "We've got to get him out of here, before the wrong people find him, Millie."

"What you talking about?" She detected the urgency in his voice.

"See them boot tracks?"

"Yes."

"Billy Hawks has been here, and not too long ago."

"You're sure those are his tracks?"

"I'm sure, he's the only one I know that wears a cowboy boot with a walking heel."

"Do you really think he means to do him harm?"

"Who knows, he doesn't appear to be the type of man that would come this far to go back empty handed," Charlie replied.

"Maybe it's not the dog he's looking for?"

"It's him."

"You seem pretty sure of yourself."

"I am, come here." She followed Charlie back to the hallway. "Hawks told us at the barbershop that the man he killed was named Shank. Look here." He bent over and showed her the markings in his ear.

"How long have you known that?"

"Since we ran into each other at Murphy's Grove this spring."

"You mean he made up with you?" There was a note of excitement in her voice.

"Oh yeah, we spent the day together."

"Why didn't you tell me?"

"Because, I figured if I didn't tell anyone, I wouldn't have to worry about anyone talking about his whereabouts."

"I guess I've got a confession to make too."

"Really."

127

"I've been feeding him here all summer."

Charlie wasn't surprise. "Did you ever see him?"

"Yes, several times, but only when he wanted me to see him."

"What do you mean by that?"

"Sometimes I felt he was here, but he wouldn't come out." She kneeled down and stroked his head.

"He certainly knows how to disappear," Charlie commented.

"That's for sure. Charlie, what are we going to do? Hawks is sure to come back."

"We need some help. Is your dad home?"

"No, everyone went to the sale over at Wilson."

"Eli Bledso would help us. If he's home."

"I guess that's our only hope. Uncle Ezra might help if we could find him," she remarked.

"I could try too call the barbershop. Tell you what, you stay here. I'm going to ride over to the Bledso's. Hopefully, Eli will be home, if he's not . . . I'll try to get hold of Uncle Ezra. Maybe, I can use the Bledso's phone . . . if I can't . . . I'll have to go over to your place."

"Why don't you just go over to our place and use the phone?"

"I'd rather not use the phone, if I can help it. The wrong people might be listening." Charlie started toward the front door.

"You be careful." Millie warned, as she followed.

"I will. Sit down and rest somewhere . . . you look tired. I'll be back as quick as I can."

Diablo was standing under the tree, content to be in the shade. He wasn't happy to see Charlie, as he half ran across the yard. It came as a surprise when he let Charlie mount him with no dancing around or acting up.

Charlie waved at Millie as they trotted down the path that lead to the road. Diablo picked up the pace as Charlie kicked him in the ribs with his work shoes. It took a second kick to bring him to a full gallop. This was no time for him to act as if he was broke.

Diablo was drawing in deep breaths by the time they reached the Bledso farm.

Charlie tied him to the nearest tree and walked the short distance to the house.

Grandma Bledso was on the porch, setting in her rocking chair. She gave Charlie a cold, unfriendly, gimlet look as he approached.

The look didn't go unnoticed. "Hi! Mrs. Bledso."

She glared at Charlie, not speaking.

"I was wondering, ah, is Eli around?"

"No," she snapped.

"How about Junior and Curly?"

"Ain't here, went to the sale with their Dad."

Charlie looked at her a moment and nervously turned to walk away, afraid to ask to use the phone.

"Your riding that pony pretty hard on such a hot day. What's your hurry?" Grandma had gotten up and was standing at the top of the porch steps, holding on to one of the square wooden post that supported the roof.

"Why you looking for Eli, anyway?"

"Well, ah, ma'am, I guess we need some help." Charlie answered, in a weak voice.

"Who's we?" She asked, in an almost civilized tongue.

"Millie Elliot and me."

"You two been up to some mischief?"

"No, no, nothing like that." Charlie could hardly talk for the lump in his throat.

"Well, what is it? Maybe, I can help you."

"Ah, well, it's kind of a secret." Charlie answered cautiously.

"Ain't nobody can keep a secret like me. I know lots of secrets." A twinkle appearing in her eye, as she spoke.

"Maybe, you could help me find Uncle Ezra."

"You look awful hot, Sonny. Set down and I'll get you a glass of water." Grandma Bledso went in the house before Charlie could respond.

She returned momentarily with a large glass of water, containing two ice cubes.

"Now tell me what this is all about?" She sat back down in the rocking chair. "I just might be able to find Uncle Ezra, but I need to know why you need him."

Charlie thought for a little bit as he downed the glass of water. Maybe she was his only hope, although it certainly would be unusual for her to offer help to anyone.

"Ah, did you hear about the dog that pulled Millie Elliot out of the river?"

"Yeah, Sonny, I know all about that."

"Well, ah, he's hurt real bad. He needs help, that's why I was looking for Eli."

"How's he hurt?" Grandma took her eyes off Charlie, looking up at the barn.

"He's all cut up, like he's been in a fight."

"Who you think he's been fightin' with?"

"Ol Razor, at least the cuts look like the one's he left on our dogs when they caught him in the river. He's unconscious from loosing so much blood."

"Tell me somethin', Sonny...does that dog have any unusual marks on his body?"

"No, not really." Charlie hesitated a moment. "He has a scar on his shoulder that looks like a upside down cross. I guess that might be a little unusual."

The old rocking chair creaked as she slowly began to rock. "So what you want to do?"

"The first thing is to get him out of there. Billy Hawks has been nosein' around over there and he's wantin' him real bad." Charlie bit one of the ice cubes in half and began to chew it up.

"Billy Hawks . . . ain't he that Injun I been hearin' 'bout?" Grandma Bledso began to rock a little faster.

"Yes ma'am, he's the one."

"I'll tell you one thing, Sonny . . . don't ever trust no Injun." She shook a bony finger in Charlie's direction. "Where's that dog at anyway?"

"The old Barnes' house."

"Hum . . . not to far away." She stuck her index finger in her mouth, in the hole created by the two missing teeth; deep in thought. "Maybe, I ought to go over there and take a look at him."

"How you going to get there, Grandma." Charlie tipped up the glass and dumped the second ice cube in his mouth.

She stopped rocking as she looked around the yard, not moving her eyes, just her head, like an old Hoot Owl setting on a tree limb. She stopped when her eyes spotted Eli Bledso's pickup setting in front of the barn. "We'll take the pickup."

"Can you drive that thing, Grandma?"

"Sure I can, used to drive all the time. Won't be nothin' for me to handle that old bucketa bolts." She stood up a strange look in her eyes.

Charlie was getting nervous and wondered if he had made a mistake, confiding in this crazy old woman.

"Sonny, you take your pony up to the barn. Put him in that corral where there's some water. He needs a drink and a chance to cool off. I'll meet ya up there." Grandma Bledso retreated into the house.

Charlie walked over to get Diablo. He had caught his breath and seemed unusually calm standing in the shade. It was several hundred yards to the barn and Charlie was surprised to find that he was leading Diablo, rather than Diablo leading him. He had just closed the corral gate, when the front door slammed. Grandma Bledso was already down the front steps by the time he turned around to see she wasn't alone. On her shoulder she was carrying the dreaded double barrel shotgun—Old Mathusula.

She made it to the pickup in record time. Her face was red and she was breathing a little hard, but eager to get on her way. She jerked the pickup door open, shoved in the shotgun and climbed in herself, slamming the door shut as she adjusted herself in the seat.

"Get in Sonny, if you're goin' with me. We got things to do," she ordered.

Reluctantly, Charlie opened the door and climbed in. "I'm not sure we really need this shotgun Grandma."

"With Redskins running 'round the country, you always need to be prepared to defend life and property. Nothin' like a little hot lead to send them pesky critters on their way." She was searching for the switch as she spoke.

"Is it loaded?"

"Hell, yes, do I look like I'm so stupid, as to be carrying a empty shotgun during a Indian war. Got plenty of ammo too." She reached into the pocket of the old cotton dress and produced a hand full of shotgun shells. She shook them in Charlie's face, making sure he got a good look.

"Where's the switch on this damn thing?"

"You sure you can drive this thing?" Charlie pointed to the switch in the middle of the dash.

"I can drive just fine . . . just need my glasses." She produced a pair of ancient wire framed glasses from another pocket in the old flowered dress.

"I didn't know you wore glasses."

"Only wear 'em when I drive." She set the glasses on her crooked nose, squinting as if trying to get them to focus.

She pushed the starter with a bony foot. The motor turned over a couple of times and took off, purring like a kitten being stroked by a child's tender hand. Grandma shoved the gas petal to the floor. The engine roared, smoke bellow out the exhaust pipe as Charlie covered his ears.

"You don't have to gun the motor, Grandma." He shouted over the deafening roar.

She let up on the petal and looked over at Charlie. "You have to blow the cobs out of these things once in awhile so they run good."

She pushed in the clutch and pulled the gear shift into low gear. Once again she pushed the accelerator wide open and released the clutch. The tires spun as the old truck lurched forward, throwing dirt and rocks for thirty feet.

Diablo nickered as they sped down the hill toward the house, thinking he would never see them again.

The pickup swerved from side to side as Grandma tried to keep it on the trail.

"Slow this thing down." Charlie shouted, as they bounced into the yard.

She slammed on the brakes, stopping in a cloud of dust, nearly throwing Charlie in the windshield. "I got a idea. I'm goin' to call Uncle Ezra and have him meet us at the Barnes' place." She bolted from the pickup and rushed to the house.

Charlie drew in a deep breath and then another, enjoying the brief reprieve. He thought about unloading Grandma's shotgun, but since he didn't know anything about the old cannon, he left it rest on the floorboard and seat of the pickup. He got out of the truck and relived his bladder behind a small shed that stood just a short distance from the house. After the trip from the barn to the house, he didn't figure it would be wise to be carrying any extra water.

Charlie had just gotten back in the truck when Grandma came storming out of the house. "He's goin' to meet us over there." She slipped under the steering wheel, repeating the gas petal to the floor rock throwing incident. She found second gear just as they reached the end of the driveway, making the turn in a cloud of dust as Grandma pushed the gas peddle to the floorboard. The truck was speeding down the road with two wheels in the right ditch. She whipped the steering wheel to the left, bringing the pickup out of the ditch and back on the road.

Charlie braced himself with one hand on the dash, the other locked in a death grip on the window frame. Grandma prepared to make a right turn at the crossroads. She cut the corner short, clipping off a mailbox that flew high in the air, clearing the cab by only inches.

Grandma never blinked an eye as she continued down the road. Trouble appeared ahead as they crested the hill that overlooked Homer Oskerimer's farm. Homer's milk cow was standing broadside in the middle of the road, looking death in the eye as the blue Ford pickup careened down the hill.

"Cow in the road!" Charlie screamed, as Old Mathusula bounced against his ribs.

"Where?" Her eyes squinted in the afternoon sun.

Charlie's life was passing right before his eyes. His hide wasn't worth the salt on a fresh fried egg.

The old Jersey cow realized she was about to be made into hamburger without ever seeing a packing plant. She bounded to the right as Grandma turned the steering wheel to the left. Homer's mailbox rumbled as it rolled under the pickup.

The truck slipped in the ditch. Dead a head a Barred Rock rooster and three Leghorn hens were feasting on grasshoppers. A cloud of feathers lifted in the air as they rolled out from under the pickup.

The engine roared as Grandma pulled out of the ditch. Charlie breathed a sigh of relief as they raced down the middle of the road.

It was a brief break, as once again Grandma headed for the ditch. A plum thicket loomed ahead. She hit it like a bulldozer, still in second gear, a covey of quail exploded in the air, while limbs and leaves covered the windshield.

Charlie released his grip on the window frame as plum bushes lashed at his hands. The trail that lead up to the Barnes' place appeared ahead.

"The turn's just ahead, Grandma!" Charlie shouted.

"I see it." She slowed down, whipping the truck in the ditch forty feet ahead of the turn. They were almost there when she pulled out of the ditch and cut across an open field with the gas petal to the floor.

Grandma slammed on the brakes as they flew into the yard. The truck came to a stop in the middle of an elderberry patch, coughed once, and died in a cloud of black smoke.

Charlie couldn't get out, his door was held shut by the elderberry bushes.

Millie came running out of the house. "Charlie, you all right?" She asked, as he climbed out the pickup window. Millie watched as Charlie clawed his way through the elderberry patch.

"You all right? You're white as a sheet."

"You'd be white to if you would have taken the ride I just been on. That old woman can't drive and she can't see either. To make matters worse, there's a loaded double barrel shotgun bouncing around the cab. I don't know how many times I looked down the barrel of that thing. How's he doin'?"

"About the same, I guess."

Grandma Bledso and Old Mathusula were just making their way out of the elderberry patch as Millie and Charlie started for the house.

"Uncle Ezra is going to come over here. Maybe he'll know what to do." Charlie told Millie.

"You kids hold up," Grandma screeched. "Have you seen anythin' of that sorry Injun, Missy?"

"No, ma'am. I don't think he's around here."

"Don't be too sure of that, them Redskins can be a sneaky lot." She replied, as they crossed the porch.

Jumbo hadn't moved, still lying sprawled out at the bottom of the staircase.

Grandma Bledso was the first to speak. "Land sakes alive, that is a big dog." She leaned her shotgun in the corner and kneeled down to stroke his head. "Ain't you a beauty." She ran her hand over the inverted cross on Jumbo's shoulder. "How long has he been like this, Missy?"

"I'm not sure, I found him about eleven this morning."

"He's been here a long time . . . too long . . . he's in bad shape. Something sure worked him over."

"Hello, anyone in there?" A voice called from outside the house.

Grandma, jumped up grabbing her shotgun. "Who's out there?" She hollered while looking at Charlie.

"It sounded like Uncle Ezra," Charlie responded. "I'll go see."

"Let me go first. It might be a trick, it could be that Redskin." She shouldered Old Mathusula and carefully snuck to the door. She was about four feet from the door, when Uncle Ezra poked his head around the corner, looking down both barrels of the old widow maker.

"Don't shoot! Don't shoot! Grandma!" He shouted, as the color left his face.

She lowered the shotgun. Uncle Ezra quickly entered the room.

"What's going on here?" His color already coming back.

Grandma Bledso grabbed his arm and lead him to the stairwell. "We want you to help us keep this dog alive."

Uncle Ezra was set back by what he saw as he entered the stairwell. "Holy smoke, I never dreamed I would see him again. What in the world happened to him?"

"We don't know. We think he got in a fight with Ol Razor," Charlie offered.

"That certainly looks like a good possibility." Uncle Ezra squatted down in front of the big hound's head. He pulled back an eye lid and looked in his eye. "Boy, he's alive but that's about all."

"There's other problems too, that Injun's been hanging around here, and he's wantin' to get his hands on him. We need to get him out of here."

"He really shouldn't be moved. Although, he's pretty well stopped bleeding, except for that cut on his neck. I think that can be stopped, pretty easy. If he doesn't have any internal injuries, he might make it." Uncle Ezra stood up.

"Ezra, I need to talk to you." Grandma spoke in a sharp voice.

They walked in the kitchen. Grandma began the conversation. "Ezra, that dog is the sign, the Master has sent the sign, it's time. You have to help me keep that dog alive until the dark of the moon . . . five days." She spoke in a whisper, her lips barely moving.

Uncle Ezra's hands began to shake, his voice quivered, beads of perspiration began to form on his forehead. "I don't know if I can . . . he's in bad shape. Grandma, you sure you want to go through with this?"

She placed her hands on Uncle Ezra's chest, grabbing his shirt and wrapping it around her clinched fist, pulling his face down as she raised up on her toes. She spoke from deep in her throat—a murmur—for Uncle Ezra's ears only. "You listen to me, Ezra Bean, I've helped you out many times . . . why I've gave you enough liquor to float a battleship, now it's time for you to help me. You don't have a choice, the Master has sent the sign, you saw the cross on his shoulder . . . all you have to do is keep him alive . . . for five days. You hear me." She released her grip on his shirt.

135

"Where do you want to take him?" Uncle Ezra agreed to help, knowing it was useless to try and change her mind.

"We'll take him over to our place, we can hide him in the barn." She stuck her head out the door to be sure Charlie and Millie weren't listening.

"I can't move that big dog around myself," Ezra complained.

"We'll get the Mayfair boy to help."

"You sure you want him to know about the barn and the still—and all that?" Uncle Ezra sat down on the three legged chair.

"He won't tell . . . he wants to save that dog . . . I can see it in his eyes. Her voice so low Uncle Ezra could barely hear the words she spoke. "And after Friday, it won't matter if he does tell."

"I don't like it." Uncle Ezra pulled a half pint of cheap whiskey from his hip pocket and took a short swig.

"Ezra, I did plenty for you, now it's your turn. I told you what's in this for me. You know I did. Now, we need to get started." Grandma stormed out of the room. Uncle Ezra reluctantly followed.

"Kids, we're going to move this dog to a safe place." Grandma announced when she returned to the stairwell.

"Where you going to take him?" Millie asked.

"I know a plenty safe place for him, Missy. A place where nobody will find him, not even that pesky Redskin."

"We've got to find something we can use as a stretcher. Anything we can put him on so we can carry him." Uncle Ezra took another sip from his bottle.

"There's a door on that little shed outside, it's about to fall off anyway." Charlie figured he better come up with something fast, a few more shots from that bottle and Uncle Ezra wouldn't be able to carry anything.

They went outside to the shed and finished breaking off the door. It wasn't too large, but big enough to carry Jumbo.

Uncle Ezra and Charlie carried the door in the house and laid it down beside Jumbo. The four of them worked together and lifted him on the make shift stretcher.

"So far, so good, it doesn't look like he's started bleeding, anywhere. Charlie, you take one end and I'll take the other. Grandma you and Millie get on the sides." They all took their positions as Uncle Ezra continued to give orders. "Now all together . . . lift."

136

Everyone lifted in unison. It was a heavy load, but they were slowly making their way to the front door. Trouble loomed ahead, the stretcher wouldn't go through the door.

"We're going to have to unload him," Uncle Ezra advised. "Set this thing down, as close to the door as we can get it. What we'll try to do is slide him through the door as we slide him off."

They slowly worked Jumbo through the door, just a few inches at a time. Once he was through the doorway, the old door was turned on its side, lifted over Jumbo and laid down beside him. They carefully reloaded him on the stretcher. He never moved or made a sound.

"I'm going to back my pickup as close as I can to this porch." Uncle Ezra crossed the porch and walked the short distance to the pickup.

He carefully backed up to the porch, now they would only have to carry Jumbo six or eight feet to have him loaded. Together they picked him up and cautiously slid him in the back of the pickup.

"Charlie, you'll have to come with us. We'll need a strong back to help us. Millie, you better go home. We'll take care of this dog for you." Uncle Ezra closed the tailgate.

"But I want to come along," Millie complained.

"It would be best if you went home, Missy." Grandma Bledso spoke in a scary, intimidating voice.

Millie dropped her head. "Well, alright, but where are you taking him?"

"Someplace where no one will ever find him. You can come and see him when we get him back on his feet." Uncle Ezra climbed in the truck. "Grandma, I guess we'll leave your pickup here and come back for it later. Charlie, you want to ride up front or back here with the dog?"

"I'll ride in the back." It was an easy decision, Charlie wanted to be as far away from Grandma Bledso and that shotgun as he could get. He waved at Millie as they left. She weakly waved back, disappointed that she wasn't going along.

Uncle Ezra braked the pickup to a stop in front of the Bledso barn just a few minutes later. Jumbo hadn't shown any sign of life since they had loaded him. The cut on his neck was bleeding more now and a small stream of blood was running down the floor of the truck.

"Charlie, open up them doors so I can drive this thing in there," Uncle Ezra ordered.

Charlie jumped out of the truck and opened the double doors. The doors were big and Uncle Ezra had no trouble driving his pickup in the barn. He drove to the back of the barn.

Grandma Bledso unloaded from the pickup, before it had come to a stop. "Leave the doors open, Sonny. We'll need the light." She scurried over to the corner of the barn and quickly climbed a ladder that went up into the hay loft. Uncle Ezra waited in the pickup as Charlie walked to the other end of the barn.

Pounding on the back wall of the barn quickly caught Charlie's attention. He took a couple of steps back when a section of the back wall began to lift in the air. It was a homemade overhead door, so well fitted that it would go unnoticed by the casual observer.

Uncle Ezra drove his truck through the door. Charlie followed behind the truck, what he was about to witness was mind-boggling. They were in a large room, the width of the barn and close to fifteen feet wide.

Charlie looked around and realized he was seeing something that only a handful of people in the whole county had ever seen. He wondered, was he really in Luther Bledso's still.

There was an old cooker with foot after foot of cooper tubing setting at one end of the room. The old black hearse—he had heard about—was parked against the rear wall; while a cooper colored coffin sat in the back closed and sealed. The place looked as if it hadn't been touched in years, everything was covered with dust.

Luther Bledso had built the barn so big that no one had ever figured out it was longer on the outside than it was on the inside. Even then, Charlie Mayfair wondered how they had kept the place so well hidden, and why had Grandma Bledso let him in on the secret.

"Charlie!" Uncle Ezra brought him back to reality. "We're going to have to unload this dog, so I can work on him. We'll put him on this table." He pointed to an old wooden homemade table that sat at the back of the barn. "Let's move this over closer to the door, where there's better light."

There were no windows in the room, the artificial light that was used came from several kerosene lanterns that were still hanging from the ceiling.

"Grandma, I'm going to need some hot water and some clean rags." Uncle Ezra informed the old woman as they move the table into the light.

She left the barn without saying a word. Grandma was in deep thought. She hadn't spoken since they had entered the barn. The dreaded shotgun had been left setting in the front seat of the pickup.

"Now lets just set the door and dog on the table." Together Uncle Ezra and Charlie carried Jumbo to the table, setting him down gently, leaving him on the stretcher.

Uncle Ezra went back to the pickup and pulled a small black bag out of the cab. He returned to the table, setting down the bag. He began examining the cut on Jumbo's neck. It was still bleeding, the blood dripping through a crack in the old door.

"I guess the first thing to do is take care of this, might have to tie that blood vessel off. I think I'll wait until she gets here with some water and clean this up." He took a step back and looked around the barn. "It's been a long time since I was back in here, Charlie."

"How many people knew about this place?" Charlie asked.

"Not very many, and if Luther Bledso ever showed it to you, one thing for certain, you better not ever tell anybody."

"Why?"

"Luther didn't trust many people, and if he took you into his confidence, it was for life. If you crossed Luther Bledso, you just might disappear from the face of the earth."

"Gee, why do you think Grandma let me see it?"

"Who knows. I guess it doesn't really matter. Luther's dead and this all took place so long ago, nobody cares about it any more. Maybe, she trusts you, Charlie."

"I can't believe the place was never found."

"Well, when the place was running full blast, they always kept a lot of hay stacked up against the wall, giving the illusion that the back of the barn was full of hay. There's a trap door in the hay loft to get you back here and that's the only way to open the doors. Another thing . . . people just didn't mess with Luther Bledso. Hell! The law was even afraid of him." Uncle Ezra reached under the seat of the pickup and pulled out an unopened pint of Jim Beam. He popped the seal and downed a couple of swallows.

"So did they really haul the liquor around in that hearse?"

"We sure did, Sonny." Grandma had slipped up behind them, carrying a small galvanized bucket of steaming hot water and an arm full of clean rags. "Ezra, you get started. I'll show the boy the car, since he's so interested."

139

Uncle Ezra took the water and rags and began cleaning the wound up on Jumbo's neck.

"Come here, Sonny." Grandma Bledso coaxed, as she took Charlie by the arm and lead him over to the back of the hearse. She twisted the door handle and pulled the door open.

"Is that a real casket?"

"Well . . . not exactly." Grandma grinned and cackled a little bit. "You see, its got a false bottom. This top part, where the body would normally lay, will lift out. That's how we filled the false bottom."

"So how much would that thing hold?"

"Oh! Not very much, maybe forty, fifty gallon."

"So, that was a load, forty or fifty gallon. Doesn't sound like very much."

"We could haul at least double that much. There's a tank built in the bottom of the hearse. That's where the real cargo was carried."

"Did most of it go to Kansas City, like I've heard?"

"Most of it, 'cept what we drank."

"You folks fix this thing up yourself?" Charlie stepped back admiring their handy work.

"Nope . . . people from Kansas City brought it out to us."

"Never did get caught?"

"We got stopped one time. We would have been caught, but we got tipped off that they were going to have a road block set up for us somewhere around Junction City. We decided it might be best if we let them catch us, and if they didn't find anything, they would leave us alone." She grinned, her missing teeth showing up plainly in the dimly lit room.

"How did you pull that off?" Charlie's question would go unanswered, at least, for the time being.

"You two come over here and give me a hand," Uncle Ezra interrupted.

Uncle Ezra was bent over Jumbo, still trying to get the bleeding to stop from the wound on his neck. He had taken a scalpel and made a small incision that run diagonally from the wound to his head.

"Charlie, come over here by his head and take your fingers and hold this incision open, for me," Uncle Ezra instructed.

"Like this." Charlie place his hands on each side of the wound and spread it open.

140

"That's good, that bleeders right here somewhere." He probed around with a pair of forceps. "There it is. That vein was almost torn in half. Still should have stopped bleeding. Maybe, I can put a stitch or two in it." He reached for his little black bag and pulled out as small suture needle that was already threaded. "Grandma, you might as well finish telling him your story, this is going to take awhile. Charlie, I need you to take hold of them forceps and steady that vein for me."

Charlie picked up the forceps.

"We borrowed a hearse from the undertaker over at Ellsworth, for luck, his looked just like ours. Oscar Welling run the funeral home and him and Luther had been good friends for a long time. In fact, Oscar liked to get his hands on some good liquor from time to time and we could always fix him up. Them two get their heads together and decided that it would look more real, if they had a body in the casket. Herman Blackmon had died just the day before. It was a good deal, even for Herman, because he had always wanted to go to Kansas City."

"That night me and the old man go into town, load Herman up in the hearse and head for Kansas City. We had just gotten through Junction City when we run into the road block they had set up for us. There must have been at least twenty men surrounded that hearse with guns drawn. It was pretty damn scary, having that many guns pointed at ya."

"The old man was wearing a black suit, he looked good, could have passed for a undertaker. He stayed pretty calm, least he looked calm. He rolled down the window."

"A big fellow with, little round glasses and a fat red face walked up to the window. He told us his name, but I don't remember it anymore, said he was a FBI agent."

"You folks get out of the vehicle, we want to search it," he ordered.

"We got out and they searched us both to see if we was carrying any guns. Which we weren't." Grandma Bledso moved an old nail keg over to the table and sat down on it. "Fat Face started asking the old man a lot of question. "What you folks doing out here this late at night? What's your name? Questions like that . . .you know what I mean."

141

"Sir, my name is Luther Bledso," the old man answered. "We got a little farm up by Kanopolis, Kansas. Things are tough on the farm and we're just about broke. Mr.Welling offered to pay us fifteen dollars if we would take this body to a funeral home in Kansas City. I just don't understand why you stopped us, all we're trying to do is make a honest living."

"He sounded like he was about to bawl. I decided that wasn't too bad of a idea, so I started crying, wailing and carrying on," Grandma continued.

Fat Face says, "We think you've got that hearse full of moonshine and your taking it to Kansas City. Now what do you have to say about that?"

"How can you even think such a thing," I screamed. "We are God fearing Christian people. We would rather be struck down dead, than to even think of passing off such vile poison to another human being. What are we going to do, Luther, the banks about to take our place and now these people are going to put us in prison for something we didn't even do. Oh! Lord have mercy." One of the fellows that was searching the car came over and whispered something in Fat Faces' ear."

"We need you to open the coffin so we can look inside," Fat Face said.

"Oh, my God, now they're going to desecrate the dead," I cried.

"Now, now don't fret about this dear," Luther says. "These people are just doing their job. God will deal with them in his own way."

"Luther went over and opened the back of the hearse. Several of the government people grabbed the casket, pulled it out and set it on the ground."

"Open it up," one of them ordered.

"Luther opened the casket. They went through that casket from top to bottom. Even rolled poor old Herman on his side, just to be sure we weren't hiding anything under him." Grandma Bledso stood up and walked around the table.

She stopped and watched as Uncle Ezra finished stitching the blood vessel.

"So they let you go?" Charlie asked.

"They let us go. Didn't have a choice. They was pretty disappointed. We left them standing there with egg on their faces."

Charlie quietly watched as Uncle Ezra continued to clean up the cuts and lacerations with soap, water, and peroxide. Sparingly, from time to time, he would put in a stitch or two.

"Let's roll him over and see what the other side looks like," Uncle Ezra ordered.

Carefully they turned him over, hoping for the best but expecting the worst. They got the worst. He had a huge gaping tear in his lower front shoulder, so deep the shoulder bone could be seen. If there was a bright side to the picture, it was the only wound he had sustained on that side of his body. The wound wasn't bleeding, but was covered with dust from lying on the dirty floor.

"It's a wonder he didn't bleed to death from that wound, Ezra," Grandma remarked.

"He most likely would have, if he hadn't laid on that side, the pressure from his own weight helped stop the bleeding. Mother nature sometimes helps animals understand things like that." Uncle Ezra went for the whisky bottle that was laying on the front seat of the pickup. He took a big shot. "This is going to take some time." He tossed the bottle back on the seat.

"The time, I need to get Diablo home and wiped down before Gramps gets home. I'm probably too late already. Can you finish without my help? I need to get that horse home."

"Well, yeah, I think we can," Uncle Ezra answered.

"Eli and the boys will be home pretty soon. They can help us if we need help," Grandma added.

Charlie was almost to the door when Grandma Bledso gave him some parting advice. "Don't tell anybody about this place, Sonny."

Her advice didn't fall on deaf ears. Charlie knew exactly what she was talking about and he didn't plan on telling anybody anything. Except the one person he could trust above all others—Possum Elliot.

Diablo was standing in the corral. He had freshened up some and looked as if he was feeling pretty good. He turned his backside to Charlie as he approached, not happy to see him. Charlie lead him out of the corral. He moved away from Charlie as he placed his foot in the stirrup. It took a second try before he pulled himself in the saddle.

They made it home in record time, but only after some serious prodding. Diablo would have just as soon walked home.

Charlie had beaten his mother and grandfather home. He quickly unsaddled Diablo and wiped him down before turning him out in the corral.

He decided to tell them about his afternoon outing. There was no way he would be able to explain all the horse tracks in the yard and on the road. Besides, someone surely saw him riding that paint stallion.

CHAPTER 18

A cloud of dust puffed up every time Jake and Luka's shod hoofs struck the hard dry roadway. Charlie Mayfair set astride the big black gelding named Jake, who effortlessly carried his rider at nothing more than a fast walk. Luka, a smaller bay filly, trotted beside him saddled, but riderless, teetered to the pommel on Jake's saddle by a six foot rope.

The entire landscape was arid, begging for moisture that would not come. The sunflowers faced the sun; their bright yellow pedals drooping, dark green leaves hung limply on strong straight stems, weakened from the lack of water and the hot morning sun.

The only plant suited for these trying conditions was the stubborn bindweed, sending long slender tenacious roots deep in the bone-dry ground in its search for water. The bindweed's small flowers bloomed in large and small patches; showing up like snow white clouds on a parched and barren land.

Charlie could see the Elliot farm in the distance, thankful that he was about to reach his destination. He was anxious to get there, Possum's call the night before sounded urgent—almost demanding. He had brought along a clean change of clothes just as Possum had suggested, stuffed in the saddle bags that bounced gently on Luka's rump. They would be wrinkled; but clean.

Possum had also suggested he bring along a couple of horses; perhaps a strange request, but Charlie never questioned Possums intent.

It had been four days since he had told Possum about Jumbo; including how Uncle Ezra and Grandma Bledso had helped him hide the near dead hound in the secret room in the Bledso's barn.

Possum was under the old Oak tree changing the oil in his W6 International tractor, as Charlie rode up.

"Morning Charlie! These the horses your granddad's breaking for Minnie Choitz?" Possum ran his hand over Luka's neck.

"They are."

"Sure are a nice pair." Possum looked Jake over from a distance, studying his conformation

"Which one do I ride?" Smoky strolled up beside the waiting mounts.

"Ride the big black, I rode him over here. Figured I better take the edge off him so you wouldn't fall off and get hurt."

"I ain't goin' to fall off." Smoky failed to see any humor in Charlie's remark.

"So where you boys figure on riding these horses off too?"

"I don't know," Charlie answered.

"Smoky, there's a couple canteens hanging in the washhouse, you better fill them with water. It's pretty hot, you're going to need 'em. And get yourself a cap or hat. You'll fool around and get a sunstroke," Possum scolded.

Possum began filling his pipe from the tobacco pouch he had pulled out of his pocket, as he waited for Smoky to get out of hearing. "Charlie, something's going on over at the Bledso's." He spoke in a low deep voice. "I don't no what . . . but somethin'. Uncle Ezra's been on a drunken binge ever since he helped you move that dog over there, hasn't opened the barbershop for three days. I went in to talk to him yesterday . . .found him in the back passed out." Possum lit his pipe—smoke bellowed from the bowl. "Another thing that's damn strange and don't make any sense at all."

"What's that?" Charlie looked up toward the windmill, where Smoky was filling the canteens.

"Grandma Bledso helping you with that dog. She ain't never helped anyone in her life, now all of a sudden. . . she's willing to help a dog, somethin's up, I bet Uncle Ezra knows what it is . . . and I'll tell you right now, she's up to no good." Possum shut down the conversation as Smoky returned.

"I'm ready, let's go." Smoky hung a canteen on each saddle.

"Not so fast, son, you better take them horses up to the tank and give 'em a drink . . . it's going to get pretty hot."

"Ah! Do I have too?"

"Yes, you do, now get goin'."

Smoky reluctantly took the reins and lead the horses to the tank.

"Charlie, I think we'll pay a little surprise visit on the Bledso's tonight. You might as well figure on spending the night here . . . I'll call your mother. The excuse we'll use for stopping is that we're going to the picture show at the drive-in and we thought maybe Junior and Curly would like to go along. If nothing else . . . maybe, we can get the boys alone and they can tell us something. For now . . . remember when we talked to Billy Hawks in the barbershop?"

"Yeah, I remember."

"Hawks told you to stop by and see him if you was ever in the area." Possum tightened the drain plug on the oil pan.

"What you gettin' at, Possum?"

"I think it might be a good day to be in the area and drop in on him."

"Why?"

"Well, it appeared to me that he kinda liked you. Go down there and nose around a little. See what he's been up too and try to find out how long he plans on stayin' around here. Also, tell Hawks that I've asked around and we'll pay him two hundred dollars if he'll take out that old boar. That should give him something to think about. Think you can do that?" Possum rested his back against the tractor tire.

"Yeah, I guess."

"I haven't told anyone, anything about this matter." Possum set down in one of his homemade seats.

"I haven't either." Charlie watched as Smoky lead Jake and Luka away from the tank.

"It's a shame not to tell Smoky and Millie, but for right now, the fewer people that know about Jumbo and his whereabouts, the better."

"That filly wouldn't drink." Smoky announced, when he got within hearing distance.

"You can lead a horse to water, but you can't make 'em drink. That's what they say, makes sense to me," Possum surmised. "Don't be runnin' 'em—too hot."

"Ready to ride, Smoky?" Charlie set his foot in the stirrup.

"I'm ready." Smoky pulled himself up in the saddle.

"No your not, I told you to get a cap or hat, don't look to me like you've got either one." Possum grumbled.

"Oh! I forgot." Smoky dismounted, making a quick dash for the house.

"Possum, I'm a little nervous about this deal." Charlie looked down on Possum from his perch on Luka's back.

Possum, hands on hips, looked up a Charlie. "Don't be—just be yourself—be a good listener. Might be surprised what people will tell ya, I learned that a long time ago. Possum watched as Smoky returned, wearing a beat up straw hat. "That's better, not much better, but better. Where did you dig that thing up? Possum held Jake's bridle as Smoky mounted.

147

"It was in that old cupboard on the porch."

"It becomes you." Possum shook his head and uttered in a soft voice. "Be careful boys."

Smoky reined Jake to a stop once they were out of sight of the Elliot farm. "I'm going to roll me a cigarette." He produced a can of Prince Albert from inside his shirt.

"Where did you get the tobacco?"

Smoky was busy trying to hold Jake still and pour tobacco into a cigarette paper at the same time. He finally gave up, "hold this horse." He dismounted and gave Charlie the reins.

"You never answered my question?"

"It's a secret."

"Don't tell me you and Becky made up."

"Heck no! Becky left town."

"What! Where'd she go?"

"You mean you haven't heard." The wind was blowing the tobacco out of Smoky's cigarette paper as fast as he poured it in.

"Heard what?"

"Becky's old man sold the store."

"When did this happen?"

"About two weeks ago. Fellow named Jamieson bought the store—already took it over. Got a daughter that's a senior in high school. Real pretty, pale red hair, nice figure, she works in the store." Smoky finally finished rolling a thin cigarette. "Dad says, 'she's a strawberry-blonde, only ever saw one like her, when he was a young man huskin' corn in Nebraska.' Now what do you thinka that?"

"I guess I've never seen one, not sure I'd know it if I did."

"Well, if you see her, I'll guarantee you'll know her. Prettiest gal that's hit this part of the country in a long time."

"Oh, I see. So is she the one that sold you the tobacco?" Charlie had a sparkle in his eye, feeling he had figured out where the tobacco had come from.

"Maybe. No!" Smoky reached in his pocket for a match. His hand came out empty, in desperation he reach in the other pocket. "You got a match?"

"Why would I have a match, I don't smoke. What's her name?"

"Carlene. Damn, I need a match." Smoky stuffed the cigarette in his shirt pocket and remounted.

"These older girls sure got a thing for you. You better be careful."
Charlie gently kicked Luka in the ribs; she easily started walking
down the road.

"What do you mean by that?" Smoky quickly rode up to Charlie's
side.

"Well, if she's good looking, with a nice figure, them older boys in
town are all going to try and give her a big rush. I don't think they're
going to put up with some fifteen year old messing around with their
prime stock."

"I'm not interested in her that way!" Smoky snapped back.

"You tell that to them older boys when they're beating the tar out
of ya," Charlie grinned.

"What are we going to do when we get to the river?" Smoky
changed the subject.

"I think we might stop in and visit that Indian . . . Billy Hawks."

"Wait a minute, I don't know if that's such a good idea." Smoky
spoke nervously.

"Why?" Charlie pulled Luka to a stop.

"Because he's a Indian."

"So."

"He might put a arrow in us and . . . take our scalps."

"Oh, come on, this is nineteen fifty- four not eighteen fifty-four.
Indians don't scalp people anymore."

"You never know. Grandma Bledso says they do." The color had
began to leave Smoky's face.

"Grandma Bledso is touched in the head. She's just tryin' to scare
you." Charlie reassured his comrade.

"I, I don't know," he stammered.

"Smoky, I'll tell you something, no self-respecting Indian would
want that rag mop head of hair you've got."

"Ha! Ha! Scalp like mine, he could trade for a squaw." Smoky
retaliated in disgust.

"She'd have to be old, fat and ugly." Charlie came back.

"I still don't like the idea."

"Oh, come on. It'll be fun. I bet he'll be interesting to talk to. He
might even have a match."

It was nearly a half hour later when they rode their horses onto the
Old Iron Bridge. Jake and Luka's ears pricked as iron clad hooves
struck hardwood planks. Jake came to a sudden stop a few feet onto

the bridge. Luka didn't stop, but put her head up and pranced sideways as she continued across the bridge. Jake's eyes opened wide as he backed off the bridge, nostrils flared as Smoky gently kicked hard heels in perspiration soaked ribs. Charlie dismounted and tied Luka to a small tree along side the road.

"Hold up, Smoky. Don't spook him!" Charlie hollered, as he started across the bridge on foot.

"He don't wanta cross. Maybe, it's a sign that we're not 'spose to talk to that Indian," Smoky offered.

"He'll come, give me the reins." Charlie took the reins and rubbed Jake's neck and shoulders. "Come on boy." He tugged on the reins. Jake cautiously followed, gaining more confidence with every step. After crossing the bridge Charlie returned the reins to Smoky.

They continued up the road west for a little ways and entered an open gate on the right hand side of the road. Riding along the edge of a field of grain sorghum, they followed a well used trail that lead back to the river. Shatter cane had come up in the grain sorghum and was trying to choke it out; the leaves of both were wilted and drooping.

The smell of smoke was drifting down the river. Shortly the trail turned into the timber and before Charlie and Smoky realized it, they had ridden into Billy Hawks' camp.

Hawks was sitting cross legged on the ground in front of a rectangular shaped canvas tent with an open flap for a door. He wasn't wearing a shirt and had traded his boots for Indian moccasins.

He stood up as they reined in their mounts. Hawks reached for a white T-shirt that hung on a tree limb nearby. He pulled the T-shirt over his head, but not before Charlie noticed the ugly red scar that started at the top of his right shoulder and run down his ribs.

They slid off their horses simultaneously. Hawks was walking toward them as he spoke. "Welcome to my camp, Charlie Mayfair." His long straight black hair hung loose on his shoulders. He extended his hand, as a robust smile formed on his face.

Charlie responded, giving him a good firm hand shake.

"Who's your friend?" Hawks extended his hand toward Smoky.

"This is my friend Smoky Elliot. You met his dad in the barbershop."

"Sure, I remember." Smoky winced as Hawks grabbed his hand and shook it vigorously.

"These your horses?" Hawks turned loose of Smoky's hand and took notice of the horses the boys had rode in on, he slid his hand over Luka's rump.

"No, my Grandfather's been breaking them for a lady named Minnie Choitz. She lives over in Lincoln county."

"They sure are a nice pair. Hawks took hold of Luka's leg, just below the knee. He pulled up on her leg and Luka lifted up her foot so Hawks could look under the hoof. "Been worked with a little."

They tied the horses to some nearby small trees.

"Maybe, we should pull these saddles off, it's pretty hot." Hawks spoke, as he was already undoing the cinch on Luka. Charlie did the same for Jake.

"Come on over here and have a seat." Hawks motioned toward the tent, as they laid the saddles beside a fallen tree.

Hawks had a large cast iron kettle hanging on a three legged tripod about six steps in front of his tent. The smoke from the fire was lazily being carried down the Smoky Hill River Valley by the slight breeze that had been blowing all morning. Hawks peered in the boiling pot.

Smoky sat down on a broken tree limb, stretching out his stocky legs. "What you cookin'?"

"My mother called it three meat stew. I just call it dinner." Hawks grinned, showing of a set of pearly white teeth, as he tossed a couple small twigs on the fire.

Charlie walked toward Hawks, who had picked up a long wooden spoon to stir his stew. The steam from the pot rolled up in Charlie's face. "That don't smell half bad, what kinda meat you put in it?"

"What ever kind I have. I bet you boys are enjoying your summer vacation. When does school start up again?"

"Early September." Charlie took a seat beside Smoky.

"Never is too soon." Smoky looked at Charlie, than back at Hawks. "Did you have to go to school?"

"Yes, I went to school. It was called the Chilocco Indian School. I didn't start school until I was about ten years old."

"How come so old?" Charlie began working his foot back and forth, cutting a small channel in the loose sand.

"I guess there was several reasons. One thing Indian children didn't get along real well in public schools, sometimes it was the language barrier, sometimes it was just the fact that there wasn't a school close around to attend. The Chilocco Indian School was a boarding school, we lived right there at the school."

"That's all you did, went to school?" Smoky stood up rubbing his hips.

"Not hardly. The school set on over eight thousand acres of land in northern Oklahoma. We had cattle, horses, sheep and even chickens. The older boys were given a garden plot and each boy tended his own garden. We went to school for half a day and worked the other half. Everyone had some kinda job. The younger children and girls would work in the dining hall, kitchen, sewing and mending rooms. We all wore uniforms so they were always in need of repair. We even had a butcher shop and a bakery that some of the children worked in," Hawks related.

"So how many kids went to this school?" Charlie asked.

"When I started school, I think around six hundred. I think there was a time that there was around twelve hundred children enrolled in the school. We came from many different tribes. I was told at one time there was almost fifty different tribes represented at the school and that's not counting children that were only part Indian. Children only had to be a quarter Indian to attend the school."

"What tribe are you from?" Smoky inquired.

"I'm Cherokee, full blooded, there were more Cherokee children enrolled in the school than any other tribe."

"Where did all these kids come from?" Smoky sat back down.

"All over the United States. The school was set up and run by the government, their idea was that they could put all these Indian tribes together and they would form one big happy family. It didn't really work that way, the children formed a lot of gangs along tribal lines. That caused some problems at times."

"How many years you stay there?" Smoky reached in his pocket and pulled out the poor excuse for a cigarette, he had rolled on the road.

"I was about eighteen years old when I left."

Hawks watched as Smoky picked up a small dead twig and laid it in the fire. The flame licked at the dried wood, it quickly ignited, Smoky lite his smoke. He took a long drag and coughed a couple times. Hawks turned his back to Smoky, trying to keep a straight face. "You been smoking long?" He turned back around to face Smoky.

"About two years, I guess, off and on." He sucked in more smoke and coughed again.

"What you mean by off and on?"

"When I got tobacco, I smoke and if I don't have tobacco I don't smoke."

"We had a young fellow back home, a little younger than you, I'd say. He liked to smoke. He was smoking in the barn one day and caught it on fire. After that everyone called him Smoky. So why they call you Smoky?"

"I set the outhouse on fire. It didn't have anything to do with smoking."

"Tell me about it," Hawks urged.

"I made a peashooter out of a clothespin. It worked pretty good for shooting peas or small rocks. One day I figured out, if you loaded it with a match head, it would shoot that too and most of the time the match would light. One day I was playing with it in the old privy. I shot a match down in the pit. There was a lot of paper down there and some of it caught fire."

"So did the outhouse burn down?" Hawks was digging in a paper sack that he had retrieved from the tent.

"Heck! Yes! Went up like a dead cedar tree."

"I'll bet you got in a lot of trouble over that." He pulled a large onion out of the paper sack.

"Yeah, got the whippin' of my life. Couldn't sit down for a week, but it got us indoor plumbing."

"Did you quit playing with matches?" Hawks started peeling the onion with his hunting knife.

"He still plays with matches, but he won't go in an outhouse." Charlie answered.

Hawks left out a robust laugh as he began chopping the onion into small chunks, and dropping it into the stew. When the last of the onion dropped in the boiling pot, he wiped his eyes with the back of his hand. "How do you make a peashooter out of a clothespin?"

"I don't know if I can tell you, but I'll show you if you've got a couple clothespins," Smoky excitedly replied.

"I think I've got some around here someplace. Let me look around a little bit." Hawks retreated into his tent.

"We'll need some tape too." Smoky called out to him.

Charlie picked up the wooden spoon, gently stirring the stew, trying to figure out what kind of meat Hawks had put in it, but everything he brought to the top was unrecognizable.

Hawks came out of the tent and handed the clothespins to Smoky.

Smoky immediately took one of them apart, taking the two sticks and turning them over. "Charlie, take that tape and tape these together." They taped the two small ends together, as Hawks watch the boys carefully put the peashooter together, when finished it looked like an upside down open clothespin.

"Now you slip one end of the spring in this little groove on the underside of the clothespin, like this." Smoky demonstrated as he slipped the other end of the spring between the two taped sticks, leaving the coil of the spring on the underside.

Hawks studied the crude peashooter, as Smoky took the second clothespin apart. "Now you use one of these sticks to cock it." He pushed the bar on the spring back until it caught in the grove that would normally hold the coil, picking up a small nearly round sandstone he pushed it down into the homemade peashooter. Smoky squeezed the coil spring and fired the sandstone across the camp site.

"That thing really works, can I try it out," Hawks asked excitedly.

Smoky handed Hawks his toy. He repeated the loading procedure and fired at a nearby can, missing by a couple of inches.

"I'm glad you boys came by this morning. Otherwise, I might have never learned how to make a peashooter out of a clothespin."

Smoky had strolled over and was peering into the stew kettle. "Just don't shoot any matches in your tent."

"I'll make it a point to be careful," he laughed.

Hawks reached back in his paper sack and produced half a dozen carrots. He started scraping the carrots and clipped off the ends.

"Did you ever have a nick name?" Smoky asked.

"No, I never did, but I did change my name once."

"What name did you use before?" Charlie asked.

"When I was younger, I used the name Billy Two Hawks. I dropped the Two when I joined the Army."

"You was in the Army?" Charlie walked over and stood beside Hawks who was chopping up the carrots and dropping them in the stew pot.

"Oh, yes, when the war started, I joined up."

"So why did you change your name?" Smoky asked curiously.

154

"I think, maybe, it had something to do with the school. I'm not sure, I guess it sounded too Indian. I think I was concerned that someone might tease me or make some smart remark. I was pretty feisty in them days and pretty short tempered. I was afraid someone would say something and I would start banging heads. Looking back on it, I wish I wouldn't have changed my name. A man's heritage is something to be proud of." He dropped the last piece of carrot in the stew pot.

"Did you do a lot of fighting in the war?" Smoky sat back down on the log.

"Not much, I'm afraid. We landed at Normandy and the second day I got my leg busted up. That pretty much ended the war for me."

"You was at Normandy?" Charlie's eyes lit up.

"I certainly was," Hawks proclaimed.

"My dad was killed at Normandy." Charlie turned away from Hawks and looked across the river.

Hawks walked over to Charlie, coming up behind him, stopping at his side. "I'm sorry to hear that, Charlie. He must have been a brave man, a lot of good men died at Normandy. Do you miss him?"

"I miss not having a dad. I barely remember him. Mom talks about him a lot. I guess I know him better through her." Charlie looked into Hawks' face.

"Your mother never remarried?"

"No."

"Think she ever will?"

"I don't know, she doesn't seem to be looking very hard."

Hawks disappeared into the tent. He came out carrying a bowl filled with potatoes, already peeled, chopped in small pieces.

"She should remarry. I think your father would have wanted her to." He dumped the potatoes in the stew.

Several crows settled in the trees across the river. They were making quite a racket as they harassed a horned owl that they had found near the top of a large cottonwood.

"She might someday. She's pretty particular, not just any man is going to do. If you know what I mean?" Charlie settled back down on the log.

"I think I understand." Hawks stood over his stew. "You boys will stay for dinner won't you?"

"Well! Ah, I don't know about that," Smoky answered nervously.

155

"You boys been on the trail all morning, you must be hungry." Hawks looked over the stew kettle at the boys.

"Exactly what's in that stew?" Smoky asked.

"You pretty well seen what I've been putting in it." Hawks had picked up the wooden spoon, stirring his lunch as they talked.

"I mean, what kind of meat?" Smoky clarified his question.

"Oh, it's just some left over meat, that I had around, it's all good fresh meat. You'll like it." Hawks picked up a tin cup that was sitting on a nearby log. He dipped out a couple spoons full of the broth and put it in the cup. "Here Smoky, try it." He walked over to Smoky and offered him the cup.

Smoky took the cup.

"Be careful, it's pretty hot," Hawk's cautioned.

Smoky looked down into the steaming cup. "You try it." He offered Charlie the cup.

"Sure I'll try it." Charlie wasn't real eager to try Hawks' stew but he didn't want to be impolite either. He cautiously sipped the broth. "It's pretty good, Smoky try it." He pushed the cup back in Smoky's hand.

He carefully took the cup and reluctantly sipped the broth. Smoky smacked his lips a couple of times and took another taste. "It's not bad."

"What do you think, shall we stay for lunch?" Charlie asked.

"I guess, might as well." Smoky handed the cup back to Hawks.

"That's good," Hawks smiled. "I'll enjoy the company. It's going to be a little while."

The crows were still making a lot of racket across the river and more of them had joined in the festivities.

Charlie decided it was time to get down to business. "Mr. Hawks, Possum wanted us to stop by and tell you that a group of farmers around here took up a collection and they will give you two hundred dollars if you'll hunt down that old rough boar. The one they call Ol Razor."

"You know I see his tracks from time to time, but I've never seen him. Same with that dog, I see his tracks, but I never see him." Hawks sat down on the log beside Charlie. "Those two are like shadows on the river. You know they're, around but you never see them, you may think you've seen them—but you're never sure. I'll tell you something else, those two are having a war on this river."

"Why do you say that?" Charlie asked.

"There can only be one King on the river and until they get it settled—they will be at war. They may have already settled it. They had a big fight the other morning about a mile up river from my camp. I could hear them fighting, lots of barking and squealing, they were really having it out. I tried to get down there but it was all over before I got there. I think that dog got the worst of it. He was loosing a lot of blood. I followed him for a ways and then he went into the river. I had a devil of a time finding where he came out of the river. He's a smart one, he had been going down river and when he went into the water, he turned around and went back the same direction he had come from. It took me all morning to figure that little trick out."

"So you never did find him?"

"Yes, and no."

"What do you mean by that?" Charlie adjusted the ball cap setting on his head.

"When I found where he had came out of the river, I started to follow him—it was easy tracking since it was a blood trail. He left the river and went up into the prairie. I found a place where he had laid down to rest under some small bushes. He didn't stay there very long. I got the feeling that he had someplace in mind, he knew where he wanted to go. I was right too, because he ended up at an old abandoned farmstead. I think they call it the Barnes' place."

Smoky had a bewildered look on his face as he asked, "So was he there?"

"No, he wasn't. Someone had loaded him up and hauled him away. There had been several people around there and one of them had ridden a horse. Also Eli Bledso's pickup was parked in an elderberry patch not too far from the house." Hawks stood up and walked over to his stew, he added a couple of dry tree limbs to the fire.

Charlie stood up as well, casually walking over to the saddles, taking a drink from the canteen hanging on the saddle horn.

Smoky had followed, "Charlie, what's going on?" He lifted the canteen off his saddle. "Is there something going on that I don't know about?" Smoky whispered, after he had taken a couple swallows of water. "You seem kinda nervous."

"Yeah, there's something going on, but I can't talk about it now. Just act dumb." He was nervous. Figuring Billy Hawks knew exactly who was over at the Barnes' place and more than likely had some idea where Jumbo was being hidden. He hoped this was a subject that wouldn't be brought up again as they returned to the camp-fire.

The crows continued with their serenade, louder than ever.

"Have you got a rifle, Mr. Hawks?" Smoky looked across the river.

"Sure, would you like to see it?"

"Yeah, you bet, I'd like to see it." Smoky was quick to reply.

Hawks once again slipped into his tent and when he returned he was carrying a old thirty-thirty Winchester. The rifle showed a lot of use, the stock was covered with nicks and scratches, while in places the bluing had worn off the barrel.

Hawks snapped the lever down exposing an empty chamber. Satisfied the gun wasn't loaded he closed the action and handed the gun to Smoky.

Smoky held the gun in his left hand while running his right hand down the barrel and then the stock. "How old is this gun?"

"I'm not sure, my father gave it to me. It's been around a long time."

"Does it still shoot straight?" Smoky raised the gun to his shoulder and sighted down the barrel.

"Just as straight as the man holding it." Hawks was standing beside Smoky, resting his weight on his good leg.

Smoky walked away from Hawks toward the river bank. He turned to face Hawks. "How about putting a shell in this gun? I want to take a crack at one of them crows."

"Oh! I don't think you want to do that."

"Why not?"

"Well, for one thing, shooting a gun that size in the air, you don't know where the bullet might come down. Besides, why would you want to shoot a crow?"

"Just to see if I can hit it." Smoky once again raised the old rifle to his shoulder and sighted down the barrel, zeroing in on a lone crow at the top of the cottonwood.

"Are you going to eat the crow?"

"Shoot no, I ain't eatin' no crow."

"If you're going to kill something, you should have a good reason, such as to protect yourself or someone else. Maybe, to protect your property—or for food."

"One less crow won't make any difference." Smoky moved toward Hawks and handed him the rifle.

"That crow is one of Mother Earth's creatures and we must respect her creatures. Smoky let me explain something to you. If we take care of Mother Earth, she will always take care of us. If we don't take care of her, we will all parish and the earth will be a barren desert. We must leave the earth as we found it. If we do that, she will always be here for future generations. Does that make sense to you?"

"I guess. What do you think about it, Charlie?" Hawks looked intimidating as his dark eyes looked down on Smoky. He took a step back.

"It makes sense to me. If that's the case, why are you here to destroy Jumbo?"

"There are evil forces on this earth and sometimes they have to be dealt with."

"You think Jumbo is a evil force? He saved Millie Elliot's life!" Charlie raised his voice a bit.

"He was perceived to me, to be an evil force, now I'm not so sure." Hawks stroked his smooth beardless chin. "Charlie, I have strange feelings about that dog, ever since I trailed him to the old house—I've felt he was more than just a stray dog." Hawks swatted a fly that had landed on his leg.

Charlie thought to himself, perhaps Hawks considered a fly an evil force, he thought about asking, but reconsidered, remembering what Possum had said about being a good listener.

Hawks continued, "I haven't seen any sign that he has returned to the river—no calls in the night, no tracks . . . perhaps he's dead, but I don't think so, my feeling is that someone is hiding him—even giving him medical attention. Someone who would be, least expected to help him." Hawks looked deep into Charlie's eyes. "What do you think, Mr. Mayfair?"

Charlie held his ground, unblinking, he met the Indians gaze. Smoky curiously watched the stand-off, not understanding, but not uttering a sound. "If this is true . . . this person that's helping him; do they mean him any harm?"

"That I can't say—one thing I will tell you—I'm almost certain he's the dog that killed Orie Shank." Hawks slowly strolled toward the camp fire.

"What makes you so sure?" Charlie followed, only a step behind.

159

"For one thing, he doesn't trust men, you stop and think about it, the way Orie Shank treated him, it's only natural that he wouldn't trust men . . . but he trusted Millie Elliot, even saved her life, she could easily pass for Shank's Granddaughter . . . at least in his eyes. And what can you tell me about the old woman—Mrs. Bledso—some say she dabbles in witchcraft, or devil worship, or blackmagic? What do you say, Charlie Mayfair?"

Charlie was somewhat bewildered by Hawks' question. "Everyone has heard them stories, we joke about it at school, but I don't think anyone knows for sure. Ah . . . what have you heard?"

"Most likely the same stories. But yesterday a pickup, with Missouri tags, stopped me on the road . . . two men in it, they were looking for Grandma Bledso, said they had a delivery too make."

"What's the matter with that?" Charlie looked across the camp-fire at Hawks.

"They were hauling a pickup load of dynamite"

"Holy smoke! What would she want with that much dynamite?"

"That's a good question, Charlie Mayfair." Billy Hawks answered, as Charlie turned to walk away. "I'll also tell you this, if she is into witchcraft or blackmagic, and if she is going to do something, it will happen tonight."

Charlie spun around on his heels facing Hawks. "Are you sure about that?"

"Yes, I am, the moon is right."

Charlie turned his back to Hawks, deep in thought, as he walked behind the tent. Smoky was right behind him. "So that's what this is all about, that dog's been hurt, and I'm bettin' you know where he's at. Right?" Smoky spoke in a low voice, almost a whisper.

"Maybe, I can't talk about it now. Let's be hospitable and eat some of Hawks' stew and then get out of here . . . I need to talk ta Possum."

Charlie looked down at a large snapping turtle shell lying on the ground behind the tent. Beside the turtle shell was a fresh muskrat skin.

"How long do you plan on staying here?" Charlie asked, as they returned to the stew pot.

"I'm not sure, I certainly won't be here when cold weather sets in. I don't want to spend the winter down here."

Not getting the answer he was looking for, Charlie decided to change the subject. "Mr. Hawks can you teach us some Indian words?"

"Sure, what Indian words would you like to know?"

"How would you say, 'hello'?" Charlie sat down on the log.

"You must understand that in the Indian language, one word or phrase can have more than one meaning. For instance, if when you rode up to my camp, you would call out 'Yeta'. That would mean 'Hello, in the camp.' If I called back 'Yeta' it would mean, 'Welcome to my camp'."

Suddenly the crows went silent, sitting quietly in the tree, watching, waiting, as if something had drawn their undivided attention. The whole area had become very serene, an unknown force had hushed the river.

Hawks walked over to the rivers edge. Smoky and Charlie followed as Hawks peering eyes scanned the opposite bank.

"What's the matter?" Smoky inquired.

"This happens ever so often down here. It gets so very quiet. I think something comes into the area that the wildlife fears."

"What do you think it is?" Smoky took a couple of steps back from the riverbank.

"I'm not sure, but I've always thought it was either Jumbo or the old boar. I'll check it out this evening. The old boar's tracks will be over there someplace. Boys, I think dinner is ready." Hawks walked back to his tent. He went inside, returning with three pie tins and as many large spoons.

He passed the plates around, the boys held out their plates as Hawks filled them with stew using a large ladle. They returned to the log after each grabbed a hand full of crackers.

Charlie was deep in thought, wondering if Billy Hawks would actually kill Jumbo if he had the chance. He liked Hawks, but in this matter, questioned how far he could trust him. Maybe he was fretting for nothing, Jumbo was in bad shape and it was quite possible he wasn't going to make it. If he died, Hawks would leave the country and it would all be over. Perhaps he had made a mistake accepting Grandma Bledso's help, Charlie pondered, had he unknowingly delivered Jumbo into the world of witchcraft or blackmagic. If so, what diabolical plan did Grandma have in mind.

"Charlie, eat your stew—it's good." Smoky brought him back to reality.

Charlie carefully took a spoonful of the stew. It was very tasty, and they both ate their fill.

They finished eating and Charlie immediately let it be known they would be leaving Hawks' camp. "I want to thank you for your hospitality and the fine meal, Mr. Hawks, but we need to be getting back home. I've got a long ride ahead of me." He set the pie plate on the log, stood up and stretched.

"Thanks for the meal, Mr. Hawks, it was real good." Smoky said, as he set his tin plate on top of Charlie's.

"I'm glad you liked it, you two are good company. I hope you stop by again sometime." He followed the boys over to their horses and helped them put on the saddles for the trip home. "I want you boys to feel free to stop in again, anytime you're in the area. I've been thinking, since we have become friends, I would like to give you boys some Indian names. Just something we can . . . keep between ourselves."

"A Indian name, that sounds wild. What are you going to call me?" Smoky asked.

"Smoky, you will be known as Sitting Crow." Hawks and Smoky shook hands.

Charlie tried to keep from laughing as Hawks extended his hand. Hawks spoke, "From this day forth you will be known as Charlie No Tell."

His word surprised Charlie as a strange look came over his face. "Time to go, Sitting Crow. Thanks again, Mr. Hawks."

They mounted up and rode out of the camp; waving good-bye as they left.

Riding side by side, they were almost to the Old Iron Bridge, when Smoky spoke the first words since they had left Hawks' camp. "Charlie No Tell, are you the one that found Jumbo at the Barnes place?"

"No, I'm not. Your sister found him, I just helped get him out of there."

"You and who else? Grandma Bledso!"

"Maybe. Did you ever figure out what kinda meat was in that stew?" Charlie steered Smoky off the subject.

"No, I didn't. You got any ideas?" Smoky asked as they started across the Old Iron Bridge.

"Yeah, I do. I think that dark meat that tasted kinda sweet was beaver and the white meat was snapping turtle." Charlie turned in the saddle to look back at Smoky. Jake had slowed down as they started across the bridge. He was coming, but still wasn't sure about the noise the wood was making under his feet.

"What about the third one?"

"You don't want too know," Charlie answered.

"Yes, I do. What was it?"

"Muskrat."

"Muskrat." His jaw was set, the color left his face, a lump was forming in his throat, and he pulled Jake to a stop, quickly dismounting, hanging his head over the bridge railing, feeding his stew to the catfish.

CHAPTER 19

Millie met the boys as they turned down the driveway, stopping a few feet in front of the sweaty horses. "Charlie, you're staying overnight. Mom called and cleared it with your mother. We're going to the movie at the drive-in. Dad says to put your horses in the back corral. Junior and Curly are going too."

"What's the movie?" Smoky asked.

"Ma and Pa Kettle." She walked beside Luka and Charlie, blue eyes sparkling under long dark lashes, bright white teeth showing through a perfect smile, blonde hair glistening under the hot afternoon sun, slender round hips playfully teasing in tight cut off blue jeans—tantalizing the imagination of the young man riding beside her. "You guy's put up your horses. They look thirsty, you look thirsty too, Charlie. I'll fix you something to drink."

Charlie and Smoky rode up to the barn, as they unsaddle the horses Smoky began to question Charlie. "When are you going to tell me about that dog?"

Charlie thought about it for a moment, and finally decided he might as well fill Smoky in on what was going on. Hawks already knew about Jumbo being injured and after their conversation, Charlie was sure he knew where he was being hidden, as well as, who had moved him from the Barnes' place. Junior, Curly and Eli Bledso surely had found out by now, but they would never tell, fearing Grandma would make them pay dearly if they let out any of her secrets.

Charlie began telling Smoky the story as they led the horses to the corral. They where about to enter the front door of the house when he finished. Charlie could see the disappointment in Smoky's face; feeling he should have taken him into his confidence sooner.

Mom Elliot was busy working in the kitchen, as they entered the house. The room was rather warm, a twelve inch fan setting on the counter, provided some relief from the heat.

"Hi! Charles," Mom Elliot gave him a little hug. "Did you have a nice ride?"

"Yeah, we did. Pretty hot though."

"Yes it is, sit down here at the table. Milacent fixed you some ice tea."

Millie appeared in the doorway. She took a seat across the table from Charlie, looking into his steel blue eyes. "So, what did you do down there on the river?"

"We visited with Billy Hawks most of the time," Smoky replied.

"Why did you go visit him? I don't trust him." Millie spoke sharply, a frown on her face.

"He treated us real nice . . . even feed us dinner." Charlie turned his head slightly, finding it hard to meet Millie's gaze.

"What did he feed you?" Mom Elliot inquired.

"Stew, he called it three meat stew, it was pretty good." The color was leaving Smoky's face as they talked about the fine cuisine they had partaken of at Billy Hawks' camp.

"Three meat stew, I never heard of such a concoction," Millie snapped. "What kinda meat was in it?"

"I think it was snapping turtle, beaver and a little muskrat." Charlie answered, as Smoky bolted for the door.

"What's the matter with him?" Millie inquired.

"I don't think that stew set to well on his stomach," Mom Elliot grinned.

"I'm not surprised, I couldn't eat anything like that," Millie surmised.

"He gave us Indian names."

"Like what?" Millie relaxed her attentive look.

"Smoky's named Sitting Crow."

Mom Elliot and Millie began to laugh.

"So, what did he name you?" Millie asked, after she stopped laughing.

"From this day forth, I shall be known as Charlie No Tell."

They laughed some more.

"That fits you," Mom Elliot concluded.

"What else did he tell you?" Millie questioned, as Charlie finished his tea.

"I'm not tellin'. Where's Possum?"

Millie picked up a dirty dishcloth and threw it at Charlie, catching him square in the face. He picked it up, preparing to toss it back—when he noticed Mom Elliot's disapproving look.

"He's around here someplace doing chores. More than likely down at the barn getting ready to milk the cows."

"I guess I'll go hunt him up. Maybe, he needs some help."

"Good idea, find Sitting Crow and take him with you." Mom Elliot laughed, shaking her head from side to side.

Charlie found Possum in the barn, just sitting down under a Jersey milk cow. "Need some help?"

Possum turned his head, looking in Charlie's direction. "I've never turned any down before an' don't plan on starting now. Grab one of them milk stools and start with Roanie." He pointed toward a big blue roan colored cow that was calmly eating grain from the manger.

Charlie picked up a milk stool, a bucket, and set down under Roanie. She turned her head, looking at Charlie as he squeezed her long slender teats, realizing these were not the hands she was used to.

"How did things go down on the river?"

"Alright I guess, Hawks knows all about that dog being hurt. He followed him up to the old Barnes' place, the same day we found him. I think he knows who hauled him out of there and might have a pretty good idea where he's at. Hawks says that Ol Razor and Jumbo got in a big fight that morning. The fight was over before he could catch up with 'em."

"Looks like he's here to stay," Possum replied.

"At least for a while, unless Jumbo dies." Old Roanie slapped Charlie in the face with her tail. "Now, here's something else that might interest you. Hawks says two fellows from Missouri delivered a pickup load of dynamite to Grandma Bledso yesterday. And another thing, he thinks she might be into witchcraft or black magic and if she's planning something—she will do it tonight, to quote Mr. Hawks 'the moon is right'."

"She's up to something, you better damn well believe that." Possum stopped milking, deep in thought. "That much dynamite— could make a heck of an explosion."

"Possum, I told Smoky what was going on."

"I guess it doesn't make much difference. I'm anxious to get over there—maybe, we can figure out what's going on."

CHAPTER 20

It was nearly seven-thirty when Possum brought the car to a stop in the Bledso's yard. Junior and Curly were standing in front of the house, looking toward the barn, dressed in overalls, dirty hands and faces—both looking worried and scared.

Possum and Millie unloaded from the front seat, Charlie and Smoky remained in the back seat. They met in front of the car.

Possum took note of their demeanor. "Hi, boys. We was going in to the movie . . . thought maybe you might like to go along."

Junior and Curly looked at one another. Junior finally spoke, "I don't think we better leave. Grandma might not like it."

"Where's she at? I'll talk to her," Possum offered.

"I don't think she wants to talk to anybody right now." Junior answered nervously, looking down at the ground, hands in his pockets.

"What's goin' on boys? Maybe I can help you." Possum put his hand on Junior's shoulder.

Charlie and Smoky had gotten out of the car and walked up to the gathering, as Junior and Curly looked at one another.

After a long pause Curly spoke—"It's Grandma, she's been acting strange all day."

"In what way?" Possum asked.

"First thing this morning she had us take thirteen white candles and paint them black," Junior continued. She says, 'Can't find no black candles, white ones painted black will have too do'."

"Just a little while ago, she had us help her move that dog up to the front of the barn," Curly had taken up the story. "Had us lay him on a red blanket with a black star in the middle of it."

"Why is she doing all that?" Millie asked.

"Say's, she's going to perform a healing seance, to keep him alive." Curly rested against the car, hands entwined in the bib of his overalls.

"What do you think this is all about, Possum." Charlie's curiosity was getting the best of him.

"This is not good. The last healing seance she performed was on Homer Oskemier's milk cow." Possum was pacing nervously, a trait he seldom displayed.

"Did she live?" Millie inquired.

"Yeah, she lived, but her milk always tasted like vinegar, after that. Her own calf wouldn't drink it. Why in the world is she so worried about that dog dying? She never worried about anything like that before."

"He can't die, that's what she said," Junior remarked.

"Oh, boy! I don't like this. Where's your dad boys?"

"He's gone until Sunday night," Curly answered.

"Any idea where he went?"

Curly hesitated a moment. "No."

Possum looked up toward the barn, the big sliding double doors that faced the house were closed. "I'm going up there, see if I can talk to her." He started the long walk to the barn. The entourage fell quietly in behind him.

He was almost to the barn door when he realized he was being followed. "You kids hide around the corner of the barn, I don't want her to know you're here, and be quiet," Possum whispered.

They did as told moving to the side of the barn.

Possum knocked on the door. "Grandma, I want to talk to you." She refused to answer. Possum knocked again. He tried the door, it was locked from the inside. "Grandma, we need to talk about this."

He waited for an answer, none came.

"Charlie, come here." Millie motioned to Charlie. "Can you see in this window." She pointed to a small window above her head.

Charlie walked up beside the window, standing on tip toes, he was still too short. "I need something to stand on," he whispered.

"There's some buckets behind the barn. I'll go get one," Junior volunteered.

He returned shortly with the metal bucket, quietly it was set under the window. Charlie stepped up on it. He could still hear Possum trying to make conversation with Grandma Bledso. Cautiously, he peeked in the window.

Grandma Bledso had set up shop about fifteen feet in front of the big double doors. She had her back to the door and was standing in front of a crudely made altar. The altar was constructed from four hay bales, two on each end, with a weather beaten two by twelve set between the bales. Two lighted black candles set on each end of the make shift altar. Setting between the candles was a Rhode Island Red rooster in a small wire cage and a butcher knife with a six inch blade, a unlit candle sat beside the knife.

Grandma was dressed in a long black shroud that run from her shoulders to the floor. She had a black scarf over her head and a thin black veil covered her wrinkled face. She seemed to be in a trance, swaying from side to side, while doing some sort of chant.

Jumbo lay behind her on a round red blanket. In the center of the blanket was a black five pointed star, just as Curly had said earlier. Ten lighted candles surrounded the star, one at each point and one between each point in the well of the star. Jumbo was unconscious, lying with his feet toward the altar.

Charlie felt a tug on his pant leg. "Can you see anything?" Millie asked.

He stepped off the bucket. "I can see plenty." Charlie was about to tell them what he had seen, when Possum came around the corner of the barn.

"What you kids doin'?"

"Charlie just looked in the window," Millie spoke up.

"What did you see?"

Charlie was about to speak when Possum interrupted. "We better go back down to the house, before you start."

Possum took the lead as they returned to the Bledso yard. Charlie sat down on the front fender of the car as he began to relate what he had seen. Possum silently listened, hands in his pockets, pipe between his teeth—unlit. Charlie slid off the fender as he finished.

"I don't know what to do, maybe we should leave her alone. I guess she won't hurt herself." Possum was talking in a low voice, almost as if he was talking to himself. "What do you boys think?" He turned to Junior and Curly who were leaning against the car.

Junior spoke, "I guess she'll be alright . . . as long as she doesn't set the dynamite off."

"Dynamite! What are you talking about son? Dynamite," Possum exclaimed.

"Yesterday afternoon, about four o'clock, two fellows drove in the yard. Grandma talked to them out in the yard. We was settin' on the porch steps. Grandma waved for us to come over to the strangers' pickup and we all rode up to the barn and unloaded some dynamite."

"How much dynamite?" Possum asked.

"Thirteen cases," Curly answered.

169

Possum lit his pipe, taking a deep drag, letting the smoke trickle out his nostrils. "Where is it at in the barn?"

"Toward the back," Curly replied.

"Covered with a tarp?" Charlie looked at Curly, then Possum.

"Yeah."

"I seen it."

"This might be worse than I thought. Maybe she's up to something else. I got a good notion to call the sheriff. We might need some help." Possum rubbed a clean shaven chin. "I need to use the phone."

"I'm not so sure Grandma would like that." Junior cautiously objected.

"I don't like her bein' locked in that barn with that much dynamite. There's enough dynamite in there to blow that barn off the face of the earth. It'll be alright boys, just trust me."

Everyone followed Possum up the steps and in the house. The front door opened up into the living room, it was spacious and fancy. A large solid oak hutch set straight across the room from the door. It had beautiful glass doors that protected countless pieces of old china and glassware. An old settee rested against the wall to the right of the door with a fancy cane back rocking chair, that was setting out from the wall. Several other chairs were scattered around the room. The real eye catcher was the crystal chandler that hung from the ceiling. It was quite old and at one time had been adorned with candles, but in more recent times had been converted to electricity, half the bulbs were burned out. A thin coat of dust covered everything in the room.

The phone was on the wall, just inside the door. Possum picked up the receiver and dialed the operator. "Get me the sheriff's office."

Possum waited for an answer, while Millie and Charlie took a seat on the settee. "Hello, Hank, this is John Elliot." There was a moment of silence as Hank Buggs spoke on the other end of the line.

"Hank I'm out here at the Eli Bledso farm. There's some things going on out here that seem a little peculiar." Possum went on to tell Sheriff Buggs what they had found when they arrived only a short time earlier. The conversation ended when the sheriff decided to come out and see what was going on for himself.

A grandfather clock began to chime in the dining room.

Possum reached in the bib pocket of his overalls for his pipe and a beat up tobacco pouch. He filled his pipe as the clock struck the ninth time. "Nine o'clock kids, I don't think we'll make it to the movie tonight."

****

Billy Hawks cast a long shadow as he curiously watched the western sky, where a small bank of clouds was beginning to form on the horizon in an otherwise azure sky.

He had been uneasy ever since Charlie Mayfair and Smoky Elliot had left his camp early that afternoon. Their conversation had left little doubt that his assumptions were correct. Charlie Mayfair knew where Jumbo was being hidden; it was written in his eyes.

He was sure Grandma Bledso had Jumbo in her clutches; but where was she keeping him, and what were her intentions?

Billy Hawks was the grandson of a Cherokee medicine man. His Grandfather had told him about the spirit world, he had talked of witchcraft, devil worship and black magic. He told of the evil forces that could be brought into play by evil beings, individuals that desire to destroy their enemy or control those that would follow them. He wondered if Grandma Bledso possessed these powers or was it the dream of a mortal man's imagination, out of control, seeing what was not there? He understood the moon and the stars, the signs were all in place, if someone had an evil plan to carry out, this night would be a sorceress's dream.

Perhaps he would check the Bledso farm later, to see if anything looked out of place; but for now he would watch in the twilight as a storm began to brew.

****

The old Grandfather clock chimed one time, as Sheriff Buggs pulled into the yard. The sheriff was a big man, well over six foot tall and a regular bathroom scale wouldn't have weighted him. Possum was waiting at the door as Buggs climbed the porch steps. He was sucking in short breaths of air as he reached the top step, small drops of perspiration were forming on his already red face.

"What time did all this start?" Buggs entered the dinning room, collapsing in a nearby chair.

"The boys can answer that question better than me," Possum advised.

Buggs looked toward Junior who was standing beside the hutch. "I guess about six o'clock, but she didn't close the doors until around seven."

"Possum, you mentioned someone looked in the window, who was that?"

"I did." Charlie raised his hand, as if, asking permission to speak.

"Tell me what you saw."

Buggs looked at Charlie with beady brown eyes, through narrow slits. Charlie related to the sheriff what he had seen in the barn.

"That's everything, can't recall anything else? Think hard son, it might be important."

Charlie was silent for a moment "No sir—I can't."

He looked toward Possum. "Possum, you said something about some dynamite?"

"Well, yeah, the boys said they unloaded thirteen cases of dynamite in the barn yesterday."

"Did she say what she was going to do with it?" Buggs asked.

Junior and Curly shook their heads, indicating she didn't tell them her intentions.

"Hard to say what she's up too," the sheriff surmised. "I wish Eli were here, he might be able to talk to her. You boys got any idea, where your dad might be?"

"No sir, we don't," Junior answered.

"Seems to me like he left a phone number at the office, once," Buggs pondered. "He told me if there ever was a emergency to try that number. He might be there. I think I gave that to one of the deputy's to file away. Maybe we can find it." Buggs got up and walked over to the phone.

He dialed the Sheriffs office. "Joe, was you there the day Eli Bledso came in an' left a envelope, with a phone number in it?" Buggs took a handkerchief out of his pocket and wiped the sweat off his brow, while deputy Joe Clark, talked on the other end of the line. "Well, see if you can find it. We need to get hold of Eli Bledso. Call me back if you find it," he ordered.

Buggs returned to the chair he had previously occupied. He looked back and forth from Junior to Curly. "Boys, did you know your Grandma, was into seances and this type of thing?"

Junior and Curly hesitated to answer. Possum intervened, "They knew...just like I did."

"How long has she been doing this witchcraft, devil worship or what ever it is she's doin'?" He looked around the room.

"As long as I can remember," Junior finally answered.

"Did she practice this herself or was there some other people involved?" Buggs again wiped the sweat off his forehead.

"I guess by herself—there's a room upstairs she used. She would go up there by herself, nobody ever went in that room but Grandma," Junior answered nervously.

"So you boys have never been in this room?"

"No sir, Grandma said, if she ever caught us in there she would skin us alive, with a buggy whip," Junior replied.

"Did your dad ever go in that room?"

"I'm not sure, but I don't think so."

"Where is this room?" Sheriff Buggs stood up.

"I'm not sure we should be messing around that room. Grandma wouldn't like it," Junior warned.

"It'll be all right, just show me where the room is," Buggs encouraged.

Junior hesitated, but finally took the lead as everyone followed him upstairs.

Sheriff Buggs stopped at the top of the stairs to catch his breath. The upstairs of the house was hot, almost unbearable.

Sheriff Buggs tried to open the door, it was locked. "You boys know where the key is?"

"Up there." Junior pointed to the sill above the door.

He run his hand along the door sill, found the key and slowly unlocked the door, without hesitation the door was pushed open. Everyone followed Buggs in the room except Junior and Curly who retreated downstairs.

The room was unbelievably cold, considering the rest of the upstairs was so hot; it was eerie, scary, and dark. Millie took hold of Charlie's hand, her heart pounding in her chest.

Possum turned on the light switch that was by the door. A small red bulb in the middle of the ceiling lit up the room. It didn't give off much light but it was enough to see what they had walked into. Everyone looked around the room in disbelief. It was a large room with two windows, both covered with heavy dark red curtains that let in very little light and the walls were painted black. In the far corner, to the right of the door, there was an altar made of limestone. Chiseled into the front of the limestone was a serpent that ran the length of the altar. To the back of the altar set an inverted gold cross. In front of the cross was a small pentagram with a five pointed star. A human skull set in the middle of the pentagram. Two figured black candles set on each side of the pentagram and skull. A gold chalice set on the right side of the altar and an incense burner was positioned on the opposite side.

"Charlie, let's get out of here, this place gives me the willies." Millie whispered, as she pulled Charlie toward the door.

He willingly followed her. The place made him feel uncomfortable, as well.

"I've seen all I want to see." Possum remarked as he and Smoky left the room.

They had just reached the bottom of the stairs when the phone rang. Possum rushed to the living room and answered the phone. "Hello!" There was silence as Possum listened. "Yeah, he's here. I'll get him."

Possum returned to the stairs and called to the sheriff. "Joe Clark is on the phone, he wants to talk to you."

The door to Grandma's secret room slammed shut. "I'll be right there." Sheriff Buggs lumbered down the stairs. He looked pale, perspiration began to soak through his shirt. He spoke into the mouth piece. "What did you find out, Joe?" He listened nodding his head up and down. "Joe, call that number and see if you can get hold of Eli Bledso. If you do, tell him there's some trouble out here at his place and he needs to get home as quick as he can. Find out what town he's at, if it's very far away, we might be able to get the highway patrol to escort him back." Buggs listened as his deputy talked on the other end of the line. "Call me back as soon as you find out anything."

"Let's go out on the porch, this heat is about to do me in." The sheriff led the way as everyone walked out on the front porch, to join Junior and Curly, who were seated on the porch steps.

The weather was beginning to change; dark clouds were building up in the southwest. Sheriff Buggs walked to the end of the porch. "Looks like we might have a storm building up, Possum."

Possum leisurely walked over beside the sheriff. "It does look like we might have something moving in. That's funny the weather man sure hasn't been talking about a storm. We could use some moisture."

"Possum, what do you make of all this?" Buggs leaned his back against the wall of the house.

"I wish I knew. Ain't no normal person ever going to figure out what's going on in Grandma's mind

"You're right, I guess, we might be jumping to conclusions, anyway. She might not be planning any harm to anyone. Maybe Eli can shine some light on this. I hope we can find him." Buggs walked across the porch. The back of his blue uniform speckled with white paint chips from the wall.

"You know," Possum rubbed his chin. "There is someone that might be able to shed a little light on this."

"Who's that?"

"Uncle Ezra . . . he knows something, hell, he's been passed out drunk the last three days."

"Hummm, you might be right. I'll call Joe. See if we can find him." Sheriff Buggs was just entering the house when the phone rang. He closed the door.

Junior and Curly were still setting on the porch steps. Junior looked to be deep in thought, while Curly worked his foot back and forth, making a small channel in the ground, at the bottom of the steps. Smoky had laid claim to Grandma's rocking chair and slowly rocked back and forth. The old chair creaked every time he rocked forward. Charlie was leaning against one of the wooden post that supported the roof. Millie paced nervously nearby.

"Dad, isn't there something we can do?"

"I'd like to do something, but I don't know what. Sometimes these kinda problems solve themselves, but I'm not so sure in this case." He put his arm around her shoulder giving her a little hug.

"That dog sure has had a rough life and it just seems to be getting worse all the time. Why you s'pose that is, Possum?" Charlie sat down on the steps beside Junior and Curly.

"Oh, I don't know, things works that way, sometimes. Just like people, some people never can get ahead and others, everything they do turns out right. Maybe some people are just born under a lucky star or something."

Sheriff Buggs pushed the front door open and stepped onto the porch, closing the door behind himself. "We found Eli. He's in Manhattan. The Kansas Highway Patrol is going to fly him to the airport in Salina. Joe is on his way to pick him up. I would think he would be leaving Manhattan in the next few minutes. I've got Freddie Matther looking for Uncle Ezra. I told him to just bring him out here if he found him."

The Grandfather clock began to chime as Buggs walked to the porch steps. Charlie stood up letting him through. The clock would chime ten times. The sheriff went over to his car and took an unopened package of cigarettes off the dash. He leaned against the car as he opened the package, lighting one up with a silver cigarette lighter. He took a deep drag and sat down in the front seat of his car; staring up at the barn.

Everyone was still sitting out on the porch as a police car, red lights flashing, turned down the Bledso drive. It was dark now and the headlights lit up the yard as the police car carrying Uncle Ezra pulled to a stop, a bolt of lightning flashed across the sky.

Freddie Matther shut off the lights and stepped out of the car. Matther was a tall, slender, good looking young man in his late twenties. He adjusted the pistol hanging on his hip as he walked around the car to help Uncle Ezra.

He took Uncle Ezra by the arm to steady him as he got out of the car. Uncle Ezra was wearing an old pair of faded overalls and a white dress shirt. Matther guided him to the front steps. Uncle Ezra stumbled up the steps; a half pint of whisky in each hip pocket to help him keep his balance. Uncle Ezra was loaded.

Smoky gave up the rocking chair so he would have a place to sit.

Sheriff Buggs stepped up in front of Uncle Ezra. "How you feeling, Ezra?"

"Pretty . . . pretty . . . damn good." Uncle Ezra slowly answered, as he looked up at the sheriff.

"That's for sure," Possum spoke in a low voice.

"You know who your talking too—don't you?"

"That badge . . . must meean . . . your some kinda . . . laaw dog."

"That's right."

"Is this a in . . . ter . . . gation?" Uncle Ezra stuck out his chin.

"Well, sort of, I want to ask you some questions."

"I ain't answerin'. . . no questions . . . fer nooo . . . law dog. You'll . . . never make . . . me talk." Uncle Ezra reached in his right hip pocket pulling out, an almost empty half pint of Old Crow.

"You don't need anymore of that stuff!" Buggs snatched the bottle from Uncle Ezra's hand, tossing it on the porch floor. The bottle broke on impact, the contents ran across the wooden floor.

"Hey, you caan't—do that," Uncle Ezra complained.

"Yes, I can. Now you need to answer my questions," Buggs demanded.

"Go ta hell. I ain't talkin' to nobody . . . that taakes my . . . liquor."

"Just a second, Hank," Possum intervened.

"Hi!" Uncle Ezra gave a half hearted wave as Possum approached from behind the sheriff. "—Possum."

Possum knelt down beside Uncle Ezra. "Ezra, can I talk to you for a minute."

"Sure . . . Possum."

"Grandma, needs your help."

"What's the matter with . . . with Grandma?" His voice taking on a tone of concern.

"We're not sure anything is wrong, but she has locked herself in the barn, she told the boys she's going to perform a healing seance on that dog."

"Healing seance, hells bells . . . is she messing around with thaat—stuff again."

"What do you mean by that?" Possum inquired.

"Possum, she's been . . . messing a, a, around with . . . black magic, devil worship, witchcraft . . . or what evver you call it for years. Seance, ha, ha, she knows just enough about that stuff to, to get herself in trouble." He reached in his left hip pocket and pulled out a full half pint of Jim Beam.

"What kinda trouble?" Possum stood up.

Uncle Ezra popped the seal and took three big swallows. "Who knows—you mess with that bl, bl, black magic, anything . . . might happen. You better know, what . . . what your doin'. If you know what I mean." He hiccuped.

"I guess your right about that, Ezra. To make matters worse, the boys told us...she's got dynamite in that barn," Sheriff Buggs remarked.

"Dynamite, dynamite, she's got dynamite in there?" Uncle Ezra cried out.

"That's what the boys say, they helped unload it." Possum struck a match on the side of the house and lit his pipe. Lightning continued to light up the sky.

"Is that right boys?" He looked at Junior and Curly.

They looked over their shoulders at Uncle Ezra. Junior spoke first, "That's right."

"How much dynamite was there?" Ezra demanded.

"Thirteen cases."

Uncle Ezra seemed overly concerned with Junior's answer. He put his hands to his head. "It's time. Oh, Lord, I hoped I would die before this day would ever come. She's gonna do it."

"There's someone walking up the drive," Millie interrupted. Lightning lit up the sky again. "There, did you see him? Looks like a man."

"We seen 'im." Sheriff Buggs peered into the darkness. Wonder who it might be?"

Silence over took the group gathered on the Bledso porch, as the form of a man entered the yard.

"It's Billy Hawks." Charlie recognized the figure as lightning fired up the sky and thunder rumbled overhead.

Billy Hawks ambled up to the porch steps. "My pickup stalled out on me about a mile up the road."

Possum turned away from Hawks. "Imagine that, and on a night like this, storm coming in and all."

"I been having a little trouble with it, guess I should have had someone look into it." Hawks walked up the steps onto the porch. "My name is Billy Hawks." He extended his hand toward Sheriff Buggs.

"Nice to meet you, I've heard about ya. They tell me your lookin' for that dog that stays down on the river." Their eyes met as they shook hands.

"Yes, I am. Any idea where he might be?" Hawks released the sheriff's hand and took a step back, resting his weight on his good leg.

"Up there." Buggs drew dirty looks from Millie, Charlie and Possum as he pointed toward the barn. Looks that didn't go unnoticed by the Sheriff.

Possum turned to face Uncle Ezra. "Tell me what you mean, when you said she's going to do it? What are you talking about, Ezra?"

"Oh, Possum you're not going to believe this. I sh, sh, shouldn't even tell you about it. But it doesn't really matter, no one is going to, to—stop what's going to happen tonight?"

"Why don't you just tell us about it," Possum encouraged.

Uncle Ezra's eyes were wide open, the color had left his face, he stood up, steady on his feet, scared sober.

"Grandma and me was drinkin' one night about a year after Luther Bledso died. Grandma drank way too much, and she told me all about Luther and some of his beliefs and a lot of other stuff, too. You see." Uncle Ezra looked at Possum and then turned toward the sheriff. "Luther Bledso was into devil worship. He had a room upstairs that he used to worship, or what ever it is they do." Uncle Ezra paced back and forth nervously.

"We was up there," Possum spoke up.

"I'm not sure I would have went in that room. I helped carry that limestone rock up there."

"Just tell us what's going on, Ezra," Possum coaxed.

"Grandma told me that when Luther was on his death bed, he told her to destroy the barn and everything that was in it. He told her to put thirteen cases of dynamite in the barn and let mother nature take care of the rest. He wrote everything down, and she was to follow his instructions to the word."

"So your telling us Luther Bledso had this all planned before his death?" Sheriff Buggs remarked.

"That's right." Uncle Ezra took a sip of whisky.

"What about Grandma?" Junior looked up at Uncle Ezra, from his perch on the porch step.

"She goes up to. Everything in the barn. You see, Luther told Grandma the barn held too many secrets. He wanted the barn leveled and buffalo grass planted on the ground where it stood. He also told her that if she carried out his wishes, her spirit would go to a special sanctuary."

"This is crazy," Sheriff Buggs exclaimed. "Secret rooms, devil worship, an old woman locking herself in a barn with dynamite. Performing some kinda ritual. I really wonder if anything is going to come of all this."

179

"You wait. You'll see Hank Buggs! You'll see! Luther Bledso is doing all this . . . and he's doing it from the grave." Uncle Ezra shook his finger at the sheriff.

Millie began to weep.

"I think I better take these kids home, this ain't no place for them." The clock chimed one time as Possum spoke.

A bolt of lightning flashed across the sky overhead, quickly followed by a loud clap of thunder. The sky opened up and rain began to fall. Lightning lit up the sky repeatedly followed by more thunder. The rain was coming down in torrents with a strong wind to whip it around the farm yard. Suddenly, it was raining so hard that one could barely see the cars when the lightning flashed.

"My gosh, this storm sure came up fast. Maybe we better move into the house." Possum held the door open as they filed into the house. "I'll take you kids home when this storm calms down a little bit."

"It all started with that dog." Uncle Ezra rambled on.

"How's that?" Possum asked, as he propped the door open with a rubber door stop.

"Luther told Grandma he would send a sign. That she would be asked to help a four legged creature that was injured and near death . . . and the animal would be marked."

Billy Hawks eyes widened as he sat down cross-legged on the floor across the room. "What type of mark?"

"A inverted cross—on his left shoulder." Uncle Ezra patted his left shoulder.

"The devil's sign." Hawks uttered, in a voice barely audible.

"I guess he left her all kinda instruction as too what she was s'pose to do and when. At least that's what she told me. She talked about the fifth day, as being the right time, or something like that."

"It was on Monday you found that dog, wasn't it Millie?" Possum turned to look at Millie, who had taken a seat on the floor between Smoky and Charlie, still sobbing.

"It was Monday, the day of the sale at Wilson." She answered, through quivering lips.

"Tuesday, Wednesday, Thursday, Friday, Saturday." Sheriff Buggs counted the days on the fingers of his left hand. "Midnight tonight starts the fifth day."

180

"Oh, Lord, strike me down, I don't want to see this." Uncle Ezra dropped to his knees as if waiting for his prayer to be answered.

"Ezra, get hold of yourself." Uncle Ezra downed more of the whisky he still clutched in his hand. Possum and Sheriff Buggs lifted Uncle Ezra to his feet and set him in a nearby chair.

"How did Luther get involved in this devil worship, anyway?" Buggs asked, as he sat down in a stout made wooden chair, near Uncle Ezra.

"I don't know about that, except it all started when he was running shine to Kansas City. Oh, he was a evil man. He used to beat Grandma and Eli. He's the reason these boys' mother left." Uncle Ezra looked over at Junior and Curly as they sat on the floor with their backs resting against the wall.

"Everyone figured Grandma run her off. At least that's what the story always was." Possum stood in the doorway, watching the storm that was raging outside.

"That's only true to a point. Grandma didn't want her around, but Luther was the reason she left."

"Maybe, you better tell us about that," Sheriff Buggs encouraged.

"You see." Uncle Ezra hesitated, the liquor was starting to take effect again. He was beginning to slur his words and stop talking from time to time. "Luther had eyes for Nancy Bledso. He wanted her to take part . . . in some of his ceremmonies. She . . .didn't want no par' . . . of it. Eli didn't like the idea eithher and, and . . . Grandma sure didn't like it. Luther was so infatuated with her and . . . he had become so deemanding . . . that Grandma knew she had to do something. One night . . . when Lutther was gone . . . Grandma told Nance . . . she better get out of here . . . before things got any worse that, that, Luther was out of conttrol . . . and there was no telling what he might do. Sc, sccared her half, to—to death. So bad in fact that she . . . left them two boys behind." He pointed at Junior and Curly. "Grandma told her she would take care of them . . . and theey would get them to her laater. Of course that never happened, Grandma wanted them boys . . . and she waasn't 'bout to give them up."

"So, where did they take her, Ezra?" Buggs asked.

"Someplace I don't know where. Eli knows, he took her away." Uncle Ezra finished off what was left of his whisky.

"How did Luther take her leaving?" Possum turned away from the door and sat down on the settee beside Freddie Matther.

"Not very well. Grandma and Eli told him that she had run . . . away during the night. Luther didn't believe them. He was really mad . . . beat Grandma up bad. That's when she lost them teeth. But she never did tell him where Nancy was. Eli run away so he, he, couldn't beat him up. He didn't come back for a long time."

"Ezra, why do you think Luther wants Grandma to destroy the barn. Just because that's where the still was hid, doesn't seem like reason enough to destroy a perfectly good barn. I mean, why not just destroy the still," Possum pondered.

"I don't want to talk—about that. I need another drink. Possum, you got anythin' to drink?"

"No, I haven't." Possum turned his head as the phone rang.

"Hello, this is Sheriff Buggs." Buggs was quiet for a little bit, nodding his head as if he understood what was being said on the other end of the line. "Keep me posted. Is it storming there in town?" He hesitated for a moment. "Yeah, it's bad here to. Call if you hear anything." He hung up the phone.

"I need some liquor," Uncle Ezra wined.

"The plane carrying Eli Bledso landed in Salina at ten-thirty. He should be here in abouta hour," Buggs announced.

"If it doesn't quit raining, they'll never get out here. Even if it does quit, the roads are going to be damn near impassable," Possum warned.

"Let's hope they can get out here." Buggs sat down beside Uncle Ezra, who had his face buried in his hands.

"Ezra tell me what else you know about that barn?"

"I bet Grandma's got something to drink in the kitchen cabinet." He staggered to his feet.

Buggs pulled him back down in his seat.

"Ezra, I'll get you something to drink, but first you have to finish telling me about the barn."

"You're lyin' . . . I ain't takin' the word . . . of no law dog."

"If I show you what I got, will you tell me about the barn?"

"Maaaybe."

Buggs reached in his pocket and pulled out a set of keys. He tossed the keys to Freddie Matther. "Go out and get that bottle that's in the trunk of my car."

"But sheriff, it's raining like crazy out there. I'll be soaked," Freddie complained.

"I know it, now get goin'," Buggs ordered.

Matther reluctantly walked out on the porch.

The liquor and the situation at hand had really loosened Uncle Ezra's tongue. Buggs wanted to take advantage of his weakened condition before he changed his mind

Freddie Matther stood in the doorway, completely soaked. He had completed his mission. In his right hand he was carrying a fifth of Old Charter. He set it on the table and posted up against the wall. A puddle of water immediately began to form around him on the hard wood floor.

The temptation was too much for Uncle Ezra. He tried to get up, but again Buggs pulled him back in his seat. "Ezra, before I let you do any more drinking, you have to tell me what else is in the barn?"

Everyone watched as Uncle Ezra's eyes moved from the whisky bottle too Hank Buggs' eyes. "The still wasn't in the barn . . . it was under the barn. Luther Bledso had dug out . . . out about the back third of the floor. He made a floor with railroad ties and then covered them with a foot of dirt. The room in the back of the barn was just a hiding place for the hearse . . . they used to move the shine to Kansas City. The only way to fill the hole under the barn . . . is to blow it up and cave in the floor. Can I have a drink now?" He looked at Buggs with pleading eyes.

"Have you told me everything." The Sheriff stood between Uncle Ezra and the whisky.

Uncle Ezra lowered his head, staring at the floor. "No."

"If there's more tell us. What else is in that barn?"

Uncle Ezra sat back, hands intertwined, twiddling his thumbs nervously, circling one another, counter-clockwise. He looked in Buggs eyes, a long hard look, answering in a whisper. "Bodies."

Billy Hawks lifted a black brow. The children looked at one another in disbelief.

"Did you say 'bodies'?" Possum took a step closer.

"Bodies, dead people." Uncle Ezra clarified his answer.

"Who are these people?" Buggs asked, as he got up and began to pace nervously.

"I . . . don't know."

"I don't have anything in my files about any missing people."

"They're not from . . . around here. Can I have a drink, now?"

"No, you have to answer a few more questions. Where did the bodies come from?"

"Kansas City."

"You better explain." Buggs towered over Uncle Ezra.

"Luther Bledso was involved with . . . a group—of mobsters in Kansas City. He would deliver a load of shine . . . in that hearse. Well . . . the old hearse didn't always come back empty."

"Ezra, are you saying the mob would murder someone an' Luther Bledso would bring the body out here an' bury it in his barn?"

"Exactly."

Sheriff Buggs handed Uncle Ezra the unopened bottle of Old Charter. Uncle Ezra waved it away with his hand. "I've had enough." He sat straight in his chair, head up, looking at Sheriff Buggs with bloodshot eyes, as if a huge burden had been lifted off his shoulders.

"Possum, we've got to stop that old woman. We've got a crime scene to secure." Buggs turned toward Possum.

"That's not a bad idea, but I don't see how you're going to do that...until this storm blows itself out." Possum stood in the doorway, watching the storm as the grandfather clock began to chime; it was eleven o'clock. Buggs set the bottle back on the table, they walked out on the porch. Freddie Matther, a disgusted look on this face, shook his head and retreated to the porch with Possum and Sheriff Buggs. Billy Hawks stood up, looked at Charlie, shaking his head, as he too walked out on the porch.

The rest remained in the living room, including Uncle Ezra. All too dumbfounded to speak. They sat there for a long time, each one living in a world of his or her own thoughts.

Uncle Ezra had gone to sleep in his chair. He was snoring vigorously.

Charlie couldn't take the silence or the snoring any longer. "I could use a drink of water."

"Me too." Smoky was quick to reply.

Curly, who had been setting on the floor got up and lead them into the kitchen, which was just off the living room. The kitchen was a mess, the table was cluttered with dirty dishes, as was the sink. Junior opened a metal kitchen cabinet and found a lone drinking glass. They took turns, all drinking fresh well water from the same glass.

"I wonder if it's ever going to stop raining?" Millie asked.

"I'm sure it'll stop, sometime," Charlie answered.

"What do you think she's doing up there?" Smoky inquired.

"Something crazy, Grandma is always doing something crazy," Curly replied.

Junior and Curly were upset, looking as if all the energy had been drained from their bodies. Charlie wanted to say something to make them feel better, but couldn't find the words.

"You guys look tired. Why don't you find a place to rest for a while." He finally suggested.

They looked at one another. "Let's go upstairs, at least until Dad gets here," Junior purposed.

Curly nodded his head in agreement. "We might as well, if anything happens we can see from the bedroom window."

Curly took the lead flipping on a light switch at the bottom of the stairs.

They were almost to the top of the stairs when the clock let them know it was eleven-thirty.

Everyone walked down a narrow hallway to a small bedroom. Junior and Curly each had their own room. They set beside each other on the east side of the house and each one had a door that opened into the hallway Curly lead them into the first room they came too. He switched on the light. The bed was unmade and dirty clothes were strewn about the room. There was an open door between the two rooms, so one could move from one room to the other without going into the hallway. The only furniture was a bed and an old chest of drawers, with half the drawers open. The walls were covered with dingy wallpaper and the only window in the room was badly in need of repair.

Junior crossed into the other room and turned on the light. The two rooms mirrored one another. The only difference being it was a corner room and had two windows, one in each wall. A dresser with a mirror set against the divider wall and an iron bed set in the corner.

Millie had walked over to the window and was watching the storm that was still raging outside. Charlie stood beside her. Lightning flashed across the sky lighting up the whole area; they could still barely see the barn through the pouring down rain.

"I've never seen it rain this hard, for so long. Have you?" Millie looked up at Charlie.

"No, I haven't." He turned away from the window, sitting down on the bed beside Curly and Smoky.

"You got anything to smoke?" Curly uttered in a low voice.

"No," Smoky answered.

"I wonder how long Uncle Ezra has known about all this stuff he told us?"

"A long time, I'd say. "Charlie answered, Curly's question.

"I bet that's why he drank so much," Millie remarked.

"You might be right, I hope I never have to carry a burden like that," Charlie replied.

"Me too." Millie was still looking out the window. "If you guys ever do anything crazy, don't tell me about it."

Curly lay back on the bed. "I'm tired, I wish I had a cigarette." He closed his eyes.

They were all tired, it had been a long day. Smoky and Charlie stretched out on the bed beside Curly. Junior remained in the other bedroom.

They rested quietly, eyes closed, dozing off for a short time, while Millie stood watch.

"Hey, you guys, its stopped raining." She finally announced.

They got up in unison and walked over to the window. The storm was over, no rain, no lightning, no thunder, and no wind. Curly raised the window. Fresh air rushed into the room, it smelled clean, refreshing and free of dust and all the other impurities that the air is known to carry. Junior open the windows in the other bedroom.

A sliver of light appeared as the double doors of the barn began to slide open. Grandma Bledso stood between them, one arm on each door.

Grandma Bledso with what seemed like super human strength, extended her arms and the doors slid completely open. The only light came from the twelve candles that were still burning around the pentagram and on the altar.

"I can't see Jumbo." Millie strained her eyes trying to see in the dim light. "Do you see him, Charlie?"

"I can't see anything."

"Here, try these." Curly opened the top dresser drawer. He handed Charlie a set of old binoculars.

The grandfather clock began to chime downstairs.

Charlie focused the binoculars as he looked in the barn door.

"You see anything?" Smoky pushed closer, looking over his sister.

The clock struck for the third time.

"All I can see is a dead chicken." Charlie watched as Grandma picked up the unlit candle that was sitting on the alter. She lit it from one of the other candles on the alter.

The old clock clanged for the fifth time.

Grandma raised the lighted candle over her head, swaying from side to side, as the clock hammered again.

A police car with red light flashing turned down the driveway.

"Pa's here!" Curly shouted, as the old time piece continued its serenade.

The melody continued for the eighth time, as the police car came to a stop in the front yard.

They turned off the lights as a strong wind came out of the west. The small amount of light from the candles disappeared as the wind snuffed out the flame, except for the one Grandma held high above her head. The old clock hammered again.

It came from the sky, a huge ball of fire riding a bolt of lightning that extended to the horizon, striking the head house of the barn, with so much force that it disappeared in an instant. The entire roof was ablaze, as the ball of fire crashed through the hay loft in route to a meeting with thirteen cases of dynamite. The thunder that accompanied the lightning was so loud that no one heard the clock toll the tenth time.

The ensuing explosion drowned out the eleventh chime as well. The barn was engulfed in a huge ball of fire. The flash so bright, the eruption so loud, that everyone turned away and fell to the floor, the whole house shook as window glass crashed to the floor around them. The clock withstood the impact and announced itself for the final time.

A loud crash came from down the hall. The children lay silently on the floor, huddled together, covered with broken glass. Millie began to cry. Charlie was the first one to get up. Millie continued to weep as he helped her to her feet. Their arms wrapped around each other as they looked out the window. The barn had been leveled and fire was taking care of what was left.

"He's . . . de, dead" Millie stammered, as she clung even tighter to Charlie.

"You kids all right?" Possum rushed up the stairs.

"I think we're all right," Charlie answered. "Just a few little cuts from the flying glass."

"What fell down, we heard a loud crash?" Sheriff Buggs entered the room.

"It came from down the hall." Junior pointed toward Grandma's secret room.

Buggs made his way down the hall. Everyone followed him, single file, except Junior and Curly who stayed in their rooms. He quickly retrieved the key and unlocked the door, switching on the light as he entered.

The limestone altar lay in a pile of rubble on the floor, broken in so many pieces it could be carried out in small buckets.

CHAPTER 21

"I think I'll go over and see the Bledso boys this afternoon." Charlie Mayfair announced, as he pushed his chair back from the dinner table.

"How they doing, anyway?" Charlie's mother picked up his plate, setting it in the sink.

"Alright, I guess, I haven't seen them since the memorial service for Grandma. I guess I should have gone over there sooner. You know, I just can't get over how hard they took her death."

"Well, Charlie." Herb Taylor turned down the radio that was playing on the counter beside the sink. "I can, after all, she was the nearest thing to a mother they ever knew."

"I know, but she treated them terrible. Never showed them any kinda love, just hollered at 'em, abused 'em.

"Well, let me explain something to ya. If someone gave you a puppy an' every morning when you get up, you give that puppy a swift kick with your barefoot, after a month or two, what do you think he would expect, first thing in the morning when he gets up?"

Charlie pondered the question for a bit. "I guess he'd expect to get kicked."

"That's right. Why?"

"Because he always got kicked."

"Right, because he didn't know no different. That's what life is to him. It's the same way with Junior and Curly—they never knew life to be any other way." He leaned over, turning up the radio as the newscast began.

The reporters baritone voice immediately caught everyone's attention. "Ellsworth county authorities, with the help of the Kansas Bureau of Investigation and the FBI, have completed their investigation at the Eli Bledso farm located east of Kanopolis, Kansas. The barn on the homestead was destroyed by an explosion and fire nearly two weeks ago. Clorisa Bledso, the owner of the farm, was killed in the explosion. An investigation was launched when a family friend reported that bodies had been buried in the dirt floor of the barn years ago. Ellsworth county sheriff Henry Buggs reports that the entire floor of the barn has been excavated and seven bodies were recovered. The only body identified at this time was that of Frank

(Dirty Hands) Sacadae, who at one time was on the FBI's ten most wanted list. Sacadea, an automobile mechanic turned hit man for the Mafia, was believed to be implicated in at least twenty-five murders in the Kansas City area, according to Sheriff Buggs. KGGN news will—."

Herb Taylor switched off the radio. "How about that, who would have ever thought something like that was going on round here."

"Certainly not me," Charlie's mother shuttered. "I, also heard they found the opening to a tunnel that went out in the pasture nearly a quarter mile."

"That's right, Hank Buggs told me that himself. Old man Bledso had everything figured out, didn't he, just in case the law came callin'!" Herb grinned as he finished off his coffee.

"I wonder if Jumbo might have escaped through that tunnel?" Charlie stood up moving toward the door.

"Maybe, but I doubt it. I don't think we'll be seeing him again." Herb followed his grandson to the door.

"Gramps, you got any idea where I might find some worms. We might decide to see if the fish are bitin'."

"Should be some along the corral fence under that old hay. You drive careful, no hot rodin', you wreck that car I'm not buyin' you another one. You just pickin' up Junior and Curly?"

"We might pick up Smoky and Millie . . . if we decide to fish."

"Have they seen your car?"

"No sir."

"I can't blame you for wanting to show it off, but you drive extra careful with them other kids in the car. Don't let 'em distract ya."

"I won't. Why do you think I'm wanting to show off my car?"

"I was your age once, an' if I would have gotten a new car I would have wanted to show it off."

"I don't think a forty-six Chevy is exactly new."

"New to you, isn't it," Herb chuckled.

"I guess, I never thought of it that way."

"Just drive careful," he cautioned.

"I'll be careful. I'm going to see if I can find some worms."

"Put on some old clothes if your going to be fooling around down there on the river." Charlie's mother ordered, as he was about to slip out the door.

He quickly went to his room, returning shortly with the worst clothes he could find.

His mother spoke again as he passed through the kitchen. "Charlie, you didn't have to put on those old rags."

"You said to put on some old clothes."

"Well, I didn't mean that old. You look like a beggar. Go see if you can't find something a little better." She pointed to the stairway.

"Mother's sure are hard to figure out." Charlie grumbled, under his breath, as he returned upstairs.

The second set of clothes was more satisfactory, at least nothing was said, as he passed through the kitchen.

"Good-bye Son." She shouted, as he pulled the door shut.

Charlie picked up a spade from the storage shed on his way to the corral.

Diablo nickered as he approached. "Wanta go for a ride?"

He turned and walked away, making it known he hadn't forgiven Charlie for the treatment he had received only a few weeks earlier.

It didn't take long to collect a can of worms. The ground was wet and the earth worms liked the half rotten hay.

Charlie put two fishing poles in the trunk and was on his way to the Bledso's. The old car ran good, it wasn't anything fancy, but certainly beat walking or riding Diablo. Deep down Charlie knew Diablo was the reason he had gotten the car. His Grandfather wasn't too happy when he found out his grandson had been riding someone's prize stallion around the country.

Junior and Curly came running out of the house before he got the engine shut off.

Charlie couldn't help noticing they were wearing new jeans and shirts along with freshly trimmed hair and new shoes.

"When did you get this thing?" Curly stuck his head in the window.

"Couple days ago." Charlie opened the door and got out.

Junior took his place under the steering wheel. "How fast will she go?"

"I don't know," Charlie replied.

"Let's find out," Curly said, as he pulled his head out of the window.

"I don't think I'll be doing that anytime soon. Gramps says if I wreck this car I'm not gettin' another one and I need wheels. I brought a couple fishin' poles, let's go get Smoky and try our luck down on the river.

"That sounds like a good idea, but before we leave there's someone you need to meet." Junior was smiling from ear to ear. "Come on." He took the lead as they walked to the front door of the house.

Curly motioned Charlie to come inside, as he opened the door. Charlie looked around as they entered the dining room, everything was neat and clean, the walls and ceiling were freshly painted, the old chandler sparkled like new, not a speck of dust on anything. Charlie was ushered into the kitchen.

A medium sized woman was standing at the sink. She turned to face them as they entered the room, long wavy dark red hair draped over her shoulders. She was an attractive lady with a few pale freckles sprinkled on her face, hazel eyes looked Charlie over.

Charlie knew who she was even before Junior made his introduction. Nancy Bledso had came home to raise her boys. "Charlie, I want you to meet our Mom. She's living with us now. Mom, this is Charlie."

"Charlie, it's nice to meet you. I've certainly heard a lot about you." She wiped her hands on a white apron that was wrapped around an attractive waist. They exchanged a firm hand shake.

"Nice to meet you. When did you come back?" Charlie asked, trying to make polite conversation.

"Let's see, must have been about ten days ago."

"Where have you been living?"

"Manhattan." She changed the subject. "Sorry about the way the place looks, but there is just so much work to do. I've been working the boys pretty hard. They'll be wanting me to leave, if I don't ease up on them."

"You'll never work us that hard." Curly spoke up quickly.

"You're here to stay." Junior was quick to state his feelings.

"I think you got the place lookin' pretty good." Charlie complimented, as he looked around the kitchen.

"It needs a lot more work, I'm afraid. So what are you boys up to?"

"I though maybe we would go fishin' down on the river, if that's alright with you, ma'am?" Charlie asked politely.

"I guess that would be alright. How are you going to get to the river?"

"Charlie's got him a car, real nice one, come and look at it." Curly took his mother's hand, trying to lead her to the door.

"Not right now, I'll look at it when you get back. I've got work to do. You boys best get going . . . it's already two o'clock."

"It was nice to meet you ma'am. I'm glad you came back. These two need someone to keep them in line."

"I don't think it'll be too hard. If I need some help I'll give you a call."

"I doubt that I'll be much help."

"Oh, that's not what I hear."

"Let's go!" Curly led Charlie by the arm toward the door.

"Put on the skillet. Fresh fish for supper, Mom." Junior said, as he followed out the door.

"You'll stay for supper, won't you, Charlie," she invited.

"We'll have to catch some fish first." Charlie called back to her, as Junior pulled the door shut.

It didn't take Junior and Curly long to gather up their fishing poles. Everything was loaded into the trunk of the car, and they were on their way to the Elliot's.

It was just past two-thirty when they parked the car on the east side of the Old Iron Bridge. Smoky and Millie, were riding in the front seat with Charlie."

"Man it's hot," Smoky made note of the situation. "I doubt the fish are going to be bitin' in this heat."

"You're probably right. We'd be better off if we went skinny-dippin'," Curly remarked.

"Sounds like a good idea to me," Smoky agreed. "We should have left this girl at home."

"I don't care what you guys do. I'll walk up to the caves and see if there's any new names carved in the walls. It'll be cool in there."

"Good idea. Why don't you do that," Smoky encouraged. "While you're there, see if any girls have carved my name in stone."

"You're dreaming big brother," Millie replied.

"What do you mean, there's a lot of girls around town looking me over." Smoky straighten up in the seat and turned sideways giving Millie a good look at his profile.

"The only reason they're looking at you is they've never seen anything so strange. Let me out." She turned her back to him as she started toward the caves.

"Anybody got anything to smoke?" Smoky asked, as she walked away.

"Not me." Junior and Curly answered in unison.

"Come on, you guys always got something to smoke."

"We quit," Junior answered.

"Why?"

Junior hesitated a second before he answered. "Oh, we wanted to play football for one thing. You know the coach doesn't allow no smoking."

"Never stopped you before," Smoky quipped.

"The other reason is Mom asked us not to smoke."

"Oh!" Smoky ended the conversation.

"Let's see what the waters like." Curly was already taking off his shirt as he made his way to the water.

The rest followed his example.

Charlie sat down on a log and began untying his shoes. He kicked off one shoe and stopped. A strange feeling had came over him, the hair stood up on the back of his neck and a cold chill ran down his spine. He sat there for a moment thinking, listening, not moving.

Smoky already had his clothes off as he spoke. "Come on, Charlie. Let's hit the water."

Charlie heard him, but didn't respond.

Smoky walked over and stood in front of him. "Charlie, what's the matter?"

Charlie didn't answer.

Junior and Curly moved over and flanked Smoky on either side, already naked.

"Charlie . . . Charlie, what's the matter?" Junior shook his arm.

"Something's not right," he finally answered.

"What do you mean?" Smoky had a bewildered look on his face.

"I'm going to check on Millie." Charlie answered, as he pulled his shoe back on.

"You're crazy, she's alright." Smoky raised his voice. "I think you would just rather be with her than us."

They all laughed, as Charlie ran up the river bank. He could have taken the car and driven at least part way up to the Ferris Caves, but instead ran up the road.

The Ferris Caves was a series of three man made caves. In the late 1800's, Charles Griffee, a Colorado miner, had moved into the area. Griffee put his mining experience to work and hand dug the caves' side by side, in the Dakota sandstone bluff that ran north and south a couple hundred feet off the river. A spring ran through one of the caves, so there was always fresh water and a cool place to keep food. Griffee and his family lived in the caves for many years. Now the caves were nothing but a landmark for people to visit and carve their initials in the sandstone walls.

Charlie was about halfway to the caves when he heard the scream; a loud piercing cry, a lump formed in his stomach.

He broke into a hard run. Millie screamed again, even louder and more bloodcurdling than the first one.

He tried to run faster as he became more terrified. The trail that led up to the caves loomed ahead. She cried out again, a loud short scream—too short.

Charlie was surprised when he saw her on the trail, running in his direction. She dropped to her knees, in front of him, tears running down her pale white face.

Charlie knelt down beside her, as a hog squealed back in the timber.

She was out of breath and still crying as she tried to talk. "The pig—Ol Razor . . . sleeping in the cave . . . I startled him. He . . . started chasing me. I fell down. He's alive." She grabbed Charlie's arm. "He's alive! He saved my life," she rambled.

"Who's alive? What are you talking about?"

"Jumbo! He's alive! She tried to wipe the tears out of her eyes with the back of her hand.

"That's impossible, nothing could have lived through that explosion." He pulled a handkerchief out of his pocket and offered it to her.

She took it wiping her face and eyes. "I tell you . . . I seen him . . . when I fell down . . . I thought I was done for. I don't know where he came from," she sobbed. "But he was there . . . standing between us. Razor tried to run past him . . . he grabbed his ear and turned him away from me."

195

"I still can't believe he's alive." Charlie stood up.

"He is or it's his twin brother. Don't you hear him and Ol Razor fighting."

Charlie listened for a second. Razor was certainly having it out with something from the sound of the grunts and squeals, the battle had moved into the river.

"You stay here, I'm going up there and see what's going on," Charlie instructed.

"I'm not staying here. I'm going with you."

He offered her his hand as she started to get up. Her knees were badly scratched and a small amount of blood was running down her legs.

"You need to stay here. Why don't you go back to the car?"

"No, I'm going."

Charlie didn't feel like arguing with her. "You'll have to keep up on your own."

"I'll keep up."

The battle raged on ahead, as they followed a trail outside the timberline of the river. Ol Razor's screams seemed to be coming closer together. The trail soon ended and the terrain became more difficult to navigate, as Charlie and Millie got farther behind.

"Let's get in the river," Charlie suggested.

"What ever you think. I'm wondering if we're ever going to catch up with them?"

"I'm not sure we will either." Millie followed, as Charlie led the way down to the rivers edge.

****

On the opposite side of the river, moccasin clad feet were moving quickly and silently in the direction of the melee. Billy Hawks cradled the well used thirty-thirty rifle in his arm like a mother carrying a sick child. He ducked and dodged low hanging tree limbs, vines, river trash, and downed trees that loomed in his path. He moved up the river in earnest, sensing a closure to the quest he had undertaken early in the summer.

****

Razor was in a fight for his life, this was not the same dog he had fought before. Razor had never felt real pain, but Jumbo was inflecting an unimaginable amount of damage every time they squared off, ripping huge mouthfuls of hide and flesh from his body, leaving gaping wounds that left a bloody trail as they battled up the river.

Razor stopped at the edge of a large sandbar. Jumbo circled his prey. This was war—war without terms, a struggle that could only end in death for one or perhaps both.

Buzzards began to gather above the battleground eager to claim the spoils of war.

Razor charged, hoping to catch Jumbo with a well sharpened tusk. Jumbo effortlessly stepped aside, leaving Razor off balance, with one quick move he locked vice like jaws on Razor's right ear. Razor roared his disapproval as Jumbo ripped off his ear along with half his face. Jumbo distastefully tossed his prize in the air. It landed in the water floating down the stream like river trash.

Razor spun in a tight circle, driven wild by the excruciating pain. He stumbled, falling down on his knees. Jumbo seized the opportunity, grabbing a hind leg just above the first joint, severing the Achilles' tendon with one quick snap of his mighty jaws. Razor was powerless to defend himself as he struggled to get back on his feet. Jumbo struck again, taking out the tendon on the opposite leg. Razor's deafening screams echoed up and down the river, as Jumbo disappeared into the timber, leaving his old nemesis to die a slow agonizing death.

****

Charlie and Millie continued their trek, stopping from time to time to catch their breath and listening to see if they were catching up to the battle that continued around the bend of the river. At one point they heard voices. Smoky, Junior, and Curly had taken up the chase as well.

A rifle shot cracked ahead. They silently looked at each other, knowing what the shot signified. Billy Hawks' rifle had hushed the river. The birds, the animals, the trees and even the river itself was peacefully quiet. The only sound was their own breathing.

They rounded the bend in the river to find Billy Hawks standing over Razor's lifeless body at the water's edge, a bewildered look on his face, as he tried to catch his breath. Hawks shot had been true, the bullet struck just above the eyes, a brain shot, death had came instantly.

Millie looked down at his body. "Oh, my God!" She turned away; horrified by what she saw.

"You got him," Charlie remarked.

"Not really," Hawks answered. "I found him like this. I just ended his suffering."

"Did you see Jumbo?" Millie asked.

"No! I figured that's who he was fighting. I don't mind telling you, something mighty strange is going on here."

"What are you talking about?" Charlie studied the carcass, as Razor's blood turned the river red.

"I'm not sure." Hawks stepped back studying Razor's mortal remains. "I don't believe any ordinary dog, even a big dog, could do this kind of damage to a tough hided old tusker like Razor. It would take a creature with demon like powers to do this."

"Maybe, it was Jumbo's ghost," Millie offered.

"I never heard of such a thing," Charlie spoke up. "I thought a ghost was like a wayward spirit or a lost soul."

"He's not a ghost. He's made of flesh and blood just like you and me."

"You sure of that?" Millie looked up at Hawks face with inquisitive eyes.

"Yes, I'm sure. The answer to that question is in the sand." Hawks pointed at a freshly made dog track.

"He leaves tracks." Charlie whispered under his breath. "So what do you make of all this, Mr. Hawks?"

"We have no way of knowing what took place in that barn the night of the storm. Nor do we have any idea of the magic the old woman possessed, or perhaps, it was Luther Bledso's powers that were at work." Hawks hesitated for a little bit—thinking. "Remember Uncle Ezra saying, Grandma Bledso's spirit would go to a special sanctuary?"

"My Grandfather was a Cherokee Medicine Man. He told my father that he thought it was possible for an animal to posses a human's soul. He felt it would be possible with black magic and the forces of nature coming together at the same time. That may have been what happened in the Bledso barn. The elements where both there." Hawks stopped talking and took another deep breath.

"Now wait a minute," Charlie interrupted. "Are you saying, we got a big dog, that's running around with Grandma Bledso's soul?"

"Perhaps, but it's only a theory."

"That's scary." Millie shuttered, a cold chill running down her spine.

"Charlie, I received a letter this morning from Lois Shank. She asked me to come back to Oklahoma. Armella Shank has regained her memory and told them everything that happened on the day Orie Shank was killed. It seems that Orie was beating Armella and Jumbo came to her rescue and accidentally killed Orie. Mrs. Shank says everyone has suffered enough, including Jumbo, and I should call off the search." Hawks extended his hand. "It was nice to meet you Charlie No Tell, but I must go."

"Same here, if you ever come back, look me up." They shook hands, a warm firm hand shake.

****

Jumbo quietly entered the graveyard late that night, head bowed, ears laid flat, tail down—showing respect for the residence in his own way. In the quiet of the night his ghostly silhouette showed up like a shadow as it moved through the headstones, it wasn't a wondering path Jumbo was following, he knew exactly where this trail would end. He stopped at the foot of Luther Bledso's grave, with head held high, he would send out a summons that would carry across the barren land, over the rolling hills and grassy plains, up and down the flowing rivers to the quiet streams and the still brooks.

This was a keen for all to hear, the man that would do good, the woman that would show compassion, the foolish and the ignorant that would do evil—both the living and the dead.

Weep not for the righteous and the godly; but shed your tears for the unjust, for they shall wonder the universe in darkness, with eyes that do not see, ears that do not hear, and minds that do not comprehend. They shall search forever—but find no peace.

THE END

ABOUT THE AUTHOR

Born at Ellsworth Kansas, Lon D. Haden, spent much of his youth exploring the rivers, streams, and prairies of Central Kansas, usually with one or two canine companions. Born to a farming family, he soon became aquainted with the vast amount of wildlife that abounded in the area. He learned their habits as well as their peculiarities.

There was a time when he thought about going west to California and entering a career in acting and comedy, but he knew he would never be happy living in a large metropolitan area. His bond with nature and the great outdoors too strong. Instead he chose to take over the family farm and raise his family in the same rural area that he investigated as a boy.

Like many who choose to till the soil, he worked off the farm at different jobs, livestock feed salesman, packing plant laborer, and recently retired from the Ellsworth Correctional Facility where he worked as a Corrections Officer for thirteen years.

Now he is prepared to take on a new career, writing fictional stories that are humorous at times, and tragic at others. He will take the reader down trails most have never followed, rivers and streams many have never known, and a sagacity into the animal world that few have ever experienced.

Printed in the United States
1360400003B/15